IN THE SHADOW OF DIABLO
Ghosts of Black Diamond

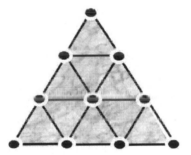

Michael,

Enjoy!

Printed in the United States of America

First Printing, 2018

ISBN-13: 978-1727739534

ISBN-10: 1727739531

CreateSpace

www.createspace.com

Cover Design by Veronica Hanel

Dedicated to historical society staff and volunteers everywhere –
without whose passion and commitment to the preservation of
local heritage this book would not be possible.

PREFACE

During the mid-19th century, coal was discovered in the Mt. Diablo foothills of eastern Contra Costa County, California. Though of relatively poor quality, the coal's proximity to San Francisco's burgeoning economy made it a much desired, and profitable, commodity. Fueling everything from steamboats and locomotives, to homes and heavy industry, the abundant *black diamond* helped California prosper.

Alongside the largest coal mining operation in the state, pioneer towns housed miners, service providers, and their families. The largest of these towns was Nortonville, drawing mostly Welsh immigrants looking for a better life in America. Along with their coal-mining acumen and unparalleled work ethic, they brought their rich culture and traditions.

In researching the history of Nortonville, Black Diamond Mines, and the adjacent Rose Hill Cemetery, I found myself tracing threads of an ever-expanding web of facts and fables, sometimes unable to distinguish between the two. It is my intent to share a bit of the fascinating story of this coal mining town, while exploring the remarkable connections to some well-known legends, and some not so well-known. I invite the reader to join in this exploration, both during the book, and after.

I hope you enjoy the journey into Black Diamond Mines.

Dan Hanel

ACKNOWLEDGMENTS

I wish to acknowledge the many individuals who so generously gave of their time and expertise:

To my wife, Jackie, whose steadfast support allows this adventure to continue; to initial editors Lisa K., Karin R., and Lindi H., who had their hands full with damage control; to my daughter, Veronica, who manages to take a few rudimentary ideas and turn them into remarkable cover art; to retired East Bay Regional Park Naturalist Traci Parent, whose thirty-plus year career at Black Diamond Mines Regional Preserve resulted in publication of the extraordinary *Rose Hill: A Comprehensive History of a Pioneer Cemetery* that documents the life and death of many of Nortonville's residents and proved an invaluable resource.

Thank you all!

CHAPTER 1

"You know this place is supposed to be haunted."

"You mean the White Witch? I've heard. You don't believe in that sort of thing, do you?"

CHRISTINA AND DONNIE PULLED their coats tightly closed and leaned into each other, fending off the cold February night air with shared body heat. The teens had been dating for two years. With high school graduation and their subsequent separation at colleges a thousand miles apart quickly approaching, they treasured their time together.

They were supposed to be at the movies, but Donnie wanted to get Christina alone to talk about their upcoming senior ball and graduation plans, but mostly about continuing their relationship during college. They both danced around the subject in the past. Now, as the end of the school year grew near, Donnie needed to know how Christina felt. Would they have a future? Christina wondered the same.

Donnie drove past the residential housing on Somersville Road and wound his way into the foothills beyond. He pulled off the road and parked at the closed gate for the Black Diamond Mines Regional Preserve. He asked Christina how she felt about trespassing in the middle of the night. When she smiled and scrambled over the fence without answering, he felt more attracted to her than ever.

The two hiked a short distance along a paved road that soon gave way to a narrow dirt trail. Donnie led them to the top of a small, yet steep, hill where he pulled off his backpack and emptied its contents. Christina spread the blanket on the ground while Donnie set out a flashlight and a thermos of hot chocolate. The air was still and countless stars sparkled brilliantly in the clear night sky. Donnie hoped for this exact setting. He fondly remembered an eighth-grade star-gazing trip to the summit of nearby Mt. Diablo. Volunteers from the Astronomical Society of the Pacific set up telescopes in the Visitor Center parking lot on weekend nights for the public to view the wonders of the universe from above city light pollution.

At this late hour, the gibbous moon was low on the horizon, providing just enough glow to light the trail during their hike. Also illuminated was the eerie, yet serene, stand of headstones scattered a hundred yards away in the old Rose Hill Cemetery.

Christina sipped the hot chocolate that Donnie handed her. The liquid heat was appreciated. He forgot to pack a second cup, so she passed it back. Donnie, too, was glad he thought about bringing something warm to drink.

They sat and cuddled in silence, Christina leaning her head on Donnie's shoulder. Blanketed by stars overhead and wrapped in the tranquil night air, neither wanted to bring up the subject. This moment felt too perfect. A serious conversation about their future together would wait a while longer. So they just sat.

"What's that?" asked Christina.

"Where?" Donnie replied, slowly awakening from a deep contentment.

"Down there, to the left of the cemetery." Christina pointed to a soft green glow in the distance that seemed to hover a few feet above the ground.

"Uh, not sure," Donnie finally answered after staring and squinting for several minutes. "But the light looks like it's moving toward the cemetery."

Christina turned toward Donnie. He felt her hand close tightly on his. "You don't think …"

"No, no," Donnie quickly replied, still intently watching the strange object. "Look, now that the thing's in the moonlight you can see it's a person. They're holding something that's giving off light."

"Do you think It's a ranger coming to get us?"

"If it is, they're heading the wrong direction. Looks like they're going straight into the cemetery. It's weird — the glowing light is not a flashlight. I wonder what's making the green glow."

The two watched for a while from atop the hill, being careful to not call attention to themselves. The figure slowly weaved through the headstones, moving closer to Christina and Donnie's perch. The green glow, now clearly visible, floated directly in front of the person. The teens agreed that the shadowy individual was a man, and not likely a park ranger.

"I know what that is," said Christina suddenly.

Donnie turned toward her, anxious for an explanation.

"My uncle uses one of those at the beach." The confused expression on Donnie's face triggered a chuckle out of Christina. "It's a metal detector. See, if you look close you can see the long wand he's waving back and forth in front of him. The green glow is the readout screen he's wearing."

Donnie squinted again. "You're right. A metal detector … in a cemetery … what an asshole."

3

Christina instinctively elbowed him for the language, but then thought a moment. "You're right. What an asshole. I can't believe someone would try to find valuable metal in an old cemetery. Should we say something?"

The thought of letting the man know he was being watched had already crossed Donnie's mind. Not knowing the response to such an encounter, and thinking first and foremost of Christina's safety, he opted against it. "Probably safest not to say anything right now. I'll call the park tomorrow and let them know."

Christina smiled. She knew that if she were not there, Donnie would act. He always stood up for what was right, whether to help a friend bullied at school or admonish a stranger littering in town. She loved that about him. But she also appreciated that he did not take unnecessary risks. And confronting a stranger at night in an isolated park was absolutely unnecessary.

They watched for thirty minutes as the man continued to walk among the upright headstones and horizontal grave markers. He paused occasionally to make an extra sweep or two in an area, only to continue on, apparently getting no indication of his desired treasure.

Then he stopped. The wand swept back and forth much faster. He circled a small area several times, looking intently at the readout strapped around his waist. Something triggered his metal detector.

A gentle nudge by Donnie recaptured the attention Christina lost in reflection. "I swear," he started. "If he starts digging up …"

But before Donnie could finish his thought, something else caught their eye. Approaching the man from behind was another light. This time, it was certainly a flashlight, and moving quickly.

"Ha," Donnie muttered, "caught by the ranger." He felt relieved that he wouldn't have to get involved.

They watched from their hill as the man with the flashlight neared the glowing detector, whose operator remained unaware. A voice called out, but neither Christina nor Donnie could make out the words. The man with the metal detector spun around and the two stopped, mere feet apart.

Harsh, yet still unintelligible words flew back and forth between the two men. The flashlight's bobbing white beam sporadically illuminated the metal detector and its owner. The detector's glowing green screen cast a ghostly hue on the scene.

As the teens watched transfixed, their anxiety grew. The argument below was escalating. Donnie gripped Christina's hand tighter when he saw the man with the metal detector shift the wand from his right hand to his left. The man slowly reached behind his back.

With a single motion, the man with the metal detector drew a long blade from his belt and thrust it at the ranger. The flashlight shook violently and then fell to the ground motionless.

Christina screamed in horror, unable to control her reaction. Donnie leapt to his feet. Without thinking, he yelled as loud as he could, "Hey!"

They saw the shadowy image of the man with the detector turn in their direction. Masked by darkness, Donnie knew the man would have a hard time seeing them. He hoped his shout would be enough.

It was. The man fled the cemetery. The glowing green light faded into the distance and disappeared. Donnie turned toward Christina, who was clearly shaken by what she had just witnessed. "Call 911," he tried to say calmly. "I'm going to see if I can help."

Christina reached for her cell phone. "Be careful!" she called out while Donnie raced down the hill toward the cemetery.

With the flashlight lying on the ground, Donnie could not see the ranger. He rushed toward the light, fearful of what he would find. But when he arrived at the light, no one was there. He stood, confused and uneasy. Where was the ranger?

Donnie picked up the light and shined it in the direction of the fleeing man with the metal detector. Nothing. He thought for a moment, and then scanned the ground. Instantly, Donnie recognized the deep red liquid trailing off to his left. A massive lump formed in his throat.

He followed the blood ten feet, then twenty feet. It seemed to be heading toward one of headstones. Donnie approached cautiously. As he lifted the light toward the headstone, he gasped. Crumpled at the base of the stone was a man, bloody and still.

Donnie hurried to the man. He struggled to remember his first-aid training from years ago, wishing he paid more attention during the week-long session in PE class. But it was too late. Donnie moved the light onto the man's face. Although he had never seen a dead person before, he knew immediately that this man was gone. The man's eyes remained partially opened in a fixed gaze, as if taking in the starlit sky one last time. The most unsettling feature to Donnie was the lack of an eye-spark. The man's eyes reflected nothing, not the stars, not even the flashlight beam. They were flat and lifeless. He was definitely dead.

Startled by his vibrating cell phone, Donnie realized by the ring tone that Christina was calling him. He grabbed the phone from his pocket and tried to calm his voice before answering, "Hi."

"Are you okay?" she asked with deep concern.

"Yeah, yeah. I'm fine. Are you alright?"

"Yes. What happened?"

"Well," replied Donnie, staring down at the body in front of him. "What we thought happened, happened."

His obscure message was enough for Christina to understand. "Oh my, gosh, that's terrible. The police are on the way. I told them to meet us at Rose Hill Cemetery. I'll be down there in a few minutes."

She hung up before Donnie could talk her into staying back, hoping to spare her the sight of a bloody corpse. He watched her flashlight as she descended the hill toward him. He cut her off before she got near the body.

"The guy was stabbed over here," he said, pointing to the blood-stained soil. He figured the initial site of blood would upset her enough to avoid seeing the rest. He was wrong.

"Then what?" Christina asked, unfazed.

"For some reason, he crawled or dragged himself over there. Not sure why he would go that way, back into the cemetery."

Christina followed the trail to the body. The dead man's face leaned against a headstone, and one arm seemed to wrap around it. She took a deep breath. "How awful."

"Something else is strange," added Donnie. "Judging by the way he's dressed, I don't think he's a ranger. Not even wearing hiking shoes. Any ranger working out here would at least wear shoes meant for dirt trails."

The two looked at each other with deep consternation. "What's that?" Christina continued, pointing her flashlight at the headstone.

Donnie shone his flashlight next to Christina's. He stepped over the body and knelt down. The dark red writing on the headstone was now obvious.

Christina could barely contain her curiosity. "What does it say? What does it say?"

Tilting his head in line with the slanted lettering, Donnie read the words.

> *"Madog near*
> *Warn Celeste Scott."*

CHAPTER II

"*Y DDRAIG GOCH ddyry gychwyn.*"

Ten of the fourteen men burst out laughing as William Gething pushed the Canadian, Dumas, to one side and passed him in the long narrow tunnel. The sun had just risen, but here, halfway down a four-hundred foot long underground tunnel, the dim glow of mining safety lanterns was the only light. A long, strenuous, and extremely dangerous day lay ahead of each man. But for now, they were in good spirits, if for no other reason than working the Upper Black Diamond mine, with its much easier walk-in access to the coal vein. The other crew assigned to Lower Black Diamond mine first descended down a four-hundred foot shaft before reaching the tunnel entrance.

Dumas glared good-naturedly at the man squeezing by him, knowing Gething did not expect to be understood. Dumas and the few other Canadians in town, along with a larger group of Italians, had a hard enough time understanding the lilting Welsh accent when speaking English. If the immigrants from Wales broke into their native language, comprehension was impossible. Fortunately, Welsh conversations were rare, and usually saved for situations such as this, when they just wanted to be annoying.

Two more Welshmen, Griffiths and Lewis, edged by Dumas, gently nudging him as they passed. Dumas spun around to prevent the next man from walking further. Most of the miners were in their late twenties to mid-forties, but the person he faced now was William Williams, only eighteen years old. "Alright, Willy, what did he say?"

Willy smiled and replied, "The Red Dragon will show the way." He lifted his lantern and pushed past Dumas.

The men chuckled. Even Reynolds, the Englishman, and the Italian, Marengo could not help but laugh. Dumas knew the Red Dragon, the ancient symbol of Wales. How could he not? The overwhelming majority of Nortonville's population were Welsh immigrants. The original settlers left South Wales coal mining towns looking for a better life. Some came overland along the California trail, but most sailed south to Panama, crossed the isthmus on horse or foot and then caught a steamship north to San Francisco.

In 1855, Noah Norton founded the first of five towns to crop up in what was termed the Mount Diablo Coal Field. Although relatively poor in quality, the coal served as a major energy source for a burgeoning Northern California economy. Twelve separate mines led to the three steeply angled coal veins – the Clark, the Little, and the Black Diamond – all providing fuel for factories, mills, steamships, and homes.

Dumas, Gething, and the others lived in Nortonville, one of the largest towns in Contra Costa County, boasting nearly one-thousand residents. Nearby Somersville served the Pittsburg, Independent, and other mines, whereas the outlying towns of Stewartville, Judsonville, and West Hartley housed operations for smaller mine shafts.

While the miners made their way through the long, dark tunnel toward the Black Diamond coal vein, on the surface, Nortonville awoke from its slumber. The wives and children of Griffiths, Lewis, and Reynolds set about their daily routines. Since yesterday was Sunday, there was much work to catch up on. The Welsh Protestants held firmly to their faith, observing the Sabbath and worshipping at church. This morning the children tended to chores - milking cows, gathering chicken eggs, fetching well water - all before heading to school.

Sometimes work took priority for Nortonville children. Griffiths, in particular, was thankful his kids were too young to work as knobbers - boys small enough to stand inside a shaft and rake coal downward. The children of other miners were not so lucky. Trailing the men into the mine this morning were two boys, nine and twelve years old. They would work in the mine today and not attend school. If done early enough, the knobbers and other working children might attend an evening session at Nortonville School to keep up with their studies. But this made for excruciatingly long days.

Nortonville's main street now bustled with activity. Hotels propped open windows to take advantage of the first few hours of cool morning air before the stifling summer heat set in. Blacksmiths, carpenters, and cooks all prepared for the day. Noakes butcher shop began morning deliveries to the hotels, while the Engler family shoe store started cobbling an order for Morgan Morgans, the Black Diamond Mine superintendent. Even the saloon on Main Street gradually opened its doors, though most patrons would not arrive until much later in the day.

Boarding houses dotted Main Street and the surrounding hills, serving as hosts to mostly single working men. The Ginochio family ran a boarding house and saloon some distance from Main Street in an area known as Italian Hill. Additional residences and stores on the hill provided a cultural respite for the Italian immigrants living among the pervasive Welsh society.

For millennia, the golden grasslands covering gently rolling hills hid untapped wealth buried deep below. Decaying swamp plants compressed and hardened over countless years to form layers of coal. Now thrust thousands of feet above sea level by shifting tectonic forces, the coal was accessible. Through the

11

Black Diamond miners' backbreaking efforts and an expanding population of support providers, Nortonville became a thriving community situated unassumingly in the shadow of Mount Diablo.

GETHING, DUMAS, AND THE REST of the crew finished eating assorted jerky, breads, and summer fruits. Griffiths and the other men with wives always ate better than the rest, usually indulging in meat and potato stuffed pastries that their spouses prepared. The men stowed their metal lunch buckets along a wall of the widened tunnel room, stretching and groaning before grabbing nearby tools.

"How 'bout one more?" Reynolds asked, directing his query to the Watts brothers, Theophilus and David.

The brothers looked over at their friend Thomas James. "Well, what say you?" asked Theophilus.

Thomas smiled, as he always did when asked to sing. He and the Watts brothers were renowned for their singing voices and often stood front and center of the popular Nortonville Welsh choir. "What shall it be, boys?" asked Thomas.

"Tell us of Myfanwy," responded Willy, still sitting against the wall, thankful for another few moments of rest.

The Watts brothers looked at each other, then at James. They began in unison and on key, as if performing for royalty at the grand Cardiff Castle of Wales.

"Paham mae dicter, O Myfanwy,
Yn llenwi'th lygaid duon di?
A'th ruddiau tirion, O Myfanwy,
Heb wrido wrth fy ngweled i?
Pa le mae'r wên oedd ar dy wefus

12

Fu'n cynnau 'nghariad ffyddlon ffôl?
Pa le mae sain dy eiriau melys,
Fu'n denu'n nghalon ar dy ôl?" [1]

The gentle ballad's perfect harmony resonated through the tunnel. The sweet tale of unrequited love from the fair maid, Myfanwy, left the men in deep, silent reflection. Even Marengo and the other non Welsh speakers stood mesmerized by the melody's haunting beauty.

The trio's last verse faded into silence. Without a word, the crew lifted their tools and slowly dispersed, allowing the final chord to linger in the chamber like a soothing caress upon a weary body.

A mule's low-pitched bray signaled Harry Mannwaring's return. Using mules to pull coal cars along the metal tracks stretching the tunnel's length was another benefit to working the upper Black Diamond mine. Many of the other mines required grueling efforts to push each one-ton coal car by hand.

Three of the crew, Davies, Smith, and James, began the agonizing crawl back into the coal vein. Each dragged a pick as they crept on hands and knees a hundred feet up the thirty-degree angled incline. The two young knobbers followed. Black Diamond's forty-inch thick coal vein allowed the boys to walk stooped over, rather than crawl. As the men chipped away at the coal, the knobbers shoved fragments downward atop oiled iron sheets to a waiting coal car. The knobber's mobility inside the cramped vein was essential to a quick and efficient process.

At the moment, the rest of the crew worked on installing additional support pillars. Several men dug footings for the thick wooden posts, while others hoisted beams overhead. The recent collapse of a small tunnel segment, though minor, had everyone especially nervous. Every miner understood that timber posts would provide little resistance should the tons of shale and sandstone above them give way. Yet, no one thought about it much. Any miner who let the possibility of collapse burden his mind would never set foot underground again.

Work continued this way for the next several hours – picking and pushing coal, loading and transporting cars, and maintaining the precarious subterranean environment – all while the crew inhaled smothering coal dust in barely lit tunnels deep beneath the earth. Today's shift was twelve hours long. The men and boys worked six days a week, breaking only on Sundays and holidays to soak in the light of day. Some had been doing this for more than ten years.

Mannwaring's lamp flickered as he approached again from afar, returning with another empty coal car. He situated the mule at the vein opening, and headed toward Meredith Lewis, the crew supervisor. Mannwaring handed Lewis a piece of paper, heavily smudged with black fingerprints.

"What's this?" asked Lewis.

"Not sure," responded Mannwaring. "Someone gave it to the foreman outside who told me to give it to you."

Lewis unfolded the note and read its contents. "Great," he said sarcastically. "Just what we needed."

Without addressing Mannwaring, Lewis headed toward the vein opening. Looking up into the angled shaft, he paused a moment, waiting for a break in the distant sound of metal picks. Lewis took a deep breath, and shouted, "Thomas, Little Robert, get down here now!" The call summoning the knobbers reverberated off the coal vein walls. Seconds later, Lewis heard the two boys shuffling as they climbed down the shaft.

Sliding out of the vein and hopping off the coal car, the knobbers stared up at Lewis. Their bright white eyes peeked through the black coal dust completely blanketing each boy's face. "Yes, sir?" said Thomas.

"Work's over boys. Something going on at church that they want you for."

The boys looked blankly at each other. "Don't know of anything at church," Thomas stated.

Lewis began shooing the boys toward the mine entrance. "Don't argue. Head home and get cleaned up. I'm sure your parents will let you know what's going on."

Tentatively, Thomas and Little Robert followed the tracks toward the mine entrance. The one thing they hated more than knobbing in the mine was going to church.

Another hour passed. The crew worked steadily, but slower than with the knobbers. Mannwaring returned once more leading the mule and empty car. As he positioned the car, Lewis noticed an odd expression cross Mannwaring's face.

"What's the matter?" asked Lewis.

"Just strange," answered Mannwaring, adjusting his safety lantern to better watch the coal tumbling from the vein.

"How's that?"

"Well," Mannwaring continued. "I swear I smelled something sweet on the way here. Near the chamber."

"Sweet?" Lewis questioned, hoping Mannwaring wasn't dazed from inhaling too much firedamp or blackdamp. Pockets of extremely flammable methane gas called firedamp or areas devoid of oxygen know as blackdamp, could suffocate a man in minutes.

Mannwaring looked toward Lewis and gave him a nod to indicate he felt fine. "Sweet, like honey."

Lewis shook his head. "Sure you did. And did you also smell a plate of fresh-baked biscuits to go with that honey?"

15

The comment hung in the air as Mannwaring considered a response. But there was none.

The first explosion was small. It came from a short distance away, toward the tunnel entrance. Mannwaring's face flushed with terror as the blast echoed down the tunnel cavity. Lewis instinctively shoved Mannwaring behind the coal car and turned toward the rest of the men. "Get down!"

It was too late.

The small amount of firedamp always present in the mines must have ignited. But that wasn't the worst of it. Fine particles of coal dust suspended in the air instantly caught fire, creating a firestorm that blazed through the tunnel in every direction.

Gething, Griffiths, and the others turned away or threw themselves on the ground as flames engulfed the room. The dust explosion reached high into the Black Diamond vein where Davies, Smith, and James lay with their picks, and the Watts brothers, acting as knobbers, hunched down on their knees. The men cringed in fear, utterly helpless.

Like the Red Dragon of Welsh lore, the inferno hissed and clawed at the miners, tearing through clothes and ripping into flesh. Then, in an instant, the beast was gone.

As the Red Dragon escaped Black Diamond Mine's underground confines, left behind was a scorched hollow filled with deadly blackdamp, devoid of light — and life.

Black Diamond Coal Miners [2]

CHAPTER 3

STUDENTS FROM THE BACK ROWS of Harrison's biology class crept toward the front for a better view. Harrison had already performed the demonstration several times during other classes. Now the last period of the day, Harrison hoped to end with an especially big bang.

A lesson on surface area and its importance in biological functions would follow the demonstration in the coming days. For now, Harrison just wanted to introduce the topic in a manner that engaged students' interest.

Harrison poured a small pile of very fine lycopodium powder onto the table top. "Flammable or not?" he asked the class.

None of the students were familiar with the yellow powder, so an array of haphazard guesses followed. "Well," Harrison continued, "only one way to find out."

He placed safety goggles over his eyes as anxious students in the front row leaned back. Dramatically, Harrison touched the powder with a butane lighter flame.

Nothing.

Students groaned, disappointed in the lack of pyrotechnics. Without explaining the result, Harrison continued. He affixed a candle to the table top and lit the wick. He then poured some lycopodium powder into a small funnel attached to the end of a two-foot long rubber tube. He aimed the funnel at the candle and, after a deep breath, blew through the other end of the tube.

The powder shot from the funnel and into the flame, creating an immense fireball. Every student in the first two rows jumped backward, startled by the intense heat and light.

"Whoa!" came the class's choral response, as Harrison expected.

"Cool! Do it again," added several students.

Harrison obliged, carefully watching the clock with one eye. The second fireball blasted from the funnel even bigger than the first.

More "whoas" filtered through the room, along with several "oohs," "cools," "awesomes," and an "excellent" or two.

"Like dragon fire," said a voice from the back.

Harrison smiled at the description, and continued, "So I ask again, flammable or not flammable?" While student hands began shooting up with a response, he added, "And why the difference?"

Most hands dropped with the added burden of explanation.

"That will be for tomorrow's discussion. Bring your thoughts." On cue, the end-of-school bell rang. Students rushed to pack up and exit, totally unaware of the time. Adept at bell to bell instruction, Harrison had mastered provocative endings that left students wanting more, anxious for the next day's follow-up lesson. He knew that some students would discuss the demonstration with friends and parents, while others would search the internet for information, even watching YouTube videos of the activity's many variations. A few students would not indulge their curiosity. These were the ones Harrison would invite the next day to blow the lid off a gallon paint can by confining the explosive reaction within.

Eventually, students would thoroughly understand the significance of increased surface area relative to combustion. Separating the lycopodium into particles that flew through the air allowed more oxygen to contact each piece. When one particle ignited, a chain reaction was created resulting in the fireball. The

19

same phenomenon explained kindling is used to start a fire, why dust-filled grain silos can explode, and ultimately why people chew their food.

An hour later, after cleaning up the lycopodium demo and finishing tomorrow's lesson preparation, Harrison walked a few doors down the hall to see his good friend and colleague, Jim Schumacher. As a fellow science teacher, the older, and in Harrison's opinion, much wiser, Schumacher was an invaluable mentor. Schu offered unpretentious advice on everything from improving instructional strategies to dealing with student behavior and handling parent complaints. The gentle guidance was often peppered with folksy adages and quotes from the likes of Nietzsche or Dr. Seuss. It wasn't long before Harrison realized that Schumacher's counsel was as applicable to life as it was to the classroom. Today, however, Harrison did not seek guidance. He simply needed a yes or no answer.

"Hey, Schu," Harrison began as he entered Schumacher's chemistry room.

"Hi, there," replied Schumacher with his usual energetic smile. "What's up?"

"Got a minute?"

Schumacher logged off the computer where he was entering grades and turned toward Harrison, "Of course."

Harrison felt uncharacteristically apprehensive. He had thought long and hard about what he was going to say, and he knew what Schu's response would be. Still, the question created a nervous anticipation.

Harrison leaned against the counter a few feet from Schu's desk. "So, Celeste and I have been talking a lot about wedding plans."

Schumacher's eyes instantly widened. He was thrilled at Harrison's engagement and had been enthusiastically waiting to hear details. "Excellent," Schumacher replied with a huge smile. "Do tell. When, where?"

"Actually, we don't have all those details yet," Harrison said. "We're trying to decide on whether we want a big ceremony or small, in a church or not … that sort of thing."

"Sounds like a good start," said Schumacher, hiding his slight disappointment at the lack of details.

"Yeah, a lot of specifics to work out still. The one thing we know is that we don't want to wait too long, so we are thinking of this summer."

"Yes!" responded Schumacher, throwing his hands up with giddy excitement. "I am so happy for you."

"Thanks, Schu. And that's what I wanted to talk to you about. Though I don't know exactly when, or where, or what kind of ceremony, I do know one thing." Harrison paused. A sudden lump formed in his throat, and he swallowed hard. "For the past fifteen years, you have not only been an amazing mentor, but an incredible friend. I have no doubt that without your support I would not be where I am, either professionally, or personally.   So …"

Harrison paused again. He lifted his head to look at Schumacher eye-to-eye. "I was wondering if …"

Schumacher fixed on Harrison's gaze, listening intently to his friend.

"You would consider …"

Harrison swallowed hard again and quickly said, "…being my best man?"

Schumacher did not respond. He simply got up from his chair, walked over to Harrison, and gave him a big hug. Schumacher was renowned with the Brentwood High teaching staff for his hugs, not just because he gave them, but because

21

they were deeply sincere and heartfelt. That's how this hug felt, though perhaps even more than usual.

After a quiet moment, Schumacher released. A grin stretched across his face, broader than ever, and he responded, "Absolutely!"

The men talked for a while longer before Harrison excused himself to allow Schumacher to finish his work. As he left the chemistry room, Harrison realized a huge grin now stretched across his face, even bigger than Schu's.

A familiar vibration rattled Harrison's pocket. He pulled out his cell phone and immediately recognized Celeste's number. The text simply read, *See me ASAP.*

Harrison already planned to stop by Celeste's classroom before heading home for the evening, as he did every day. They stayed together on weekends, but usually spent weeknights at their respective homes. Gradually, Celeste moved belongings into Harrison's house where they planned to live once married. Celeste's house would be rented out, possibly to a couple of rookie teachers who had already inquired once they heard news of the engagement.

Seeing Celeste's text requesting him to come as soon as possible made Harrison both curious and nervous. She knew he was coming over shortly, so why the need to see him now? Was she alright?

Brushing speculations from his mind, Harrison quickly slid papers to grade into his messenger bag. He headed out the door and sped across campus to Celeste's classroom. "Everything okay?" he said, slightly winded from the quick pace.

"Yes, yes. Fine."

Celeste's half-smile and subdued tone indicated that her answer was not entirely accurate. Harrison understood her facial and vocal expressions better than he did his own. After years as friends, and more recently lovers, Harrison was a master in discerning Celeste's state of mind. He realized that he began studying her from the very first time they met, paying attention to the nuances of her voice, the subtle gestures of her hands, and the expressive gaze of her eyes.

During a recent fishing trip with Schumacher, Harrison remembered describing his relationship with Celeste as harmonious. Life together felt like a perfect chord, resonating with love. The slightest dissonance was discernable, but a slight tuning by one or both of them always restored harmony.

Celeste's current discord was noticeable but, to Harrison's relief, did not seem serious. He waited for Celeste to form her thoughts.

"Detective Lawlor just left," she said with some unease.

The comment caught Harrison completely off guard. His mind quickly flashed back to the last time the Brentwood Police Detective came to Celeste's classroom. Her translation of a message found on a mummified corpse led to their most recent adventure together. Could the detective need another translation? It seemed unlikely, but Harrison's pulse suddenly quicken.

"And …?" Harrison prodded.

Celeste, still half lost in thought, responded. "The detective is investigating a murder that happened last night."

A wave of concern washed over Harrison. "Was it someone you knew?"

"No, no. Nothing like that."

"Phew," responded Harrison. "That's good. Well … I mean … not for the victim …but good …well, you know what I mean."

Harrison's awkward comment seemed to refocus Celeste. "Sit down a minute and I'll tell you what Detective Lawlor told me."

They slid two student desks next to each other and sat. Harrison listened intently as Celeste recounted Lawlor's story. "Apparently," she started. "Someone was killed out in Antioch, up at the Black Diamond Mines Regional Park. You know that place, right?"

"Of course," Harrison answered. "Been there many times."

"Two teenagers witnessed the murder, however, in the darkness, they could not see the perpetrator."

The story intrigued and confused Harrison. "So, what does this have to do with you?"

"Well, the murder actually happened in the Rose Hill Cemetery. Do you know it?" Celeste asked.

"I know of it, but not much more. It's where the miners and their families are buried, I think."

"I guess," said Celeste. "I'm not familiar with it, which is what makes the rest of the story so strange."

Harrison now slid so close to Celeste's desk that he was barely in his chair. "Go on ..."

"Just before the victim died, he managed to crawl over to a headstone and write something with his own blood."

"And . . . what did it say?" said an astonished Harrison.

Celeste handed Harrison a folded paper given to her by Lawlor. Harrison unfolded the note and read it aloud. "Madog near. Warn Celeste Scott."

The message sent a chill racing through Harrison. "What is that supposed to mean?"

"No idea," answered Celeste.

"Could be a coincidence," added Harrison incredulously.

"Could be."

"Well, no need to worry. I'm sure there's a simple explanation having nothing to do with you."

24

"Yeah, you're probably right."

Harrison took Celeste's hand, understanding that the message clearly shook her. She squeezed his hand and smiled.

"There was one other odd thing, though," said Celeste.

Harrison swallowed hard.

"The man who was murdered ... who wrote that strange message on a tombstone as his final words on earth ..."

"Yes?

Celeste furrowed her brow, drifting into her own thoughts again. "He's from Wales."

CHAPTER IV

July 26, 1876

"HERE ARE A FEW MORE CANDLES I made last night."

"Thank you, Ann," said Sarah Norton. She took half of the bee's wax candles and the two women added their lights to the dozen nearly-spent tapers scattered throughout the room. With the morning sun peeking through cracked window shutters, the candles' orange glow and sweet smell filled the space with soothing warmth.

White curtains draped the walls and mirror inside George Reynold's small house. Another Nortonville woman busily set out mugs and plates and added water to a vase of fresh-cut flowers. In the kitchen, several other neighbors mixed flour, eggs, and butter, while sprinkling in nutmeg, almonds, raisins, and other candied fruit. A nearby wood stove radiated intense heat in preparation for baking.

The women continued with their tasks in earnest. They spoke quietly as they scurried about. Not once, however, in the cramped confines of the Reynold's home, did any of them look at the large table situated in the exact center of the main room. Resting upon the table lay an open wooden coffin displaying the body of George Reynolds.

Though Reynolds was not as badly burned as some of the other miners, seared flesh on his face and hands was easily visible. His body had been washed and dressed in his only suit, the one he wore to Sunday church. He was then placed upon the table for viewing by friends and neighbors who visited the home over the past day and a half. Mourners now had one last opportunity to

26

pay their respects before the funeral later in the day. Cake and spiced wine would greet them as they shared stories and offered solemn condolences to the family.

Tragically, this scene was repeated all over Nortonville — in five other homes today and in three more tomorrow. Six miners died immediately from the blast - William Gething, George Reynolds, David Griffiths, Theophilus Watts, Meredith Lewis, and William Williams – either by fire, by suffocation, or both. Three others lingered for a day before succumbing - Theophile Dumas, David Watts, and Thomas James. Evan Smith and Evan Davies were both badly burned. Smith would likely not last much longer. Watkins Williams, Harry Mannwaring, and Marengo managed to escape with less severe injuries Mannwaring knew that his life was spared by Meredith Lewis's quick actions. And he made sure the town knew, too. Fortunately — miraculously some said — the two knobber boys had left the mine just minutes before the explosion.

Nortonville citizens were accustomed to death. Loss of human life swept through the town as regularly as the delta breeze. Mining accidents and occasional mishaps with surface machinery took an especially hard toll on the men. Much more common, though, were waves of illness whose typical victims were the youngest Nortonville residents. Small pox, scarlet fever, and diphtheria resulted in heartbreaking child and infant deaths. It was not uncommon for one family to lose two or three children from an outbreak.

While a single unfortunate death unsettled tightknit community members, the magnitude of so much loss all at once devastated them. During the next two days, residents would attend nine separate wakes, carry nine separate coffins to the cemetery hill, and bear witness at nine separate funerals. Sorrow draped the town like the mourning cloth on George Reynold's mirror.

"How are they doing?" Ann whispered to Sarah.

Sarah glanced into the bedroom where Reynolds' wife and three young children sat on the bed. The oldest daughter slowly brushed her little sister's hair while their mother straightened a slightly oversized suit borrowed for their brother. The boy fidgeted continuously and tugged on each sister's white dress until they squealed. Reynolds' wife, clad in black crepe, gently reprimanded the boy. She no longer tried to hide her red, weeping eyes from the children. Soon grieving guests would arrive and unrelenting tears would flow.

"As well as can be expected," answered Sarah in her normal, pragmatic tone. "How are the others doing?"

Ann delivered candles to the other wakes before arriving at the Reynolds' that morning. Four of the miners lived in single-family homes, while the rest stayed at two different boarding houses. The miners' corpses now lay in various parts of town awaiting a last viewing and slow procession to their final resting place.

"As you said," replied Ann, "as well as can be expected."

"Did you see any of the Cambrian Mutual Aid Society at Griffiths' house? They were the last of the coffin-bearers to arrive."

Ann nodded. "Yes, Abel Vaughn and Hugh Jones were there. They said the others were on the way."

Sarah turned toward the kitchen. "Ladies, I'll be back. It will be a few hours by the time we are finished with services for Mr. Griffiths and the others. Keep the candles burning and mind the rising sun. No light on the body."

To some, Sarah's matter-of-fact attitude in such somber circumstances appeared callous. To all in Nortonville who knew her, however, hers was a calming, welcoming manner. Widow of the town's founder, the sixty-five year old Sarah Norton was deeply respected. For the past decade, she served as midwife to Nortonville and the surrounding towns, traveling as far as Clayton, a seven mile journey to the west, to birth babies. Of the hundreds of newborns Sarah had delivered, word was that not one was lost during childbirth.

The staunchly independent and practical Sarah was highly regarded not just for her medical skills, but also for her ability to organize and influence the Nortonville people. When Sarah talked, the town listened.

As expected, during the past twenty-four hours of misery, Sarah took over coordinating the multiple wakes and services. She dispersed neighbors to the widows and children first, then to the single men, ensuring each body was properly prepared, food and drink were well-stocked, and all manner of religious customs attended to, even though she, herself, was not at all religious.

She coordinated processions to the cemetery with the community's various fraternal orders. In Welsh tradition, only men went to the cemetery. Women and children watched the coffins carried through the streets, but did not make the trek out of town. Sarah even orchestrated arrangements for Reverend Parry so the many services over the next two days would not overwhelm the elderly minister.

Outside the Reynolds house, Sarah untied the horse and climbed into her buggy. With a deep sigh, she spoke softly to her horse. "Steady now, Mabel. It is going to be a long, sad day." She gave the horse a gentle tap of the riding crop and headed off toward David Griffiths' home.

THOMAS OLIVER SLOWLY WALKED across the boarding house room toward the window. Creaking wooden floorboards announced his entrance in the dimly lit space.

"It's alright," said Evan Davies from his bed. "I'm awake."

Though he survived the mine explosion, thirty-year old Davies was badly injured. Burns covered much of his face, chest, and hands. Doctors from nearby Somersville and further down the hill in Antioch, arrived to assess and treat his wounds. The Somersville physician spread a layer of honey onto the damaged skin before loosely wrapping the wound with cloth bandages.

Outside, the setting sun dipped behind Mount Diablo, leaving a fiery-orange sky. Oliver lit a kerosene lantern, set it by the bed, and slid a chair next to Davies. "How are you, my friend?"

Davies grimaced with pain as he struggled to sit up. Oliver propped pillows under his head and back and straightened the blanket. "I am ..." Davies paused, staring down at his bandaged hands. "... alive."

"Thankfully, the good Lord spared you," responded Oliver.

"Yes," said Davies. He looked up at Oliver. The agony of talking was evident in Davies' face, but he appreciated the company. "How were the services?"

"All quite nice. The weather was calm and clear, though a bit warm. Reverend Parry did a fine job reflecting on each man. His words brought much needed perspective to such a horrible calamity. God's will is often difficult to understand."

Davies looked down again at his hands. "Yes, difficult. And the families? How are they?"

"Mrs. Norton is making sure they are all cared for, especially the children. Soon we will meet with the lodges to discuss additional support."

"Yes, yes," said Davies, wincing with each word. "I want to help however I can. I ... I should have died, too."

Oliver gently put his hand on Davies' shoulder. "Nonsense. God has other plans for you. Soon you will heal, and you will see."

The words did not comfort Davies. He turned again toward Oliver. "Gething and Reynolds. We must do something for their headstones."

"Yes," Oliver responded. "I am meeting with the stone-carver, Pioneer Steam Marble Works, in San Francisco next week to make arrangements."

"And the symbol? It will be included?"

Oliver removed a small white cloth from his breast pocket. He unfolded it, displaying an embroidered image — a knight's helmet sitting atop a shield with crossed battle axes. The shield contained the letters F, C, and B. Davies reached out a bandaged hand and ran an exposed finger across the raised thread.

"Of course," replied Oliver. "Of course."

THE NORTONVILLE DISASTER

The terrible disaster at Nortonville Monday afternoon is the most fatal and distressing that has ever been experienced here in mining operations always subject to great hazards. Up to this writing seven deaths have resulted from the disaster, and it is feared that one or two more may occur. Among those killed were several men of family, and who were among the most useful and highly respected members of the community in which they lived. A correspondent writing the morning after the sad occurence indicates the anxiety and distress which the first rumors of the disaster occasioned among those who had fathers, husbands, brothers or friends in the mine. He writes: "About 3 o'clock P.M. of Monday, July 24th, rumors of a terrible catastrophe spread through the village. Crowds began to gather around the mines, very anxious to know what the matter was. Women — wives and mothers — anxious for their loved ones, children trembling for the safety of their fathers, friends in fearful suspense for friends, thronged the approaches to the mines. The suspense was not long. It was broken by a terrible revelation. No less than six dead bodies were brought up from the mines in the course of an hour or two, together with eight persons more or less severely injured. The cause of the accident was a powder explosion, let off in the ordinary operation of mining, and that igniting sulphur gas and raising large volumes of what the miners call black damp or fine coal dust. Those who were brought up dead were smothered by the black damp — their death was almost instantaneous. Most of those who survived have been terribly scorched by the fire, and are understood as being in a very critical condition."

Contra Costa Gazette, July 29, 1876 [3]

32

CHAPTER 5

HARRISON RELEASED CELESTE'S HAND to place both of his on the steering wheel. "Road gets a little curvy up here."

A strong winter breeze buffeted the car on a cool, clear morning. Green grass-covered hills rose and fell, reaching higher as Harrison and Celeste made their way toward Black Diamond Mines Regional Preserve. Huge oak trees dotted the landscape, each mass of twisting branches a unique work of art.

"So beautiful out here," said Celeste. I love how green everything is this time of year."

"Me, too," Harrison replied. "Enjoy it while it lasts, though. Another month or two and the green will fade back to dry golden-brown. We'll have to come back out here in the spring. I know how you love wildflowers; and since we got some decent rainfall this winter, the display should be spectacular."

"That sounds great. Is the park much further?" added Celeste.

"Nope. There's the main gate. That building on the left is one of the visitor's centers, but I thought we would go straight to the other one. You'll see why when we get there."

Harrison soon reached the road's end and turned into a gravel parking lot. He and Celeste pulled on coats and wool hats and began trekking toward the second visitor center. They followed the gradual ascent of a well-worn trail into the hills.

After a short walk, Celeste paused. "Uh, are you sure you know where you're going? I don't see any buildings."

"Nor will you," said Harrison with a smile. He took Celeste by the hand and led her to an angled concrete wall that fronted a steep slope. A large arched doorway opened through the wall's center panel. Open metal doors stood as sentries, inviting guests to enter. Bold letters atop the doorway read, Greathouse Portal.

"Greathouse Portal?" asked Celeste.

"Right. It is a portal into the Greathouse Visitor Center," Harrison responded.

"Underground?"

"Correct."

"Cool," said Celeste, now leading Harrison by the hand through the portal. "Is there actually a great house inside?"

"Yes and no. There is a great room, but that's not the reason for the name. R. Marvin Greathouse was the first owner of the sand mine."

The portal opened into a long, narrow tunnel lit only by strings of small lights hanging overhead. Both teachers succumbed to an unmistakable perception of stepping from present to past as they traversed the underground corridor.

Celeste's hand ran along the gray concrete-reinforced wall as they progressed. "Hey, I just realized you said that Greathouse owned a sand mine. I thought Black Diamond was a coal mine."

"It was a coal mine. They stopped mining coal in about 1920, and Greathouse began mining sand for making glass. Apparently, this sand has high silica content, which makes for good glass."

"I see," said Celeste. "And how do you remember all this?"

Harrison stopped, now at the end of the tunnel. "I'd like to say that I remembered it all from previous visits, but to be honest, I looked it up last night."

He knew that Celeste heard him, but she did not respond. Her mouth froze agape as she stared into the sprawling underground chamber before her. "Awesome!"

Carved out of solid rock, the huge room opened two-stories high and nearly two-hundred feet long. Feathery bands of rust-colored minerals weaved through light-gray sandstone. Sparkling flecks of quartz saturated the walls, highlighting the coveted silica mineral's abundance. Black splotches peppered the arched ceiling, a remnant of pre-park days when bonfires burned in the chamber warming all manner of teenager and transient.

Harrison and Celeste toured the exhibits. Interpretive panels explained both the area's geologic and human history. Quaint displays housed inside vintage wooden cabinets and cases held artifacts from days gone by – historic photographs, mining tools for both coal and sand, and various nineteenth-century household objects commonly used when the towns thrived. One showcase contained crystal clear honey and vinegar glass jars, manufactured from the local sand.

For the next hour, the two studied the exhibits inside the Greathouse Visitor Center. As they perused the requisite gift shop, they were suddenly interrupted. "Harrison, Celeste ..."

The familiar voice surprised them. Harrison spun around to see his old friend, Richard Dix, the East Bay Regional Park District ranger. Celeste met him while touring nearby Vasco Caves two years ago. He was also the ranger that guided her and the police to save Harrison during their John Marsh gold adventure.

"Rick," said Harrison with a big grin. "Long time, no see." Harrison reached for a handshake.

"It's been a while," Rick replied. He bent his lanky six-foot four-inch frame down to give Celeste a hug. "It is great to see you guys, and congratulations. I haven't seen you since I heard about your engagement."

"Thanks," said Celeste. "It is always great to see you, too. I hope everything is going well."

"Yup, all good."

"Hey … ," Harrison began. "I didn't know you worked this park."

Rick tucked a pen into his olive green park district shirt pocket. "Not usually. But I'm doing a special tour for a Boy Scout troop since the regular ranger is on vacation. We'll meet here for a bit, and then I'll lead them on the Hazel-Atlas mine tour."

"Hazel-Atlas mine tour?" asked Celeste.

"Sure. Back outside and around the corner is the portal to the Hazel-Atlas sand mine. This room is actually part of that mining operation. I'm sure Harrison has been on the tour, but if you have not, Celeste, I encourage you to go. I know you'd enjoy it," said Rick.

"I have," responded Harrison. "A couple times. Really interesting. You get a hardhat and a flashlight and learn about the history and geology of the area while getting a sense of what underground mining life was like."

"How far down does it go?" Celeste asked.

Harrison referred to Rick. "About a quarter-mile walk. Mostly level until you descend a very long flight of stairs that leads back to this visitor center." Rick explained. "You two are welcome to join my tour today, if you like."

Celeste glanced at Harrison and then back at Rick. "That sounds incredible, but we actually have another reason for being out here today."

"Did you hear about the guy murdered at the cemetery last week?" asked Harrison.

"Of course," said Rick, looking slightly perplexed at the question. "That was big news in the park district. But that didn't have anything to do with either of you, did it?"

"That's what we're trying to find out," continued Harrison. "Do you know about the writing on the headstone?"

"I do not. We did not get much detail, other than someone was murdered. Stabbed, I think. What writing?"

"Before he died, the guy managed to write with his own blood, 'Madog near. Warn Celeste Scott.'" Harrison gently squeezed Celeste's hand, knowing how much the message disturbed her.

"Oh my, gosh," said Rick, looking at Celeste with sincere concern. "Any idea what that means?"

"No, none," said Celeste. "But I wanted to take a look at the cemetery anyway."

"How bizarre," said Rick. "I can tell you, there are no mad dogs out here. Some coyotes, a few foxes, but no dogs."

"I figured," said Harrison. "But it's worth a look."

Rick checked his watch. "You can't argue with that. It has been great to see you guys, but I better get going to meet the scouts. Let me know if you want that mine tour some other time."

"Will do," said Harrison. "Take care." He shook Rick's hand and Celeste gave another hug. The two then headed back through the tunnel, out the Greathouse Portal, and into the open air.

"Wow, the wind is really blowing," exclaimed Celeste.

Harrison pulled his hat tighter onto his head. "Yeah, that's pretty common here. The weather comes off the ocean in the west and funnels through the delta, so these hills can get breezy. Are you warm enough?"

"I'm fine. Which way to the cemetery?"

"This way." Harrison took Celeste's hand. "It's not too far."

They walked along the dirt trail leading to Rose Hill Cemetery. From the Greathouse Portal, the path meandered down a steep hillside and headed back up another. Halfway up the hill, Celeste suddenly stopped.

"Are you okay?" Harrison asked. "Need to take a rest?"

Celeste looked anxious. "It's not that. Something just doesn't feel right. How far to the cemetery?"

"It's close, just at the top of this ridge."

Celeste took a deep breath and continued. As the trail crested the hill, the scattered Rose Hill Cemetery headstones and memorials came into view. A small sign denoted the cemetery, and a modest wire fence marked its boundaries. Harrison led Celeste toward strips of yellow caution tape wrapped around grave markers further inside the burial ground. He noticed her tightened grip and heavier breathing and knew she was still struggling.

"I assume that is the crime scene over there. Looks like the police still have it taped off," said Harrison.

"Detective Lawlor said the writing on the headstone would be here for just one or two more days while they investigate and then they'll clean it off. That's why we needed to get out here quickly," added Celeste.

The couple wound their way through grave markers, some standing upright, others lying cracked or broken on the ground. Celeste's anxiety grew with each step. She glanced at passing epitaphs.

Mary
Wife of
David Powel
Died
April 7, 1878
Aged 60 yrs.
Gone but not forgotten

Julia Etta
Daughter of
John H. & Julia Piercy
Died Dec. 7, 1870
Aged 2 years 11 Mo's & 8 days
Too sweet a flower to bloom on Earth
She is gone to bloom in Heaven

Katie
Dau. Of
J. & B. Aitken,
Died
Dec. 24, 1879
Aged
8 yrs. 4 ms. 12 ds.
Weep not Father and Mother for me
For I am waiting in glory for thee

Celeste could not understand why she felt so uneasy.
Nervous pressure knotted her stomach. Her breathing grew rapid
and shallow.

Now steps away from the taped-off headstone, Celeste
suddenly spun around.

"What was that?" she exclaimed.

Her unexpected comment startled Harrison. "What? What is it?"

She paused, looking around and behind. "I thought I saw ... nothing. It's nothing."

To Harrison, Celeste almost seemed afraid. But afraid of what?

Celeste took a few more steps, and then stopped. She leaned in toward Harrison. "I ... I can't go any further. I'm sorry. I don't know what's the matter with me, but this place is creeping me out. Can we leave? Can we leave now?"

Harrison wrapped his arm around Celeste and pulled her close. He had never seen her like this. The tension in her voice was palpable, and worry hit him like a bucket of cold water. "Yes, of course . . . of course."

He immediately turned and led her out of the cemetery and back onto the trail. The stiff wind blew colder as they walked quickly toward the parking lot. Harrison's mind raced. What just happened? Is she going to be okay? How can I help her? Confused and concerned, Harrison focused on just one thing – getting her out of here . . . now.

CHAPTER VI

December 23, 1876

Evan Davies expected the knock on his bedroom door inside the Main Street boarding house.

"Come in, Ann."

Following the horrendous mine disaster five months ago, Ann helped tend to Davies. At first, she treated wounds and brought meals. Then, as he healed, she stopped by with tea on Saturdays and the two chatted to pass the time. Davies was not been able to work since the accident, so he appreciated Ann's company. She not only comforted him with conversation, but asked endless questions about his life, providing an intimate connection absent since coming to Nortonville.

She queried Davies about his family back in Wales, his plans to return to work after the New Year, and about his participation in a fraternal order – the Knights of Pythias, whose lodge members collected donations to help bury deceased members and support the injured. Ann moved to Nortonville just six months ago to set up a candle-making shop. Though Davies did not know her before the incident, she now knew him better than anyone he had met in America.

Ann entered Davies' room carrying a teapot and single cup and saucer. As always, she wore a blue button-down, ankle-length dress. She, like most Nortonville women, owned just two dresses – a simple one for everyday use and a fancier, heavily pleated one for church. Over the months, Davies grew fond of that blue dress. Each time she entered, it was as if a bright, cloudless sky poured into his room. Accompanying the uplifting vision was always the sweetest of aromas. Davies could not be sure if Ann added a touch of perfume before visiting, or whether the scent came from her work handling beeswax candles and associated honey. It did not matter.

"Just one cup?" said Davies. "Won't you be joining me?"

Ann set the saucer and cup on the side table and began pouring the tea. "I can't today. I'm sorry. I have so much to do before Christmas service on Monday. I have only finished making half of the candles needed for the *Plygain*. Will you be joining them?"

Davies considered participating in the traditional church caroling at 3:00 a.m. Christmas Day, but the thought of singing with the Welsh Men's Choir without his friends, Thomas James and the Watt's brothers, was more than he could bear at this time. "No, I don't think so," he replied.

"I understand," said Ann. She smiled and handed him the tea. "It is a bittersweet occasion. This *Nadolig* we celebrate the birth of Our Savior while still mourning the death of our loved ones."

"How are the other *Nadolig* festivities coming along?" asked Davies, hoping Ann would stay a bit longer.

"Quite nicely. Sarah Norton sent some of the knobbers climbing into the nearby oak trees to gather mistletoe and they returned with loads. Enough for the whole town and then some. Mistletoe and holly decorate nearly every home and business on Main Street."

Ann previously offered to decorate Davies' room, but he declined. The vision of seeing her fair skin, long blonde hair, and warm brown eyes standing beneath a mistletoe sprig would make it far too tempting to resist stealing a kiss, and revealing his unspoken affection. But how could she ever love him? Each time he glimpsed his reflection in a mirror, he saw the grotesquely scarred face of the man he had become. How could any woman ever love him?

The morning sun now engulfed Mt. Diablo and the foothills to the west. Ann pulled open the curtains to better capture any warmth able to penetrate the small boarding room window. "Many of the women are also preparing for *Noson Gyflaith*," she continued.

For the first time in weeks, she noticed Davies' smile. "My favorite tradition," he said. "As a child I fondly remember spending hours the evening before *Nadolig* making toffee and playing games with my mother and sisters."

"As do I," said Ann. "I loved mixing the brown sugar, butter, and water, and watching it boil. We added lemon before pulling. How about you?"

"Usually peppermint oil," said Davies.

"Sounds wonderful. While I never got as good as my mother at pulling and twisting, my toffee still tasted delicious."

Davies' smile broadened at the reminiscence until the stretched scars prevented further physical or emotional expression.

"And guess who will carry the *Mari Lwyd* this New Year's Day?" Ann asked.

Davies pictured in his mind the traditional *Mari Lwyd*, a horse's skull with false eyes and ears, decorated with ribbons and bells, and mounted on a pole. Carrying the skull and draped in a white sheet, the *Mari Lwyd* and his merry band travelled the town knocking on doors. When someone answered, a member of the group began a Welsh poetic verse or insult, whichever they felt most appropriate for the residents. Someone inside would then respond in verse or insult. This battle of words continued back-and-forth until a winner was declared. If the *Mari Lwyd* was deemed victorious, the group would be invited inside to eat, drink, and sing before heading off to the next encounter. Last New Year's visit by the *Mari Lwyd* to the boarding house was still a vivid memory for Davies. The resulting joyful drunkenness as he joined the party on its subsequent travels through town was the most fun he had in America.

"I'm sure I do not know," Davies finally replied.

"Thomas Oliver, from your lodge."

"Is that so? He did not tell me. He will make a fine *Mari Lwyd*."

The smile quickly faded from Davies. He touched his scarred face and turned away from Ann.

"You know," said Ann. "You really should get out today. A group is heading into San Francisco this morning. It is a beautiful, clear day out. A bit cold, but very pleasant. You should join them. The Black Diamond Railroad is making a special trip for the passengers from here down to the wharf at New York Landing. They are catching a steamer from there."

"Do you know how many people are going?"

"I heard fifteen to twenty. But I believe Stewartville and Somersville residents are also going. Stewartville is taking the Empire Railroad into Antioch and Somersville is catching the Pittsburg Railroad down to Pittsburg Landing. The steamer is picking them all up, so it should be a fun outing."

Davies stared out the window. The thought of crowds made him nauseous. So many people gawking at him, pointing and whispering about the man with the burned face, would not make an enjoyable outing.

"No," he said softly. "Thank you for letting me know, but no."

Ann gently patted him on the arm. "Drink your tea, you'll feel better."

44

Davies sat in the only chair in his sparsely furnished room and took a sip. "Tastes a bit different," he noted.

"Yes," said Ann. "Made with Toyon berries. I thought you might enjoy a change. Do you like it?"

"Delicious," responded Davies. "Toyon berries?"

"Sorry, that's what Dr. Clement calls them. It is the plant that we use for holly this time of year. Not shiny English holly like we had back in Wales, but Toyon is a very good substitute. You see the shrub growing all over the hills out here, with its berries turning bright red in the winter. Some of the others call it Christmas berry."

"Thank you, Ann. As always, I appreciate your kindness."

"Sunday mass tomorrow and Christmas service the following day. Will I see you there?"

"Yes, of course," said Davies.

"Until then," said Ann. She quietly shut the door behind her as she left Davies' room. He sat in silence, gazing out the window and sipping the Toyon berry tea.

"SO WHAT DID YOU LIKE BEST?" Thomas Oliver asked Harry Mannwaring.

"The Palace Hotel. An astounding place. Though, I could never afford to stay there, it was quite remarkable to visit. I have never before seen such luxury. That seven-story tall Grand Court with its carriage entrance, palm trees, statues, fountains, and glass ceiling was spectacular," responded Mannwaring.

"And the Christmas decorations made it all the more beautiful. Very majestic. I understand that it opened just last year, but already appears quite popular," added Oliver.

The two men, along with a dozen other Nortonville residents, stepped off the steamer *Parthenius*, and onto the New

45

York Landing wharf. Having just returned from their San Francisco outing, the group headed toward the waiting Black Diamond Railroad passenger car. The sun dipped behind Mt. Diablo, so the engineer and brakeman carried lanterns, guiding the way through the twilight.

Unburdened by heavy coal cars, the steam train quickly traversed the nearly six-mile track into the Nortonville foothills. The travelers, excited and exhausted from the trip, disembarked and headed their separate ways.

"Thought I would get a drink," said Mannwaring. "Care to join me?"

"Perhaps in a bit," Oliver answered. "I want to check on Davies. Maybe I can get him to come with."

The men shuffled along the compact dirt of Main Street until Mannwaring veered off toward the saloon. Oliver continued to the boarding house.

"Evening, Mrs. Dawkins," said Oliver, as the outer door opened to his knock.

"Good evening, Mr. Oliver. Come in. How are you today?" Mrs. Dawkins asked.

"Excellent. Just returning from San Francisco."

Blanche Dawkins, a stocky, middle-aged woman with weathered skin and tight hair bun, ran the Main Street boarding house in Nortonville for the past decade. The first few years she assisted her husband. After he died in a horse-riding accident, she continued by herself, hiring extra help only when essential. As much as she would like to see San Francisco, she never seemed to find the time to visit. "How exciting. I bet it was wonderful."

Oliver removed his hat and hooked it on the rack. "Yes, incredible. You really need to visit one day. The buildings are astounding. Even the hills are impressive."

"I would like to. As soon as I find someone to run this place when I'm out," she added. "You'll have to excuse me. I am just cleaning up the kitchen. A bit of *cawl* left if you'd like."

The aroma of traditional Welsh mutton stew hung thick in the air. If Oliver had not stuffed himself with bread he picked up at the wharf, he would surely take Mrs. Dawkins up on her offer. "No, thank you. Just came to check on Evan. How is he doing today?"

Mrs. Dawkins shook her head. "Haven't seen him today. Did not join us for lunch or supper. Not sure if he's in his room or not."

"Well, I'll just look in on him. Thank you," said Oliver. He bounded up the stairs and knocked on the closed bedroom door.

No answer.

Oliver knocked again. "Davies, it's me. You in there?"

He opened the door and stepped into the dark room. Oliver could see Davies' silhouette stretched out face-down on the bed. "Hey, Davies. Wake up."

Oliver lit the room's kerosene lantern and propped it on the side table. "Davies, wake up!" Oliver shouted.

Davies did not move.

"The bloke is good and corned," Oliver said to himself. "Probably drinking all day."

Oliver scanned the room for whiskey bottles, but saw only an empty teapot. He shook Davies. "Hey, wake up. You're missing out on supper."

Davies did not move.

Deep concern engulfed Oliver. He grabbed Davies' shoulder and slowly rolled him over. Illuminated by the flickering lantern, Davies' scarred face startled Oliver. His skin was ashen gray and his eyes stared lifelessly toward the ceiling. Oliver gently touched his friend's ice cold skin. Oliver knew instantly that Evan Davies was dead.

Nortonville, California. [4]

CHAPTER 7

HARRISON'S MONDAY AFTERNOON class finished a few minutes earlier than expected, so he used these rare extra moments to build personal connections with his students. This most often involved discussion about recent sporting events, movies, or weekend outings. Harrison made mental notes about his students' interests and shared his own personal stories as well. Helping students see their teacher as a regular person and relating to them beyond academics were both enjoyable and essential to forming the trust necessary to meet each student's needs, particularly those who struggled.

After ensuring the room was straightened up, Harrison addressed the class: "Alright, we have a few minutes before the bell. Who's got a story from last weekend?"

A few hands shot up. Harrison immediately selected a typically quiet student from the group. "Anthony, do tell."

"I won my division in a wrestling tournament on Saturday," said Anthony.

"Outstanding," replied Harrison. He lifted his hands to clap, but the class had already burst into applause for the soft-spoken student.

"He was a beast," added a wrestling teammate. "He's pretty quiet in class, but on the mat ... he's an animal."

The comment brought a round of laughter and smiles from the class, as Anthony's face reddened with embarrassment.

"Well, congratulations, Anthony. I'll be sure to make it to your next meet," said Harrison.

"How about you, Mr. Barrett? Do anything exciting last weekend?" asked a girl in the front.

49

"Actually, I did. I took a hike at Black Diamond Regional Park over in Antioch with Ms. Scott."

By now, there was not a student on campus unaware of Mr. Barrett and Ms. Scott's engagement. News about the school's most popular teachers getting married spread through social media like a coal dust explosion. Thankfully, this meant that neither Harrison nor Celeste felt they needed to continue with their previous discretion.

"Any of you ever been there?" Harrison added. A third of the class raised their hand. "The cave is pretty cool," said one student.

"You mean the mine," he was corrected by another. "Whatever. It was cool."

"I camped there a couple times for a summer program I used to do," added a third student.

"Did you see the White Witch?" asked the girl in front. The student did not seem surprised by the question. "No, but one of the other guys swore he did. Freaked him out."

"The White Witch?" interrupted Harrison.

"Yeah, the White Witch that haunts the cemetery there," the student replied.

Harrison turned to the class: "Anyone else heard of the White Witch?"

Several student hands lifted. "If you ever lived in Antioch or Pittsburg, you know about the White Witch," one student said. "My mom grew up in Antioch and said she knew the place was haunted even when she was a kid."

"Really …" said Harrison. "What do you know about this witch?"

The student continued. "My mom said that the White Witch is the ghost of Sarah Norton, who lived there back in the

50

day. I think she was killed somehow and now haunts the cemetery and the mines."

"My grandpa grew up Pittsburg," added the girl in the front. "He said he saw the White Witch more than once when he was young. Teenagers used to hang out and party at the mines before it became a park."

"Your grandfather actually saw a ghost up there?" came the voice of a skeptic from the back. "So what did it look like?"

The girl in the front spun around to reply directly to the inquest. "He said it was a white, glowing woman who sometimes hovered at the mine's entrance or the cemetery."

"Hey, Mr. Barrett, sounds like we need to take a field trip. You know, scientific investigation and all."

"Nice try," responded Harrison. At that moment, the bell rang and students quickly packed up and filed out of the classroom. "See you all tomorrow, and thanks for the creepy ghost story."

Not one to let his curiosity linger longer than absolutely necessary, Harrison immediately headed to his computer. He Googled White Witch of Black Diamond Mines and watched thousands of results appear in a fraction of a second. He spent the next hour scanning various articles and posts referencing the White Witch. Not until a custodian entered the classroom, interrupting Harrison's concentration, did he notice the time. Tomorrow's lesson still required preparation, and with plans to meet Celeste at her home for an early dinner, he needed to get back to schoolwork.

Harrison closed his search, chatted a moment with the custodian, and then began setting up for the next day's instruction. As always, he looked forward to catching up with Celeste. Not only would they get to share a rare school night together, but he was anxious to tell her all about the White Witch.

51

Nothing like a good ghost story to spice up a dinner-date, thought Harrison while printing directions on the dry-erase board.

STILL NOT COMFORTABLE ENTERING Celeste's house unannounced, Harrison knocked several times as he unlocked her front door. He and Celeste exchanged house keys several months ago, but he felt it best to respect her space.

"In the kitchen," Celeste called out.

"Sorry I'm late," replied Harrison. "Stayed later than expected at school, then of course, I had to swing by my place to feed Cousteau."

"No problem. I'm just starting to make dinner," said Celeste stirring a sauce over the stove. "How did Cousteau like you leaving this evening?"

"Same goofy lab as always. Probably wondering why he's not getting a walk after dinner, though. I'll take him for a stroll later.

Harrison walked up behind Celeste, wrapped his arms around her waist and kissed her neck. Celeste smiled and leaned back into him. "Mmm," said Harrison. "You smell delicious."

"I think that's the spaghetti sauce," said Celeste.

"Oh, I thought you might be wearing that new perfume I saw advertised, Essence de Marinara."

Celeste elbowed him gently. She turned around and they kissed. "How about pouring us some wine, and I'll join you on the couch after getting the sauce simmering," she continued.

"Any preference?" Harrison asked.

"No, you pick. Just having spaghetti with meat sauce.

"We'll do a Sangiovese from one of the Sierra foothill wineries," responded Harrison.

"Sounds great."

Harrison handed Celeste her glass of wine as she sat next to him. She lifted her glass to toast. "Here's to the rare weeknight together."

Harrison touched his glass to hers. "And here's to the day when they will be common."

"I'll definitely drink to that."

Celeste rested her stocking feet on Harrison's lap. He massaged her feet as she sank into the cushions. "Oh my, gosh," purred Celeste. "That feels wonderful."

After a long, relaxing silence, Harrison and Celeste both spoke at once. "Did you know …?" began Harrison. "Guess what I found out …?" started Celeste.

"You first," said Celeste.

"No, no. You go."

"You're my guest, so you start," she insisted.

Harrison nodded. "Okay. Well, did you know that Black Diamond Mines is haunted?"

As Harrison expected, Celeste just glared at him. "What are you talking about?"

"The mines and cemetery where we just went hiking, they're haunted — at least according to some of my students."

Celeste smirked. "You don't believe in ghosts, do you?"

"No, of course not. But a lot of people do. You should see how much there is on the internet about the White Witch of Black Diamond Mines," said Harrison.

"The White Witch?"

"That's what the locals call the apparition that supposedly haunts the area. They describe what looks like a glowing white light drifting around the mine or cemetery, sometimes taking the form of a woman," continued Harrison.

Celeste suddenly sat upright. Both hands tightly gripped her wine glass. "You say it looks like a floating white light?" her tone unexpectedly serious.

"That's the most common description," said Harrison. "Why?"

"It's just that ... when we were walking through the cemetery ..."

"What?" Harrison gently prodded. "What is it?"

"I thought I ..." Celeste paused. She turned toward Harrison. "Nothing. It was nothing. So, did you learn anything about this White Witch?"

Harrison was not convinced that it was nothing, but he chose not to pursue the questioning for now. "Yes, supposedly it is the spirit of Sarah Norton, wife of Nortonville's founder. She was a midwife for the area in the 1860s to 1870s. One day she was making a house call when her horse got spooked. She fell out of the buggy, tumbled down a cliff and died from her injuries."

"How awful."

"As the legend goes, she now she roams the hills, protecting the spirits of all the children buried at Rose Hill cemetery. I sent a message to Rick, the park ranger, to ask what he knew about the story. He said he was well aware of the White Witch tale, but the rangers never mention her."

"Why is that?" Celeste asked.

"He said that thrill-seekers trying to catch a glimpse of a ghost drew people to the cemetery before it became a regional preserve. Sadly, some of these folks vandalized the graves, damaging or stealing headstones. Very sad. So now the East Bay Regional Park District doesn't want to do anything to encourage the myth."

"I can see why," said Celeste. "But it is a fascinating story."

Celeste set her glass on the coffee table and stood up. "Now it's time for my story. She walked into the next room and out of sight. Whatever bothered her about the White Witch description seemed to be forgotten. She returned a moment later carrying a laptop. In a single graceful motion, she scooped up her glass, took a sip, and settled onto the couch close to Harrison.

"Your story needs a computer?" Harrison asked.

"I got an email this afternoon that the results from my 23andMe genetic test are in. Didn't you get yours today?"

Harrison quickly leaned forward, nearly spilling his drink. "How exciting! I did not get a chance to look at my personal email yet. Ever since you suggested it'd be fun to get our testing done, I've been anxious to see the results. The details should be fascinating and I can use my results for class."

"I figured," Celeste responded with a smile. "That's one of the reasons I recommended it. Though, admittedly, I'm intrigued to learn more about my past, if possible."

"And . . . ? Did you read your results?" Harrison asked enthusiastically.

"I did. And I have to say, I got some surprising information. I was hoping a science teacher might help explain some of the specifics."

"Well, fortunately, I happen to know a science teacher that would be more than happy to assist," said Harrison, sliding closer to Celeste. "Let me take a look."

Celeste logged into the website and opened her results summary. She set the laptop on the coffee table and Harrison scrolled through the data, landing at pie charts and color-coded DNA images.

"So the first thing to remember," he began, "is that this is all just an estimate of your ethnic makeup. By comparing specific segments of your DNA to samples taken from around the world, they are presenting the proportion of your genetic information that comes from the thirty-one populations represented. And those populations are associated with a geographic area from over five-hundred years ago, before ocean-crossing ships and planes allowed humans to move around so much."

"Got it," responded Celeste as she watched Harrison intensely scan the screen.

"So, my dear, I assume you viewed your ethnic percentages. Looks like a grand mixture of Northwestern and Southern European: 30% British and Irish, 20% Iberian, 20% Balkan, 10% French and German, 9% broadly Northwestern European, and 8% Italian. Then you have about 2% Ashkenazi Jew, and a percent of Native American. You are quite the European mix. Anything surprise you about the results?" Harrison asked.

"Since I still have family in England and Wales, I knew about the British and other Northwestern European connection. My mother's side has Spanish and Greek to explain the Iberian and Balkan results, along with Italian. I was not aware of the Ashkenazi Jew, but given that group's geographic distribution in Europe, it is not surprising. But what did amaze me, was the trace amount of Native American."

"Why is that?"

"My mother did this test a year ago and never mentioned any Native American ancestry. Her parents immigrated to the U.S., so not much time to intermingle."

"So it must be from your dad's side," offered Harrison.

"Actually, that is even less likely. My father came to America in his early twenties as the first of his family to do so. How, then, could he have Native American DNA to pass on to me?"

Harrison took a sip of wine and leaned back on the sofa. "Sounds to me, Ms. Scott, that we have another mystery on our hands."

CHAPTER VIII

January 2, 1877

"IT IS MY WILL THAT Lodge Number 29, Knights of Pythias, now come to order for the dispatch of such business as may be brought before it. Inner Guard, order the Outer Guard to clear the area, close the door, and allow no one to enter."

The silver and gold-plated medal pinned to Thomas Oliver's chest glinted in the candlelight. Its knight's helmet, shield, and crossed battle axes symbolized the fraternal order; the blue F, yellow C, and red B indicated the organization's founding principles of Friendship, Charity, and Benevolence; and the jewel's size and intricate design represented the lodge's highest office. Oliver took his seat in a high-backed central chair next to the altar.

The Inner Guard, a lanky miner named Williams standing near the door, spoke to a man outside. "Outer Guard, it is the order of the Chancellor Commander that you clear the area, close the door and allow no one to enter."

"The order of the Chancellor Commander shall be obeyed," said a young shopkeeper who hoped to soon be initiated into the order and join the secretive activities within the hall. For now, he closed the door and perched in front, steering away curious passers-by on a cold Tuesday evening. The lodge itself held a prominent place among the row of buildings on Nortonville's Main Street. However, unlike the shops, saloons, and boarding houses, few Nortonville residents knew what conversations took place within the Knights of Pythias walls.

The Inner Guard turned toward Oliver. "Chancellor Commander, the Outer Guard has received your order."

Oliver rapped a small wooden mallet twice. "Master at Arms, approach my station and communicate to me the semi-annual password, and examine all present in the same."

DANIEL ABRAHAM APPROACHED Oliver, bent down, and whispered in his ear. Oliver nodded. Abraham then walked to each of the two dozen members seated in the chamber. One-by-one, they whispered to Abraham, "*Deg pwynt.*"

"Chancellor Commander, I have obeyed your order, and have found all present in possession of the semi-annual password." Abraham then proceeded to the altar, opened the Book of Law, and saluted Oliver.

Oliver rapped his mallet three times. "Master at Arms, where is your station and what are your duties in this lodge?"

Abraham responded, "My station is at the right and front of the Chancellor Commander. My duties are to examine all present prior to the opening of the lodge, and to report the result to the Chancellor Commander; to prepare and accompany candidates; and to obey the orders of the Chancellor Commander. He then took his seat.

"Treasurer, where is your station and what are your duties in this lodge?" said Oliver.

"My station is at the left of the Chancellor Commander. My duties are to receive from the Financial Secretary all moneys collected by him and to disburse them only on an order from the Chancellor Commander, attested by the Secretary; to present to this lodge, at the end of every semi-annual term, a written report of all receipts and disbursements during the term; and to perform all other services required of me by the laws of the order and the by-laws of this lodge." The treasurer took his seat.

Oliver continued this ritual for the Secretary, Prelate, and other officers. "To aid us in our work, the Prelate will invoke divine assistance," Oliver continued.

Evan Davies had been the Prelate. Following his death, Oliver appointed an elderly member of the order to serve until a formal selection was consecrated. The Prelate offered the Knight's traditional prayer: "Supreme Ruler of the Universe, we humbly ask thy blessing upon the officers and members of this lodge and visiting brothers. Aid us to avoid anger and dissension, help us to work together in the spirit of fraternity, and inspire us to exemplify the friendship of Damon and Pythias. Hear and answer us, we beseech thee. Amen."

"Amen," responded all.

Led by Oliver, the members continued with the opening ode.

> "God bless our knightly band,
> Firm may it ever stand,
> Through storm and night;
> When the wild tempests rave,
> Ruler of wind and wave,
> Do thou our order save
> By thy great might.
>
> "For this our prayers ascend,
> God bless, protect, defend,
> God guard our rights;
> Thou who art ever nigh,
> Viewing with watchful eye,
> To thee aloud we cry:
> God save the knights!"

Oliver proceeded with the meeting's agenda, largely addressing the needs of Evan Davies' memorial. Belonging to the Pythian brotherhood assured that a deceased member would be cared for, including a proper burial, as well as food, clothing, and shelter assistance for the immediate family. Since Davies had no family in Nortonville, the Knights focused on appropriate funeral services and his memorial headstone. Each member contributed what he could, while the officers sought additional resources from the community.

The discussion of Davies' headstone took longer than Oliver anticipated since everyone had an opinion about wording and format. The one thing they all immediately agreed upon was including an engraved Knights of Pythias symbol on the gravestone.

The Secretary read off the eventual consensus of a simple, straightforward pronouncement.

In
Memory Of
EVAN DAVIES
Born
July 24, 1846
At Cwm-Bach
Glanmorgenshire
South Wales
Died
Dec. 23, 1876

"With that settled," said Oliver. "Brother Pane, please read the memorial resolution previously approved."

"Yes, Chancellor Commander." A.A. Pane pulled a paper from a folder leaning against his chair. He stood, affixed a small pair of glasses, and began reading:

"*In Memoriam.*

"*Whereas: — It has pleased the Supreme Chancellor of the universe to remove from our midst our late Brother, Evan Davies, and . . .*

"*Whereas: - It is but just that a fitting acknowledgement of his many virtues and noble example should be made, therefore be it . . .*

"*Resolved — By Black Diamond Lodge. 29, Knights of Pythias, that while we humbly bow to the will of the Supreme Ruler, we do the not less mourn for our Brother who has been taken from us.*

"*Resolved — That in the loss of Brother Evan Davies this Lodge mourns the loss of one whose hand and heart was ever open to render assistance and give aid and sympathy whenever and wherever needed, a Brother to whom the prosperity and welfare of our Lodge and Order was the incentive to strong and unwearied exertion, a friend dear to us all and one in whom the feelings of friendship for those he loved was strong as life itself: one whose life was a fitting exemplification of the great principles of our Order, Friendship, Charity, and Benevolence and whose many virtues are worthy of emulation by us all.*

"*Resolved — That as a slight testimonial to the worth and character of our deceased Brother, the Charter of this Lodge be draped in mourning for a period of thirty days. And be it further*

"*Resolved — That a copy of these resolutions, under the seal of the Lodge be forwarded to his relatives, a copy spread upon the minutes of the Lodge and a copy furnished to the 'Antioch Ledger' for publication.*" [5]

"Excellent, Brother Pane. Thank you. If there are no additional comments on the matter of Brother Davies at this time, we will continue with our agenda," Oliver announced.

The group debriefed the recent Christmas and New Year's activities, confirmed arrangements for the upcoming initiation ceremony for a new member, and debated fundraising events for the year.

Following a loud mallet rap, Oliver announced, "Master at Arms, return the flag of our country to its resting place."

Abraham saluted the flag. He removed it from the altar and stretched the cloth for display on the wall, carefully smoothing the thirty-seven white stars.

"Master of Arms," continued Oliver. "Remove the shield, close the Book of Law, secure the Sword of Defense, and collect the jewels."

Oliver waited for Abraham to comply. "By virtue of the power vested in me, I now declare Lodge Number 29 duly closed. Inner Guard, inform the Outer Guard."

The Pythian brothers rose from their seats and slowly meandered toward the door. "Brother Abraham," said Oliver.

"Yes, Chancellor Commander?"

"Please stay for a moment, if you will."

"Of course," replied Abraham. He stirred ash in the wood-burning stove used to heat the lodge, and then bolted the outer door once the final member left. Abraham dowsed three of the four kerosene lanterns lighting the hall. He carried the remaining light to the high-back chair where Oliver sat. "How might I be of service Chancellor Commander?"

"Please sit, Daniel."

Oliver's casual use of Abraham's name signified the formal meeting's conclusion. "I'm worried, Daniel," Oliver continued.

Abraham slid a chair next to Oliver and sat. "What troubles you Thomas?"

"You and I are the last, Daniel," said Oliver with a solemn gaze.

Abraham nodded as he stroked his thick brown beard. "I share your concern. With the loss of Gething and Reynolds, and now brother Davies gone, we are the only DOKK left."

"As you know," said Oliver. "The Dramatic Order of the Knights of Khorasan have been chosen to fulfill a great and honorable task. Rathbone's message was clear: we must protect, at any cost, the location of the sacred object with which we are entrusted. At this moment, you and I are the only members of the Knights anywhere in the country that know its location."

Oliver paused.

"And if something happens to us . . . ?" added Abraham.

"Precisely," said Oliver. He rose slowly from the high-back chair and began pacing. The wooden floorboards creaked with each step as Oliver considered their predicament. The stove fire was now out and the winter night's chill began permeating the lodge.

To help fend off the cold, Abraham stood and buttoned his coat. "What is it you are proposing?"

Oliver continued to walk the room as he spoke. "Should something happen to us, we cannot let the resting place of the sacred object be lost forever. We must impart others with the knowledge."

"Agreed," said Abraham. "But in whom may we trust. While the other members of the Order are fine men, I do not know if any are ready to become DOKK."

"And that is what I fear," said Oliver, now standing with arms crossed, staring at the colorful Knights of Pythias banner. "We know that dissent within the Order out east created division and threatens to undo a decade of work unifying this country. If the wrong person obtains possession of the Order's most sacred

64

object, the Knights will be finished. Chaos will reign and our just and democratic society may be lost forever. Above all else, we must keep the object hidden."

"Is there a man you have in mind to join us in this noble effort?" asked Abraham.

Oliver again began pacing. "Since the mine explosion, I have considered the possibilities. I closely observed all officers of the Order, as well as, the lower ranks. Conversations, both direct and overheard, have been contemplated. I scrutinized all manner of behavior over the past months, looking for one or more individuals worthy to join the most secretive rank within the Knights of Pythias."

"And . . . ?" Abraham asked, anxious for another brother to share the burden of their sworn duty.

"As you said," Oliver continued. "They are all fine, upstanding men; men of benevolence and honor; men with an unyielding faith in a Supreme Being and heartfelt devotion to their country. Yet, would any of them sacrifice as did Pythias – without hesitation offer his own life for that of his brother? Of that, I am not confident."

Abraham stood silently. He continued to stroke his beard as he reflected on Oliver's words. "So what can we do?" said Abraham with deep concern. "Is there no man in Nortonville whom we can trust?"

"I am afraid that is the truth of the matter," said Oliver, now running his fingers over the Sword of Defense. "But perhaps all is not lost."

Abraham waited for Oliver to finish his thought, but the delay was unbearable. "Do tell, Thomas, what man in Nortonville can be trusted with the secret that we carry?"

Oliver put his hand on Abraham's shoulder. "Perhaps, Daniel, the better question is . . . what woman?"

Knights of Pythias emblem [6]

CHAPTER 9

"ARE YOU SURE YOU ARE OKAY heading back there?" Harrison asked.

"Yes, yes. I'm fine," said Celeste. "I don't know what my problem was last time. I do know that I really want to see the cemetery and the headstone where that poor man was killed. Whether the name written in blood referred to me or not, I feel obligated to at least take a look."

Harrison and Celeste gathered their coats and water bottles from the car's back seat and began the hike from the Black Diamond Mines Regional Preserve parking lot to the Rose Hill Cemetery.

"You forgot your hat," said Harrison.

"No need," Celeste responded as she quickened her pace. "No wind at all, so it's really pleasant."

The two walked along the dirt trail that wound down, around, then back up toward the cemetery. Harrison paid close attention to Celeste's expressions. So far, there was no indication of the overwhelming anxiety that engulfed her during their previous visit.

"Any word back from your mom about the Native American DNA?" asked Harrison.

"Not yet. She's out of town and has not yet responded to my voicemail or text. When she returns, I may just make a trip out to see her so we can discuss the issue in person. Care to come along?"

Harrison answered without hesitation. "Of course. I love to see your mom. She's great."

"Yes, she is. And she thinks you're pretty great, too," Celeste added with a playful nudge.

"Awe, shucks," he said, smiling broadly as he took Celeste's hand.

Reaching the uphill stretch slowed the hike. A portion of the cemetery's fencing was visible in the distance. Thankfully, Harrison saw no change in Celeste's demeanor. She still seemed eager to reach the crime scene, and showed none of the strange sense of fear that she felt before.

"I meant to ask you," Celeste continued. "How was your field trip to the wind farms yesterday? With your environmental club, right?"

"That's right. We had a nice time."

"Remind me where you went, again?" said Celeste, pausing briefly to catch her breath before proceeding on the trail's steepest incline.

Jogging to catch up, Harrison replied. "The Shiloh Wind Power Plant in the Montezuma Hills. It's near the city of Rio Vista, over on the other side of the Delta. Since the club is doing a promotional project on renewable energy, I wanted to get them out to see some options first hand, and those are a little more accessible than the wind farms on the Altamont Pass. The power company that owns them gave us an informative tour."

"How did the students like the trip?" asked Celeste.

"They thought it was interesting. You don't know just how big those windmills are until you see them up close. They learned about the importance of a suitable location, obviously where there is consistent wind and wide-open space, not unlike these hills if you recall our last hike out here."

Celeste nodded. "Oh yes, I remember, and I really appreciate today's calm weather."

"Yeah, the kids got lots of good information, and the stop for ice cream on the way home was an added bonus," said Harrison.

"For you or your students?" smirked Celeste.

Harrison just smiled.

"So no problems?"

Harrison shrugged. "Nothing major. We had a slight conflict with the tour guide, and I had to intervene."

Celeste cocked her head and furrowed her brow.

"You know Mitchell Conder, right?" he continued, understanding Celeste required more details.

"I sure do."

"Then you know he can be a handful sometimes. A little too smart for his own good."

Celeste nodded in agreement. "Exactly. So what happened?"

"During the Q and A session with the guide, he asked what the power company is doing about wind turbine syndrome."

"Wind turbine syndrome?" said Celeste. "What's that?"

"Precisely, I didn't know either. But the guide definitely did, and she clearly didn't want to talk about it. Yet, Mitchell pushed her on the issue. Apparently, there is some concern that people living near wind farms, or even a single large windmill, can be subjected to infrasound effects caused by the spinning blades. Especially on newer, larger windmills, the huge blades create a swooshing sound with so low a frequency you might not hear it, but can still feel it."

"I'm sorry," said Celeste. "Feel the sound from the blades?"

"Right. Just like you felt the pounding beat from bass woofers when you played that hard rock as a teenager," Harrison explained with a grin. "Now keep the volume cranked up, but lower the bass note so low, that your ears cannot detect the sound. The thing is, the noise vibration is still traveling through the air and hitting your body. Your body senses that sound, even

69

though you can't hear it. The vibrations pound against your internal organs causing headaches, nausea, and all kinds of uneasy feelings."

"That's awful," Celeste said, now slowing her pace to better listen to Harrison's story.

"Of course, the power company guide denied it all. Said the syndrome is a bunch of b.s., though not quite in those terms. Their explanation for anyone who lives near the wind farms with those symptoms is that the person suffers from a psychosomatic disorder, or nocebo effect."

"You lost me again. No-ce-bo effect?"

"Yup. These people, so the explanation goes, being aware of the supposedly negative windmill effects, have the perception that they feel ill, though there's no apparent cause. It's the opposite of a placebo having a positive effect due only to a person's belief that they should feel better."

Celeste stopped at the top of the hill and stared at the entrance to Rose Hill Cemetery. "Sounds pretty difficult to prove . . . or disprove."

"True," replied Harrison. "That's why there is some controversy about wind turbine syndrome; a controversy which Mitchell was only too glad to debate. I finally had to rein him in so we could continue the tour. I was afraid the guide was ready to leave us out there with the windmills and the sheep."

"That sounds like Mitchell, alright." Celeste stepped through the gate opening and into the cemetery grounds. She stared out among the standing and toppled headstones. "So here we are. Detective Lawlor mentioned that the caution tape and writing would be removed by now. Do you remember where the headstone is located?" she asked Harrison.

"Not exactly," he replied. "But there is a display map here, and over there is a box with brochures that indicates each gravesite and known occupants. If you grab a brochure, we can look up the headstone name. Was it Gething?"

Celeste unfolded the brochure and scanned the cemetery map. "Yes, William Gething."

Harrison began walking though the graves. "I remember from last time that the caution tape was in this direction."

Celeste followed. "Here he is," she said, pointing at the map she carried. "Should be one of those to the left."

The couple moved toward a rectangular row of bricks outlining a plot. A white marble headstone stood at one end. Three large cracks ran horizontally across the stone's face, obvious repair scars from a once-broken marker. Harrison bent down to read the inscription. "Yup, this is him - William Gething. Died July 24, 1876. Aged 36 years."

"Is that all it says?" asked Celeste.

"Yes. You can see that the stone is a little cleaner where the rangers washed off the murder victim's words."

Celeste eased closer to the headstone. "Madog near," she whispered. "Warn Celeste Scott."

"C, are you okay?" asked Harrison.

"Yes, fine," Celeste responded immediately. "I'm fine. I just don't understand. Why my name? Why this headstone? Why murder? What could possibly connect it all?"

"If anything," Harrison added.

Celeste carefully stepped over the brick border and knelt in front of the marker. She slowly ran her fingers over the engraved words. "What do you suppose this symbol is at the top?"

Harrison squatted next to her looking intensely at the shield, knight's helmet, and crossed battle axes etched into the marble. "Not sure, but we can try to find out."

71

He reached into his fanny packed and removed a piece of blank newsprint and a fat crayon. "Here, hold this paper over the symbol while I do a rubbing." The two quickly created an imprint of the symbol which Harrison rolled up and stuffed back into his fanny pack.

"Let's check with the park staff to see whether they know anything about the symbol's significance. If not, maybe we can find something online."

"Sounds good," said Celeste. "I guess I'm done here. Thanks for coming back with me."

"Of course," said Harrison as he squeezed her hand.

Celeste stood and stepped out of Gething's plot. "Shall we wander some more?"

"Sure," responded Harrison. "Though there is one more plot I want to check out. Can I see the map?"

Harrison scanned the brochure's cemetery diagram and led Celeste to a far corner. "Yes, this is it," he said, stopping in front of a much larger marble headstone.

A tall Italian cypress grew directly behind the plot, as if standing guard over the departed soul buried below. Celeste leaned in and read the engraving. "In memory of Mrs. Sarah Norton. A native of Canada. Died October 5, 1879. Aged 68 years. Our head and stay has left us, and we are left alone. Our mother dear who was so near, is fled away and gone. It breaks our heart, it is hard to part, with one who was so kind. Where shall we go to ease our woe, or soothe our troubled mind?"

Celeste sighed. "So touching. This is the supposed White Witch you told me about, right?"

"Right. Clearly loved and respected. Nothing very witchy in the epitaph. I wonder why the ghost stories focused on her. Probably just the most recognized name buried here."

"Probably," said Celeste. "Shall we keep walking?"

Celeste seemed anxious to leave Sarah Norton's grave and continue exploring the cemetery, so Harrison obliged. They spent the next hour weaving through the headstones, reading epitaphs and lamenting the disproportionate number of infants and children. Harrison created rubbings of the helmet-shield-ax symbol they found engraved on several more headstones.

"We should probably head back down to the visitor center to see if we can find a ranger to interpret this symbol," said Harrison.

"How about afterward I treat you to a coffee to help take the chill off?" added Celeste.

Harrison took her hand and started the downhill trek. "You're on."

After returning to the parking lot, they drove a short distance to the front gate visitor center. "I figured we'd check out this visitor center rather than the Greathouse Portal since you have not been here. These buildings are all original to the towns that were once here. The Park District was able to save a few homes which were moved here and refurbished."

"Very impressive," Celeste replied. "Another step back in time."

"I'll see if I can track down a ranger if you want to check out the displays for a minute." Harrison stepped inside the main building and disappeared around a corner. Celeste wandered through the cute little, wood-sided outer buildings until she heard her name.

"Celeste, over here," called Harrison. She met him at the main building. Harrison gestured toward a petit women leaning over the gravestone tracing. Her khaki-colored uniform contrasted sharply with jet-black hair pulled into a tight bun. "This is Alma, a ranger here. She may be able to help us."

"Hi," said Alma, greeting Celeste. "Come on inside. I don't know the meaning of the symbol myself, but I know where we might find out."

She led them to a desktop displaying a huge book. "This one-thousand-plus page book documents pretty much everything there is to know about Rose Hill Cemetery. For thirty-years, the author, a former naturalist here at the preserve, researched the people buried up there. She put together all of her findings into this one text."

"That's incredible," said Celeste. "What amazing dedication to the area's history."

"I think," Alma continued, "if we turn toward the back, there are images of all the headstones that include interpretations." She flipped through several sections before landing on a page titled Fraternal Organizations. "Here we have the Masons, the Odd Fellows, and this one, with the shield, helmet, and axes, looks like the rubbing you showed me."

"Yes," said Harrison enthusiastically. "That's it."

"That . . ." said Alma, pausing briefly, ". . . represents the fraternal order of the Knights of Pythias."

Harrison and Celeste turned toward each and responded simultaneously. "Who?"

CHAPTER X

"OH, THANK GOODNESS, Sarah is here," said one of three women shuffling around Elizabeth Jones' bedside. "I'll let her in."

The woman, Elizabeth's older cousin, opened the door to the small boarding house just off Somersville's Main Street. Nineteen-year-old Elizabeth moved into the house after marrying the previous year. Her thirty-five-year-old husband worked the Pittsburg mine and would not return home until after dark. The pain and pressure in Elizabeth's swollen belly were severe enough to warrant a call for Sarah Norton, even though the baby was not due for several more weeks.

When the sharp, irregular twinges failed to subside, Elizabeth's cousin ran to the nearby livery stable. The stable-master quickly hitched a two-horse team to a buggy and sent his son to retrieve Mrs. Norton from Nortonville. Muddy trails made the mile-long journey slower than usual, so by the time Sarah arrived, Elizabeth, her cousin, and the two neighbors, were deeply concerned.

Sarah stepped through the front door. Heat from a single wood-burning stove seeped into her body, providing relief from the cold, damp ride. She removed the black overcoat from her stout body and stomped a few times, freeing as much mud as possible before proceeding. A few strands of graying hair slipped out from underneath her bonnet. She tucked them back under and continued into Elizabeth's room.

"The pains began last night," Elizabeth's cousin began.

Sarah paid no attention to the cousin and walked directly past her to Elizabeth, who lay in bed with her head and shoulders propped on down pillows. "Please, ladies," Sarah said, without formally acknowledging them. "Let me speak with Elizabeth alone."

"Of course," they said. The three women left the bedroom and kept busy in the kitchen – stoking the fire, making tea, and pacing nervously.

As Sarah approached Elizabeth, she reached out and gently took the cross Elizabeth clutched. To make room for her bag on the bedside table, Sarah pushed aside a bible and set the cross on the floor.

Sarah Norton's age and sometimes prickly demeanor were not the only things that set her apart from the residents in these mining towns. Her patient, like most of Nortonville and Somersville, was Welsh or English. Sarah, however, hailed from Canada. Born at sea, her parents immigrated to the United States. With the six children by her now-deceased first husband grown and dispersed throughout the Midwest, Sarah married the much older Noah Norton and followed him to the slopes of Mt. Diablo.

Upon Noah's passing, Sarah expanded her dedication to the mining towns, not just as a midwife, but as an advisor, organizer, and community leader . . . with one exception. Sarah Norton was a non-believer. Her lack of faith stemmed not from an open shunning of God, but rather from the assertion that she simply had no use for organized religion. To Sarah, so much time spent each week in church and other religious observances was impractical and pointless. Sarah made it absolutely clear to the Nortonville residents that upon her death, there should be no Christian burial or religious service of any kind.

76

Community members understood and accepted this about Sarah, though often, and in secret, they prayed for her soul.

"How long have you had the pains?" Sarah asked, now sitting bedside.

"About a day," replied Elizabeth. "At first I felt only pressure, but then with the pressure came a sharp pain that seemed to get worse."

With both hands, Sarah palpated Elizabeth's abdomen. Decades of experience from hundreds of pregnant bellies oozed through her fingertips. Position, size, and even the baby's health were derived from the midwife's touch. "Does anything ease the pain?" Sarah continued.

"Sometimes when I walk around I feel better."

"Does the pressure come on at regular intervals or sporadically?"

Elizabeth thought for a moment. "Just comes and goes, but not regular"

Sarah questioned Elizabeth for a few more minutes. She patted Elizabeth on the shoulder. "Everything is fine," said Sarah. "False labor. When the pain comes again, get up and move around and that should help. If the pain starts occurring during regular periods, send for me. Drink plenty of the tea that I brought last time."

"I will, Mrs. Norton. Thank you so much for coming, and God bless you" said Elizabeth.

Sarah forced a smile. "Get some rest now. I will check on you again soon."

Sarah rose quickly from the bed and headed out of the room toward the anxious ladies. She explained the diagnosis to Elizabeth's cousin and neighbors. They sighed with relief and thanked Sarah. "I will be back next week at the latest to check on her," said Sarah, heading out the boarding house door.

The stable-master's son helped Sarah into the buggy, and they headed west, back toward Nortonville. As the buggy pulled up to Sarah's home, one of the few single-family houses in town, she noticed a male figure sitting on her front porch.

"Good afternoon, Sarah."

She recognized the voice. "Good afternoon, Thomas."

Helping Sarah down from the buggy, Thomas Oliver carried her bag toward the front door. "Mary Tully told me where you were, so I thought I would wait for your return. Was everything alright with the Jones girl?" asked Oliver.

"Yes, yes. All is well. What can I do for you?" Sarah replied.

She headed inside her house and motioned Oliver to follow, but he declined. "I don't want to bother you now, as I'm sure you are tired from your trip. However, I would like to talk to you … in private. If possible, I would like to come by tonight, perhaps ten o'clock?"

Oliver waited for Sarah's questioning look, which he immediately received. "I apologize for requesting such a late meeting, but I assure you, there is an important reason," continued Oliver.

"Very well," said Sarah, without much concern. She respected Oliver's integrity and understood must have a good reason the unusual request.

"Excellent. I will see you tonight. Good afternoon." Oliver turned and headed back toward Main Street.

Sarah removed her overcoat and bonnet. She had left for Somersville before eating breakfast and was starving. Bread and tea should suffice, she thought.

"COME IN THOMAS," SAID SARAH, responding to the knock on her front door.

"Thank you," Oliver responded. "Again, I am sorry for the late hour."

Oliver stepped through the door and into a small sitting room. An ornately-carved cuckoo clock immediately caught his attention as it finished its eighth, ninth, and tenth chirp. "Delightful," said Oliver, surprised by the unexpected sound.

"A wedding gift from Mr. Norton," replied Sarah. "The little bird reminds me of my husband and keeps me company with its hourly declaration. Though, I must admit, there are nights when I have thought to squelch the noise with a suitably placed fry pan . . . not unlike for Mr. Norton's snoring."

Sarah muttered the last statement to herself. Oliver noticed a slight smile expand and then quickly fade from his host.

"Please sit," Sarah continued. "I will bring us some tea."

She returned quickly, poured the tea, and sat in a wooden rocking chair adjacent to Oliver. The uneven glow from a kerosene lantern and two candles were all that lit the house. "Now, Thomas, what is it you want to discuss?"

Oliver sipped his tea and leaned forward. Though he knew Sarah and he were completely alone, he lowered his voice as he spoke. "As you know, I am a dedicated member of the Knights of Pythias." He hesitated, waiting for Sarah to react to a presumably unforeseen subject. She did not.

"Unknown to all but a very few select members, the Knights of Pythias Supreme Lodge in Washington, D.C. charged our Nortonville lodge with a task of extreme importance, not just to the Order, but to the entire country."

"I see," said Sarah, noticing beads of sweat on his furrowed brow.

Oliver was unsure whether her tone was one of intrigue or suspicion. "The Knights of Pythias brotherhood is spreading throughout the country. Its members are some of the most influential men of our times and include politicians and businessmen who direct the vision of this great nation. There is, however, a deep divide among some of these members over a struggle for power."

Oliver waited again, allowing Sarah time to absorb his words. "Go on," she said.

"You see, Sarah, those controlling the Order have access to more wealth and power than you or I can imagine. How this power is wielded, and for what purpose, will determine the fate of this great country. Our Order was founded on the ideals of friendship, charity, and benevolence. We helped spread these ideals throughout the nation, hoping to unite a divided country following the War Between the States.

"But there are some who seek to disrupt our mission, Sarah. These dark forces intend to use the Knight's powerful influence for their own selfish interests, greedily enriching themselves, while promoting chaos and discord that drive this nation toward their ultimate goal — a land ruled by a single infallible leader.

"We must, therefore, be diligent in our protection of the Order's sacred tenets. Realizing the grand vision of a moral and just America, united in goodwill, may depend upon our actions."

"I am aware of the Knight's benevolent activities," Sarah responded. "This town and others owe a debt of gratitude for the Order's support of the poor, sick, and injured. I also understand that there are individuals in this world whose selfish, greedy nature would be at odds with the Knight's vision for this country. What I do not understand, Thomas, is what this has to do with me?"

"Of course, please allow me to explain." Oliver set down his tea and clasped his hands tightly, trying to conceal his anxiety about sharing the Order's most revered secret with a non-member. "When the Knights of Pythias was created, the founder was in possession of an object used to represent the Order's tenets and bestow leadership. This object is more than just a valuable artifact. Control of it has consequences not just for the Knights, but for the entire country. As factions within the Order challenged the founder's leadership and philosophy, desperate actions became necessary. The artifact was hidden to prevent its possession by unscrupulous individuals who would undermine the Order and our vision for this great land."

Sarah quietly rocked while listening with interest.

"Only the most dedicated members of the Knights know of the existence of this most significant item. Fewer still know its location, a location that changed over the years as followers of the corrupt faction searched in vain. This small group of trustworthy members is known as the Dramatic Order of the Knights of Khorassan. Other Pythians believe that the DOKK exist as leaders and organizers within the brotherhood. They do not know our true purpose.

Last year, only the DOKK within Sacramento's Knights of Pythias lodge knew the object's hiding place. When the lodge leaders suspected the location was compromised, the object was relocated. The artifact's safety then became the principal mission of a small Knights of Pythias lodge tucked discreetly into the Northern California hills."

Sarah nodded knowingly. "So you belong to the Dramatic Order of the Knights of Khorassan? And this artifact is here, with you?"

"It is."

"And why tell me?"

"Following the mine explosion, and then the untimely passing of Evan Davies, only two DOKK remain that know of the object's existence and location, Daniel Abraham and me. My fear is that should anything happen to the two of us, the blessed symbol of the Knights of Pythias will be lost forever, and with it, a most powerful deterrent against evil, dormant now, but ready to be wielded when needed."

"Certainly there must be other members of the Order in whom you can confide?" asked Sarah.

Oliver shook his head. "None that have our absolute trust. We realized we must find someone outside the Order, someone with the utmost integrity and resolute character. A person no one would give a thought to being associated with the Knights."

Sarah stopped rocking. She reflected on Oliver's words for several minutes before responding. "Very well, Thomas. What is this object and where is it?"

A wave of relief overtook Oliver. "Thank you, Sarah. I pray that your services are never needed, but if they are, I know you will do right by the Knights. Now, if you indulge me, I have something to show you. Please come with me."

Sarah fastened her bonnet as Oliver assisted with her overcoat. He grabbed the kerosene lantern and, just before leaving the house, extinguished the flame. "We'll need this later, but better that we are not seen," said Oliver.

He led Sarah through the damp, murky night. Coyotes yelped to each other as Oliver guided Sarah into the hills. "Not much further," he said. "Do you know where the powder magazine is?"

"I believe so," she replied, intrigued by the destination.

The narrow dirt trail ended at a cave burrowed into the hillside. For safety reasons, barrels filled with gunpowder and cases of dynamite were stored a significant distance from town. Outside the entrance, Oliver used a parlor match to relight the lantern. He replaced the safety screen before entering the shadowy passage. Sarah followed closely behind as they wound around boxes and barrels toward the back wall.

"Would you mind?" asked Oliver, handing Sarah the lantern.

She complied while cautiously eyeing the nearby stockpile of explosives. Oliver rolled a gunpowder barrel away from the rear wall, and grabbed a pick-ax from a pile of tools. He inserted the pick behind a large rock imbedded low in the sandstone surface, and forced the rock out. A small chamber appeared behind the stone.

Sarah lowered the lantern near the cavity. Oliver knelt down, reached behind the stone, and slowly pulled out a long wooden box. The box, four feet long and a foot wide, was nailed tightly shut. With the pick-ax, Oliver methodically pried open the top, one nail at a time. He set aside the pick-ax and squatted next to the box.

Sarah could not imagine what the box might contain. She bent down next to Oliver but could only see what appeared to be wood shavings. He reached into the shavings and pulled out a long, thin object wrapped in white cloth.

Gradually, with the tenderness of a mother unbundling a swaddled infant, Oliver removed the cloth, careful to avoid touching the object within.

Sarah stared. "So the most sacred object of the Knights of Pythias, the artifact whose possession could impact the whole country, is ..."

She paused, considering a suitable description for what she saw. ". . . an old sword?"

Sarah Norton (on right) [7]

CHAPTER 11

HARRISON LEANED AGAINST his classroom desk. His index finger darted around the cell phone keypad. He admired students who two-thumb texted as fast as he could type on a computer keyboard. Knowing he would never become a proficient thumb-texter, he continued to poke carefully at each letter.

Hey, C. 4:30 today? He hit the send button and waited for a response.

A reply immediately popped up on the phone's screen. *Sure. Where?*

Ur room.

(Thumb-up emoji). *Might be able to start* (shovel and dirt emoji) *into it early.* (Knight emoji) *of Pythias, right?*

Yup. See you soon. (Winky-face emoji)

(Blowing kiss emoji). Harrison smiled at the screen.

"No texting in class, Mr. B."

The student comment caught Harrison by surprise. "Class hasn't started, yet," he said quickly. He offered a head nod as the student grinned and headed to her seat. The school bell chimed while the last couple of students dashed into the room.

"Okay, let's get started," Harrison announced to the class. "Cell phones out." He walked between rows, checking for compliance. In a sublimely discreet motion, Harrison slid his own cell phone onto one student's desk, an arrangement made earlier in the year to ensure everyone participated, even if they could not afford a phone.

Most students were so accustomed to being told to turn phones off and put them away, that when Mr. Barrett requested their use, many felt apprehensive. This particular activity required students to text question responses using a cell phone app that instantly projected the results through the teacher's computer. Harrison used the information to rapidly check for understanding of previous material, and students gradually grew accustomed to working with their most precious possession.

Occasionally a teacher, usually a long-time veteran – a member of the Old Guard, as Harrison referred to them – would glare disapprovingly into the classroom while walking by. Harrison ignored the judgment. Even he had to overcome initial bias on student cell phone use for educational purposes. But just as he taught in his biology classes, one must adapt or go extinct. With the technological environment changing at warp speed, making use of the pocket computers students carried around only seemed logical. Besides, thought Harrison, tech tools made learning fun.

"I'M HERE," ANNOUNCED HARRISON stepping through Celeste's classroom door. "Sorry I'm late. I needed to finish up some grading." He walked up behind Celeste and kissed her cheek.

Celeste sat at her desk staring at the computer screen. She leaned into Harrison's kiss and squeezed the hand he placed on her shoulder. "No problem."

"Anything interesting?" asked Harrison.

"You better pull up a chair. After researching this for the past hour, I found a fascinating story."

Harrison slid a chair next to Celeste. He spun it backward, straddled the seat, and sat down.

"So far, I've just been reading about the origin of the Knights of Pythias," Celeste began.

"Do tell."

Celeste flipped through the notebook she used to keep track of details. "I pulled information from several different websites. The Knights of Pythias is a secretive fraternal society founded in 1864 by Justus Rathbone."

"Justice?" asked Harrison. "Like a judge?"

"No. Justus is his name. He was a teacher and worked for the government. Also a musician and wrote plays. Well-educated and multi-talented." Celeste playfully elbowed Harrison. "Kind of like you."

Harrison smiled. "Well, thank you."

Celeste scanned her notes. "He was distraught over the country becoming so divided during the Civil War and wanted to help reunite Americans. He decided to create an organization dedicated to friendship, charity, and benevolence based on the story of Damon and Pythias."

"Who?"

"That's what I said," answered Celeste. "There's an ancient Greek legend about two friends, Damon and Pythias. They traveled to a foreign land ruled by a tyrannical king. Pythias plotted against the king in order to help the people, but he was caught, and the king sentenced him to death. Pythias pleaded for the king to let him return home to settle his affairs and say goodbye to his family. Naturally, the king figured if he let Pythias go, he just wouldn't return."

"Naturally," said Harrison.

"So, Damon spoke up and offered a deal. If the king let Pythias go, he would stay in his friend's place. If Pythias did not return by the deadline, then the king could execute him instead. I guess the king thought this would be an interesting test of loyalty, so he agreed and Pythias left. When Pythias got home, he told his family what happened. Of course they pleaded with him to stay, but Pythias refused to break his vow of friendship with Damon, so he headed back. Unfortunately, the deadline the king had given for the execution had come, and still no Pythias. The king berated Damon for trusting his friend, but Damon was not deterred and insisted that Pythias would return. Sure enough, just as the executioner was about to lower the ax, into the castle bursts Pythias. The king asks Pythias why he was so late as to nearly lose his friend. Pythias tells him it was . . ."

"What? What?" asked Harrison.

Celeste had to pause to turn the page of her notes. "Sorry, I couldn't quite remember. It was pirates."

"Of course," said Harrison sarcastically, ". . . pirates."

"Pirates captured the ship carrying Pythias and threw him overboard, so Pythias had to swim the rest of the way, then run as fast as he could to get to the castle just in time. Well, the king was so impressed by the code of friendship by which the two lived, that he decided to free them both and make the friends his royal advisors."

"And everyone lived happily ever after."

"Something like that," replied Celeste. "But that's just the story that inspired Rathbone."

"I can't wait to hear the rest."

"After Rathbone founded the Knights of Pythias, guess who he discussed it with?"

Harrison thought for a moment. "Hmm . . . pirates?"

"No, silly . . . Abraham Lincoln"

"You're kidding?" said Harrison.

"Lincoln liked the Knights of Pythias mission so much," said Celeste, "that he recommended Rathbone take it to congress for formal recognition. That's how the Knights of Pythias became the very first fraternal order ever chartered by an Act of Congress. Here, read this."

Celeste opened a tab on her computer screen. Harrison read out loud.

"The purposes of your organization are most wonderful. If we could but bring its spirit to all our citizenry, what a wonderful thing it would be. It breathes the spirit of Friendship, Charity and Benevolence. It is one of the best agencies conceived for the upholding of government, honoring the flag, for the reuniting of our brethren of the North and of the South, for teaching the people to love one another, and portraying the sanctity of the home and loved ones. I would suggest that these great principles be perpetuated and that you go to the Congress of the United States and ask for a charter, and so organize on a great scale throughout this nation, and disseminate this wonderful work that you have so nobly started. I will do all in my power to assist you in this application and with your work. – Abraham Lincoln" [8]

"Pretty interesting," said Harrison. "Then what happened?"

"Knights of Pythias lodges began popping up all over the country. By nineteen-hundred, there were more than half-a-million members. It was the fastest growing fraternal organization in the country. A bunch of influential people joined the order, including businessmen like Nelson Rockefeller, congressmen, and several presidents – Harding, McKinley, and FDR."

"I am still amazed that I was not aware of this group's existence. Maybe because it is relatively young, unlike the Knights Templar and the Freemasons who have been around for multiple centuries and are associated with all those intriguing conspiracy theories."

"Also, the Pythians are not nearly as popular today as they were," added Celeste.

"Find out anything else?" asked Harrison.

"Even though they are a secretive order, there was some information about Knights of Pythias rituals. For example, the sword is a very significant symbol. New inductees receive a ceremonial sword that usually is inscribed with the letters F, C, and B."

"Don't tell me," said Harrison. "Friendship, charity, and benevolence."

"Exactly . . ." responded Celeste, ". . . the Knights of Pythias motto. I'm not sure why a sword is so significant, though, since the Damon and Pythias legend did not involve one."

"And what is this?" Harrison asked, pointing at a line on Celeste's notes. "The Dramatic Order of the Knights of Khorassan?"

"From what I can tell, the DOKK is a secret order within the secret order. Only special members of the Knights of Pythias belonged to the Dramatic Order of the Knights of Khorassan."

"For what purpose?"

"I'm not sure. Some of the websites said the DOKK just got together to have fun, but I got the sense there was more to it than that."

Harrison leaned back. "So, a bunch of the Welsh miners from Nortonville were Knights of Pythias members whose basic philosophy is to do good for your fellow man. Intriguing history, but I see no hidden conspiracies or mysterious connections to the poor guy murdered at the cemetery, or to you. You're not a member of a secret society that I don't know about, are you?"

Celeste glared at Harrison. "I couldn't tell you if I was, now could I?"

Harrison nodded. "It's getting dark. How about we wrap up, and I'll walk you to your car."

"Sounds good." Celeste closed her notebook, shut down her computer, and grabbed her coat and purse. "I'll come by your classroom tomorrow to see what else you discovered since I know you're going to continue researching this stuff tonight."

Harrison just smiled.

WITH THE SUN LOW BEHIND Mt. Diablo, twilight engulfed the city. Having said goodnight to Harrison, Celeste drove out of the school parking lot and headed for home. She felt more tired than usual after an emotional day dealing with several student issues. Her short commute home, avoiding the heavy freeway traffic, was especially appreciated tonight.

As Celeste wound through the residential streets, a subtle anxiety crept over her. At first she dismissed the feeling to exhaustion, but the growing sense that something was not right did not subside. She noted the headlights in her rear view mirror. It was too dark to make out details of the vehicle – perhaps a black, or maybe dark blue, SUV. Was it following her?

Celeste shook off the notion of being followed as utterly ridiculous. Why would anyone follow her? She turned on the radio to distract her overactive mind. At the next stoplight, she turned left. She thought about ignoring her rear view mirror altogether, but finally, with trepidation, she took a glance. The SUV was still there.

The hairs on Celeste's arms immediately stood up as a chill shot through her body. Just a coincidence, she thought. At the next stop sign, she turned right. So did the SUV. Then another right, and a left, as she navigated the side streets toward her house. With each turn, the SUV stayed directly behind Celeste's car, never approaching too close or fading back too far.

Celeste continued to rationalize the circumstance. It must be a neighbor, heading home at the same time. But she knew her neighbors, and she did not recognize the SUV. The closer she got to her house, the more anxious she became. Now, just two blocks from home, Celeste decided to find out for sure. She sped into the intersection and made a quick U-turn. She looked into the dark window of the SUV as she passed it heading the opposite direction. The SUV slowed, then paused in the intersection. Celeste held her breath while watching in her side-view mirror.

The SUV continued on its way.

Celeste exhaled. "Oh my, gosh," she whispered to herself. "What is the matter with me?" She turned her car back around and drove the remaining stretch to her home. There was no SUV in sight. She parked in her garage, unlocked the side door and went inside, thankful to be home. "I need a long, hot bath," she said aloud. She flipped on the light switch, dropped her purse and bag on the kitchen table, and walked into the living room. Immediately, Celeste froze.

HARRISON RECOGNIZED THE RING TONE on his cell phone. He trotted into his bedroom where he had left it. "Hey, C. Miss me already?"

"More than you know," said Celeste. "Can you come over right away?"

The request and her tone caught Harrison off guard. "Of course. I'll be right there. Is anything the matter?"

"First of all, I am fine. And second, I've already called the police."

A huge lump formed in Harrison's throat, nearly rendering him mute. He managed to eke out words while he raced to grab his car keys. "What? What happened?"

Celeste's voice trembled. "My ... my house . . . was broken into."

CHAPTER XII

June 20, 1878

WHETHER DUE TO AGE, a hot summer night, or the myriad responsibilities weighing on her mind, Sarah Norton tossed in her bed, awaiting the respite of sleep. The Knights of Pythias origin sword flashed into view every time she closed her eyes. A blade tarnished so severely had to be very old, she thought. The hilt appeared to be carved from bone with a metal cross-guard. She could not make out the details of the round, finely engraved pommel fixed to the hilt end. Certainly, this was a regal sword, but worth dying over?

Finally, as the hours slowly passed, her body and mind calmed enough to accept desperately needed rest. Only the sound of a strong breeze buffeting her home penetrated the peaceful night, until . . . "cuckoo!"

Although the clock's single one a.m. call came from another room, the sound echoed through Sarah's head like exploding dynamite. She opened her eyes and grimaced. "That damn . . ."

She immediately caught herself. A wave of guilt gripped her, as it did every time she thought ill of the clock her late husband had given her. Sleep would not come easily tonight. Sarah rose from bed and headed to the kitchen. A cup of tea, she thought, perhaps that will help. As she passed the bedroom window, an unusual light caught her eye through the lace curtain. She slid open the drapery and peered into the night.

Her window faced Nortonville's Main Street. In the distance, a flickering orange glow lit the darkness. Sarah gasped. "Oh, dear God."

NOT ANOTHER EARLY MORNING MASS, thought Thomas Oliver. The faint ringing of the Catholic Church bell reverberated through Oliver's boarding house room waking him from a deep slumber. What can they possibly be celebrating now, he wondered?

Oliver rolled onto his stomach and covered his head with the pillow. Just as he closed his eyes, a second bell rang, this time closer, and louder. Is that . . . the Protestant Church chiming in? Still half-asleep, Oliver could not imagine why both church bells were ringing in the middle of the night. He ignored the annoyance, certain the late-night disturbance would soon abate.

"Now what is that?" Oliver muttered minutes later. A third bell rang even louder than the others. This one, however, was getting closer. Oliver sat up. Not a bell, he realized. Sounds like someone clanging a pot. What the . . . ?

Oliver shook himself awake and rolled out of bed. He straightened his long underwear, staggered to his bedroom door and swung it open, ready to holler at the inconsiderate imbecile. But then he heard it. In the dark, Oliver could not make out who made the noise, but he clearly heard what they yelled . . . "Fire!"

"Main Street's on fire!" cried the shadowed figure. The unknown man ran through the boarding house banging a pot and shouting. "Fire! Main Street's on fire! Grab a bucket!"

Oliver watched in stunned silence as the man circled the boarding house interior, rousting its residents. "Looks bad," he said to Oliver matter-of-factly, and then dashed out the door heading for the next building.

The comment sent a chill through Oliver. Now wide-awake, he rushed back into his room, pulled on suspendered

94

pants, and slid into his boots. He ran toward the front door shouting back at the other residents. "Let's go, boys!"

Oliver grabbed two wooden milking buckets from the side of the house, and ran toward Main Street. Townsfolk, illuminated by the growing orange glow, headed toward the fire from all directions. Flames began rising from the roof of one building. Instantly caught by the stiff westerly wind, sparks flew into adjacent structures. Two, three, and then four buildings all ignited.

The bucket brigade dousing water onto the first building knew by now their efforts were useless. Oliver took a position in line at the fourth building. Morgan Morgans, the mine superintendent, took charge of coordinating the men, women, and children passing water-filled buckets toward and empty buckets away from the flames. Runners from the nearest well, a hundred yards away carried water to the end of the human chain. Sadly, when a bucket finally made its way to the front man, the splash of water onto the roaring blaze had little effect.

The firefighting battle was losing ground. Flames spread into the fifth, sixth, and seventh buildings. The situation was desperate. If they could not stop the inferno soon, all of Nortonville would be lost. Sweat poured from Oliver's face in the intense heat. Nortonville's scorching summer days dried the wooden structures into ideal kindling, igniting from the smallest spark. Three more buildings caught afire.

Morgans shouted at the bucket brigade to abandon the building on which they worked and move down. As the night went on, the possibility of saving any buildings grew less and less likely. Fatigue grew as Oliver and the others tried frantically to keep ahead of the rapidly spreading blaze.

Oliver noticed Sarah Norton speaking firmly to Morgans. She pointed at the bakery, several buildings away. Morgans

95

nodded, then mounted a nearby horse and sprinted into the hills. The action confounded Oliver, but there was no time to think, just grab a bucket and pass a bucket.

Minutes later Morgans returned. He called to Oliver and several other miners as he flew by them on horseback. The men met at the bakery and Oliver realized what Morgans had in mind. The mine superintendent jumped off his horse and quickly untied a wooden box strapped to the saddle.

"Four sticks at each corner," barked Morgans. "Run the fuse six feet."

Oliver and the others lifted dynamite sticks and fuse from the box Morgans retrieved from the powder magazine. Each man rushed to a corner of the bakery. Oliver wrapped together his dynamite with twine, and braided the individual fuses into the single long strand. To his left, the fire reached more buildings. Just one structure separated the bakery from the crackling roar and blistering heat.

Oliver intensified his efforts. He positioned the dynamite sticks and ran the fuse away from the building. Nearby, Sarah Norton and others sent the bucket brigade and onlookers away. Morgans continued to circle the bakery, checking on progress and keeping a watchful eye on the encroaching flames. With explosives in place at each corner, Morgans handed Oliver and the men a small burning stick to ignite the fuses. "On my word, boys!" he shouted.

Oliver and Morgans shared a telling glance. If this did not work, the town was lost.

"Light 'em up!" Morgans ordered.

Oliver and the three other miners immediately lit the fuses and ran from the bakery. Oliver turned back to see the building adjacent to the bakery now ablaze. He kept running.

Oliver, Morgans, and the others took cover behind a wagon. Morgans stood staring at his pocket watch. With decades of experience handling mining explosions, Morgans knew precisely how long the fuses would burn. The delay felt like forever to Oliver, but lasted less than a minute. Finally, "Fire in the hole!" hollered Morgans, as he dropped behind the wagon.

The explosion sent splintered wood in all directions. Oliver watched anxiously as a large wooden plank sailed over his head. Seconds later, the raining debris subsided. Oliver stood and cautiously peered over the wagon. Through an enormous dirt cloud, Oliver saw the initial burning buildings still on fire, though most were reduced to blackened skeletons. The building next door to the bakery was damaged from the blast, and still on fire. The bakery, however, was obliterated.

"All clear!" shouted Morgans. "Let's move!"

Thirty men rushed to the scattered pile of wood that once was the Nortonville bakery. Using rakes, shovels, and pick-axes, they scraped and cleared the debris away from the adjacent burning building. If they could create a firebreak in time, no further damage should occur. Sarah Norton reassembled the bucket brigade and aimed them at the former bakery site, determined to keep flames from jumping the gap.

For the next two hours, Nortonville residents and their Somersville neighbors worked to squelch sparks until the fire burned itself out. Sacrificing the bakery had the desired effect and the blaze spread no further. In the darkness of night, the total devastation was difficult to determine. Morgans sent most residents home until sunrise, while Sarah made arrangements for the newly homeless.

With sleeping accommodations secured for the last Main Street tenants, Sarah began considering the needs of those who lost everything. She sighed deeply, that will have to wait until tomorrow. For now, she thought, I'm exhausted and may finally get some sleep.

THE MORNING SUN HIGHLIGHTED Mt. Diablo's eastern slopes. Though still early, summer heat already warmed the air. Basking lizards perched on every large rock, flashing their blue-striped bellies at neighboring rivals. Thomas Oliver managed to grab a bite to eat and wash-up before heading back to survey the damage. He wondered how long his hair and thick mustache would smell like smoke.

Teams of men sifted through Main Street's burned-out buildings. Morgans had been supervising all night. His graying beard and rumpled clothes were peppered with ash and debris. Dark soot streaked his face and hands. Noticing an exhausted Morgans, Oliver detoured into a nearby boarding house and returned with biscuits and tea.

"Here you are, Morgan," said Oliver.

Morgans looked gratefully at Oliver. "Thank you, Thomas." Morgans devoured the biscuits and sipped on the tea as the two stood staring at the scorched section now devoid of buildings. "Such a tragic shame," added Morgans.

"If not for your quick action, it would have been much worse."

Morgans shook his head. "Not me. It was Sarah's idea."

"Of course," responded Oliver. "Well, thank the Lord no one was hurt."

"Young Tom, the knobber, happened to be returning home after he and a couple Somersville boys snuck out to catch frogs in the creek. Said that when he saw the flames, he ran into the boarding house and woke his parents. By the time they got everyone out, it was too late to stop the fire."

"How many buildings lost?" asked Oliver.

"Fourteen in all, including the bakery: Noakes' butcher shop, the Italian barber, the Jones' boarding house, the lodging house and candy store, and of course, your Knights of Pythias hall."

Oliver froze. While he knew the lodge's disastrous fate, this was the first time he considered the heartbreaking consequences. Along with the meeting hall, the Knights of Pythias Lodge #29 lost its history. All of the Order's records, artifacts, and sacred symbols were destroyed. Everything that represented the Knights was stored in that building, a building that no longer existed. Everything, thought Oliver, with one exception.

"Tell me," Oliver said, turning toward Morgans, "any idea how it started?"

"Not yet. But we do know where it started. Young Tom saw the first flames inside your place, the Knight's hall."

Oliver swallowed hard. A dozen scenarios raced through his mind. Why would a fire start inside the lodge? Or perhaps a more accurate question, who would start a fire inside the lodge?

"The boy said one other strange thing."

"What's that?" Oliver asked.

"When he walked past the Knight's hall, before he noticed the fire, he smelled . . . honey."

Nortonville Main Street [9]

CHAPTER 13

"How's Cousteau?" Celeste asked Harrison, who just returned from an early morning trip home to check on his dog and change clothes.

"All good."

"Thanks for staying over and helping me cleanup from the break-in last night, but you don't have to miss work today. I'll be okay," said Celeste.

Harrison poured coffee and handed a cup to Celeste. "Nonsense. That's what emergency lesson plans are for. You're staying home, so I'm staying home. Our classes will be fine without us for a day . . . hopefully."

Celeste smiled. Still shaken from the break-in, she appreciated Harrison's company. "It is so odd that nothing was taken. Detective Lawlor said the thief or thieves may have been spooked and fled before getting what they wanted, especially if it was something big, like a TV. But they sure had time to ransack my house, looking in every cabinet and drawer, so I'm not sure I believe that explanation."

"I agree," said Harrison, taking a seat next to Celeste at the kitchen table. "His other explanation about teenage vandals seems more plausible, especially considering your profession. How many hundreds of students have you encountered over the past years? It's possible one of them developed an unhealthy obsession."

"The idea that someone went through all my stuff really creeps me out," Celeste shuddered.

"I know." Harrison touched Celeste's hand. "Maybe we should consider moving in together sooner than later."

Celeste gently squeezed Harrison's hand. "Let's talk about it this weekend when my head is a little clearer."

Still in her pajamas and cotton robe, Celeste wore no make-up and her dark, wavy hair hung haphazardly down her neck. Harrison could not wait to welcome this vision each morning. Originally, they decided to move into Harrison's house after getting married, but if doing so now helped Celeste feel more secure, he was all for the change of plans.

"I need to get my mind off the break-in. Maybe some more research," added Celeste.

"The Pythians?" queried Harrison.

"I'll grab my laptop, you grab some more coffee."

The two settled back at the table. "What I'd like to learn more about," said Harrison, "is the Damon and Pythias story. Was that just a story about friendship?"

Celeste began typing. Her Google search instantly took her to a Wikipedia page. "Well, that's interesting," said Celeste.

"What's that?" asked Harrison, sliding his chair to better view the laptop screen.

"First of all, the legend has Pythias in trouble with the king, and Damon offering to stay in his place. When we read the tale from the Knights of Pythias webpage, it was the other way around. I guess it doesn't really matter. The story's premise is the same."

"I can see how a story might get mixed up a bit after nearly twenty-four hundred years. These guys lived in the 4th century BC, right?" Harrison continued.

"That's what it says. But here's another interesting thing. Oh, you're going to love this," Celeste added. "The friendship and loyalty values professed in the story did not originate with Damon and Pythias."

"No?"

"Apparently, they were devoted followers of an earlier philosopher. Some guy you may have heard of named – Pythagoras."

"Wait, what? Pythagoras? The geometry theorem guy?" said Harrison. "I didn't realize he was a philosopher, as well as, a mathematician."

"Me either," said Celeste. Her computer jumped to the history of Pythagoras link. She quickly scanned the screen. "Whoa. He was involved in a lot of diverse stuff. This will take some serious reading. How about I make us some breakfast while you dig into the life and times of Pythagoras?"

"That sounds great," Harrison replied. Celeste slid him her laptop. She prepped omelets while Harrison studied the website with increasing interest.

Soon, Harrison savored his first bite of breakfast. The perfectly cooked eggs hugging chopped ham, mixed vegetables, and melted cheese with a side of bacon, tasted incredible. Harrison had not realized how hungry he was until Celeste set the plate in front of him. He devoured his meal. Celeste joined him at the table, and the two ate quietly while Harrison read.

"That was delicious," said Harrison, leaning back in his chair and staring at an empty plate. "Best restaurant in Brentwood. I'll take care of the dishes when we're finished."

"Well, thank you," Celeste responded. "So, what have you found out so far?"

"I am actually amazed. Somehow I missed the whole Pythagoras-the-ancient-philosopher thing. I mean, before Aristotle, before Plato, even before Socrates, there was Pythagoras in 500 BC. Along with his Greek upbringing, he studied with the Egyptians, Phoenicians, Chaledans, and Magians. He was a mathematician, an accomplished musician, and some say his theories on the nature of reality made him the very first philosopher."

"I wonder why he is not as well-known a philosopher as those others?" asked Celeste.

"Likely because he never wrote anything down," answered Harrison.

"Excuse me?"

"It says Pythagoras is not known to have written anything, not even his famous theorem. The Pythagorean Theorem is attributed to him by his followers even though there's no written evidence."

"Interesting. Anything describing his philosophy?" continued Celeste.

"Numbers," said Harrison.

"Is that his math or his philosophy?"

"Yes."

Celeste glared. "You're going to have to do better than that, Barre."

"No, really," Harrison said half-smiling. "Pythagoras' philosophy about the nature of reality was that the universe is mathematical. All things are numbers. Here is a quote from Aristotle in 350 BC," he said, reading from the computer. "The so-called Pythagoreans, who were the first to take up mathematics, not only advanced this subject, but saturated with it, they fancied that the principles of mathematics were the principles of all things."

"What does that mean?" asked Celeste as she rose from the table to refresh her coffee.

"Pythagoras, for example, was the first to describe music in mathematical terms. It's commonplace now to associate music and math, be it note type, like quarter or eighth notes, or the actual tonal relationship of notes." Harrison quickly scrolled through the computer's description. "I'm reading here about how it was Pythagoras who discovered that notes played on a string, like a guitar, have a proportional relationship to the length of the string."

Celeste rejoined Harrison at the table. "Not sure I understand that."

"Have a rubber band?" Harrison asked.

"Sure, second drawer down in the desk."

"Scissors?"

"Same drawer," said Celeste.

Harrison instantly switched into teacher-mode. When the opportunity arose to explain, model, demonstrate, or guide, Harrison's urge to help develop understanding ignited an uncontrollable passion. Celeste loved watching the science educator enthusiastically improvise an impromptu lesson. She sipped her coffee while Harrison cut a large rubber band and tied each end tightly around a pen.

"Here," he said. "Hold each pen and stretch out the rubber band."

Celeste did as instructed.

"If I pluck the rubber band, you hear a note." Harrison demonstrated.

Celeste nodded.

"Now if I divide this length of rubber band in half, like so." Harrison gripped the center of the stretched-out band. "And then pluck either side of the now-shortened band, you get a different sound."

"It's a lot higher," said Celeste.

"Correct. The same note, but one octave higher. So, Pythagoras said that the sound of notes separated by an octave is created by a ratio of 1 to 2. That is, one whole string, or rubber band in this case, divided into two parts."

"I understand," said Celeste.

"Another example would be if I separated the band into three parts." Harrison marked the thirds with the salt and pepper shakers. "First let's again hear the note made by the whole length," said Harrison as he plucked the taught rubber band.

"Now, if I hold the band at the salt shaker and pluck the longer side, you get this note." Harrison demonstrated.

"I can definitely hear the difference," responded Celeste. "Not an octave."

"No. These notes are separated by only five steps on an eight-note scale, so it is called a fifth." Harrison repeated the example. "Do those two notes sound familiar?"

Celeste thought for a moment. "How so?"

"My middle school band teacher helped us remember the sound a fifth makes because they are the first two notes to the theme from Star Wars."

Harrison played the notes several more times while humming the extended version of the Star Wars theme song.

"Of course, I hear it now."

"Pythagoras defined this proportion as 2 to 3, for the ratio of string lengths required to make those notes. Another example is 3 to 4."

"Wait, let me figure it out," said Celeste eagerly. She handed the two pens to Harrison, who stretched them apart. "First divide the whole length into fourths." She slid the salt and pepper shakers into approximate positions, then pointed Harrison's unused knife at a third node in between the two. "I pluck the whole band and get this pitch. Then, I grab the band at either the salt or pepper shaker near one end, so one-fourth the length is on one side, and three-fourths is on the other."

Celeste plucked the longer side of the rubber band. "And now I get this pitch." She repeated the two notes several times.

"Recognize that tune?" Harrison asked with a widening grin.

"You'll have to give me a hint."

"Well, I expect that you and I will soon be listening to that whole song and . . ."

"Got it," interrupted Celeste. She played the two notes in succession once again. "It's the first two notes of . . . Here Comes the Bride!"

Harrison winked. "That interval is a called a fourth. Actually, Pythagoras called it a perfect fourth. And the previous interval was termed a perfect fifth."

"Why perfect?" Celeste asked, while continuing to strum the rubber band to create the first few notes of the well-known wedding march song.

"He noticed that the sound made by intervals of a fourth, fifth, or octave, are especially pleasing to the ear. Not all intervals are. Slide your fingers down a bit to change the length of the band."

Celeste plucked the whole length of the rubber band, then slid her fingers to a different spot and plucked again. She immediately winced at the harsh tone. "I see what you mean, or, I guess what Pythagoras meant. Some notes harmonize better together than others."

"Exactly!" responded Harrison, nearly shouting. "Harmony. That is key to the Pythagorean view of reality. Everything has a frequency. The relationship between those frequencies defines the mathematical beauty that governs the universe. And, in fact, we know that everything really does have a frequency. Next week I am teaching my science club about the concept of an object's resonant frequency. Good stuff."

"So not just music?"

"Nope," said Harrison. "Everything. Next to music, his most famous example is the harmony of the spheres, or *Musica universalis.*"

"Universal music," translated Celeste.

"Right. I had heard about it before, but did not associate the concept with Pythagoras. It is a belief that the sun, moon, and planets are imbedded in orbs that circle the earth, each at its own frequency. That frequency creates a pitch, just like the rubber band or guitar string. However, only the enlightened can hear the music created by their movement. And because the orbital frequency relationships of one celestial body to another are in the perfect ratios, like we just demonstrated, the *Musica universalis* is perfect and beautiful."

"That is quite a lovely philosophy. If only we could all hear the beautiful music of the universe." Celeste smiled. "Very mystical for a mathematician."

"That was pretty much all science was those days. Very much blending the observable with the spiritual. Here is another example," said Harrison, reading through another webpage. "The tetractys."

"The what?"

"The tetractys was Pythagoras' most sacred symbol, a triangular figure consisting of ten points arranged in four rows: one, two, three, and four points in each row, like bowling pins."

"Not sure I get the significance of bowling pins," mused Celeste.

"Oh, no?" Harrison replied. "Well try this, not only is the tetractys composed of the first four digit's summation - one plus two, plus three, plus four, equals ten, but the ratio of the top two rows is one pin to two pins, an octave like the rubber band. The next two rows have a ratio of two pins to three pins . . ."

"A perfect fifth," added Celeste. "And the bottom two rows are a ratio of three pins to four pins – a perfect fourth."

"That's right," said Harrison. "And there is a bunch more symbolism to it, as well. Everything from the divine creator to spatial dimensions are represented by one tetractys aspect or another."

"I admit," said Celeste. "The Pythagoras story is all very fascinating, but I'm not seeing the connection to the Damon and Pythias tale."

Harrison continued to scan the computer screen as he spoke. "Good point. For that we have to thank his school of followers, the Pythagoreans. These individuals actually wrote down his teachings. Some say, they may have even created many of the mathematical formulas attributed to Pythagoras. Not only did they ascribe to Pythagoras' philosophy of a universe governed by numbers, swearing an oath on the sacred tetractys, but they followed his tenets for living a purified life. It says here there were more trivial dictates, as well, such as not eating meat or beans, or wearing wool," said Harrison.

Harrison yawned and rubbed his still-tired eyes. Celeste slid the laptop in front of her. "You take a break. I'll finish reading through this. Aside from those tenets, this website says the Pythagorean Brotherhood was famous for their friendship, unselfishness, honesty, and of course, code of secrecy. Now that's more like it. Fits right in with the Damon and Pythias story."

"I read earlier that even the Freemasons and Rosecrucians claimed to have evolved out of the Pythagorean Brotherhood," added Harrison. "That Knights of Pythias motto of Friendship, Charity, and Benevolence, seems to be integrated through centuries of discourse on morality. Likely, many more fraternal orders got their primary dogmas from the original

Pythagoreans. So, we've gone from the Knights of Pythias, to Damon and Pythias, to Pythagoras; and from the mathematical resonance of the universe to the charity, benevolence, and friendship of man. I have just one question left."

Celeste leaned forward listening intently. "What's that?"

"Is there any more bacon?"

CHAPTER XIV

October 30, 1878

DANIEL ABRAHAMS READ the note again.

Urgent - Meet me at Watson's Saloon. 8:00 p.m.
Come alone.
T.O.

He walked quickly through the cool, dim night, carefully checking that no one followed. When the boy delivered the note to Abraham's house earlier that evening, an anxious pall swept over him. The responsibility assigned to Abraham, Oliver, and now, Sarah Norton, was crucial to the Knights of Pythias, and to the country. Being urgently summoned by Oliver, alone and at night, was cause for alarm.

Thankfully, Abraham could ease his mind about one concern . . . his wife. Married just one week ago, Abraham would have had a difficult time explaining to his new bride where he was going and why. Tonight, however, Rebecca was already at the church with the women's bible study group. They were scheduled to stay late planning for upcoming holiday festivities. Rebecca, just eighteen years old, conveyed a joyous energy that inspired Abraham. When she agreed to marry him after a brief but intense courtship, he felt as though his entire body suddenly lifted from the ground, weightless with delight. The daily drudgery of the mines grew much more tolerable knowing that Rebecca - young, beautiful, and full of life - would be there to lovingly welcome him home each day.

Abraham walked along Nortonville's deserted Main Street. Just four months after the devastating fire, rebuilding proceeded quickly. Rectangular foundations for reconstructed buildings stretched along one side of town. Their stacked brick walls showcased an obvious attempt to prevent similar disasters, a condition the Nortonville community insisted upon, regardless of the expense.

Just beyond the new construction stood Watson's Saloon. In the darkness, Abraham recognized Thomas Oliver leaning against the front door, his silhouette highlighted by the saloon's glowing kerosene lanterns. Abraham swallowed hard and approached quickly.

"Thanks for coming," said Oliver.

"Of course, Thomas," responded Abraham. "What is it? What is the matter?"

"Not here," replied Oliver. He looked cautiously in both directions. "Let's go inside."

Oliver's serious tone and somber expression added to Abraham's growing distress. As Oliver entered the saloon, Abraham slowly followed. Abraham closed the front door and turned into the room. Facing him were at least forty men, sitting in chairs and on tables, standing at the bar and leaning against walls – men that Abraham knew. The saloon was filled with Abraham's friends: his mining crew, Welsh choir members, Knights of Pythias brothers. Abraham did not understand.

Suddenly, as if directed by a choir master, every man in the saloon raised a glass and shouted, "*Iechyd da!*"

"Cheers," repeated Oliver to Abraham. "With the disastrous fire and all, we never celebrated your nuptials. Congratulations, my friend."

The realization of what was happening gradually seeped into Abraham. "A celebration? For me? I thought . . ."

112

"I know," interrupted Oliver. "Sorry."

Finally, Abraham allowed the fearful tension to drain from his body and a broad smile spread across his face. He wrapped an arm around Oliver. "Thank you, Thomas."

"That did it, boys," said Oliver to the crowd.

Samuel Watson slid from behind the bar and shoved a beer into Abraham, who enthusiastically grabbed the glass and hoisted it in the air. "*Iechyd da!*" toasted Abraham.

"What say you, boys?" continued Oliver. "Let's have one for Daniel and his new bride."

On cue, a solitary voice from the back of the room rang out in song.

"Pe cawn i hon yn eiddo i mi
O galon yn fy ngharu;
Ni fynnwn ddim o'i chyfoeth hi
Rhag ofn i'm serch glaearu"

The church choir tenor, who served as Nortonville's blacksmith, filled the room with the sweet, well-known Welsh tune, *If She Were Mine*. As the lyrics resonated off wooden walls, Abraham closed his eyes and soaked in the story about a desired love more valuable than gold or any earthly treasure. And then, with the precision of a well-rehearsed recital, forty odd-assorted men joined in, belting out multi-part harmonies in familiar Welsh fashion.

"Mae rhywbeth yn ei gwisg a'i gwedd
Ac yn ei hadgwedd hygar,
Rhaid iddi fod yn eiddo yn eiddo i mi
Tra byddom ar y ddaear."

The men sang of a love endowed with such winning ways and laughing eyes that they cannot live without her. Abraham

113

took another gulp of beer, inhaled deeply, and burst into song with his room full of friends. He felt blessed that he no longer related to this tale of desire. Abraham had married his love and, he thought blissfully, she is mine.

MUFFLED CHATTER ECHOED through the church nave. With bible study over, the Nortonville women rearranged benches and altar chairs into small groups. Each committee began discussing assigned responsibilities for the extensive Christmas, New Year, and Twelfth Night festivities.

In one corner, friendly bickering erupted about whose wassail recipe to use following Christmas service. Whether the traditional festive drink included mulled wine, ale, or both, always spurred intense debate among the older women, each promoting her particular blend of alcohol, fruit, and spices. Conversation in another corner centered on the *Mari Lwyd* selection. Though the churchmen appeared to make the final decision, this women's committee had substantial sway over which Nortonville gentleman they trusted to lead the New Year door-to-door merry-making without becoming too inebriated or overly obnoxious.

The decoration committee included young Rebecca Abraham. Just minutes into their discussion, the group already strayed off task. The other women peppered Rebecca with questions about her recent marriage. They wanted to know everything – details about the proposal, how she felt on her wedding day, and how her life changed since moving in with Daniel Abraham. Rebecca was only too glad to indulge. She loved talking about her well-respected husband.

When the probing turned to gifts, a woman asked whether Rebecca had received a love spoon. Rebecca's eyes instantly lit up. "Daniel carved the most beautiful love spoon I have ever seen. Would you like to see it? Oh, you have to see it," Rebecca said before any women could comment. "Let me just run to the house to fetch it. It won't take but a minute."

Without waiting for a response, Rebecca was off, sprinting out the church door toward the home she and Abraham now shared.

"I have seen a hundred love spoons," muttered one committee member. "I don't imagine hers is more beautiful than any other."

"True," smiled another member. "But to her it is, and that is all that matters."

Rebecca trotted the short distance toward her new home, oblivious to the cool night breeze. Abraham had been living in the small three-room house alone for the past few months, since his most recent boarder left town. Though she only recently moved in, Rebecca already imbued the home with incredible warmth, for which Abraham was grateful. The lingering aroma of fresh-baked pastries and colorful sight of dried flowers fronting newly-crocheted window coverings, all deepened Abraham's content.

In the dark, Rebecca stepped through the front door. She knew her exact destination, so didn't bother with a candle or lantern. The foot-long spoon hung formally on the bedroom wall where she could admire it each night.

The centuries-old tradition of young Welsh men gifting an ornately-carved wooden spoon to their love was transported across ocean and continent with the miners. Immediately following his first formal introduction to Rebecca during a church function, Abraham began designing and carving the thick redwood branch he had acquired. While some suitors offer a spoon as a sign of affection during courtship, Abraham hoped to offer his as a wedding gift. Every night, after long, grueling days in the mine, Abraham chipped away at the branch, revealing carefully considered symbols.

Thick clouds obstructed any hint of moon or starlight in the night sky. The resulting darkness required Rebecca to feel her way through the front room toward the bedroom and the hanging spoon. She stumbled several times over furniture that seemed slightly out of place. Bumping into the end table, she knew she was close. An unusual scent of honey caught her by surprise, unsure whether this was something new or just increased sensitivity due to the darkness. As she blindly ran her hand along the bedroom wall, she touched the smooth wooden sculpture.

Unable to see, Rebecca concentrated on the spoon's texture unlike she ever had before. She outlined each detail with her fingers. At the handle top, a dragon symbolized the profound connection with their homeland; in the middle, a cross denoted faith and marriage; at the handle bottom, a knot signified love entwined forever; finally, the scooped spoon-head itself, recounting a by-gone time when a spoon represented the ability to provide for a family. Rebecca sighed and lifted the spoon from the wall.

Then she froze.

"What's that? Who's there?!" said Rebecca into the blackness.

The noise came from the other side of the bedroom. She stood motionless, startled and confused. Was someone inside the room with her this whole time? Who? Why?

She needed light. Rebecca cautiously moved toward the dresser where she left a kerosene lantern the previous night. A stifling pain suddenly shot through her leg, and Rebecca bit her lip to keep from crying out. She reached down to feel what her knee hit. Why were her dresser drawers open?

With increasing distress, she swept her hand across the dresser and found the lantern. She fumbled with a nearby matchstick until it lit, and nervously inserted it into the lantern. As the flame took hold, she slowly raised the lantern in her trembling hand toward the source of the noise.

A silhouette appeared. The shadowy figure stood against the far wall. Rebecca was terrified. She squinted as her eyes adjusted to the light. Did she recognize this intruder? Why didn't the person say something?

Rebecca steadied her nerves. She stepped toward the figure.

"Is . . . is that . . ."

Before Rebecca could finish her accusation, an object came hurling at her. The vase hit Rebecca in the stomach, and she dropped the lantern, which shattered on the floor. Stunned, Rebecca watched as the intruder dashed past her and out of the room. Rebecca tried to follow, but something was wrong.

She looked down. Her fear turned to terror. Kerosene had spilled onto the bedroom floor . . . and onto her dress.

In an instant, flames jumped from the broken lantern onto her clothing. Rebecca swatted at the growing blaze with no effect. She was on fire.

Rebecca tore at her dress, desperately trying to remove the burning fabric. The flames engulfed her outer garment and took hold of the layers of cloth underneath. Rebecca screamed.

A searing pain consumed her body. Rebecca ran from the house shrieking in agony. She raised her hands to cover her face, but her sleeves were ablaze. Flames wrapped around the back of her dress as she staggered toward the church.

A terrifying wail pierced the serene night air and reverberated through the hills.

Church women and neighbors burst from their buildings, bracing themselves to encounter whomever, or whatever, could be suffering so. Neither their greatest fears nor most gruesome nightmares prepared anyone for what they saw.

From a distance, the image of glowing flames drifting through the night was indiscernible as a human. When the nearest residents realized what they were witnessing, stunned disbelief quickly turned to action. The first man to reach Rebecca tackled her to the ground. Unhindered by the scorching blaze, he yanked off his shirt and batted at the flames. Two other men grabbed blankets from their homes and raced toward her. They smothered the fire as Rebecca continued to flail uncontrollably and cry out in unimaginable pain.

With the flames finally extinguished, Rebecca lay on her back, quivering from shock. A sickening smell of scorched fabric and singed flesh hung in the air. The church women arrived and gazed in horror upon Rebecca's disfigured body.

One woman knelt down and kissed the cross dangling from her neck. "Oh, dear God. She's still alive," said the woman. She looked up at the growing crowd. "Someone get the doctor." Two neighbors dashed off toward the local physician's home on the other end of town.

She turned to one of the knobber boys peeking through the adults. "Find Daniel Abraham. Now!"

Nortonville Main Street — rebuilt [10]

CHAPTER 15

CELESTE SIPPED THROUGH the open door to Harrison's classroom. She quietly moved to the back of the room where Harrison sat at a student desk.

"We'll be done in a few minutes," said Harrison. "You can have a seat and watch, if you like."

Sinking into the adjacent desk, Celeste continued. "I thought this was your environmental club meeting."

"It is," replied Harrison. "We finished the planning part, and now Mitchell is doing some demonstrations for the group."

With great enthusiasm, Mitchell Conder stood behind Harrison's demonstration table in front of twenty club members. Celeste watched as he pulled objects from a box and placed them on the table. Harrison leaned toward Celeste and lowered his voice. "After our field trip to the wind farm, I talked with Mitchell about wind turbine syndrome. I figured if he was going to bring up the disorder, he should make sure the rest of the club knew what he was talking about. I suggested that rather than simply explain wind turbine syndrome to the group, he should try to demonstrate it. We are about to witness the result."

"How exciting," exclaimed Celeste. "I love when students lead lessons."

"Me, too," said Harrison. "I wish I could incorporate more peer teaching into my classes, but . . ."

Before Harrison could finish his thought, a voice interrupted from the front of the room. "Okay, I think I'm ready, Mr. B."

"Great," said Harrison. "Enlighten us."

Mitchell lifted a trumpet from the table, placed it to his lips, and blasted a long, loud note. Students closest to him flinched. Everyone knew Mitchell was first chair trumpet in the school jazz band, but they did not expect the sudden, intense volume from his instrument.

Calmly, and without saying a word, Mitchell set down his trumpet and dipped his finger in a cup of water. He slid an empty wine glass to the table's center and began running his wet finger along the rim. Within seconds, the glass began to sing. The sweet, pure tone from the vibrating glass spread through the classroom. While the demonstration's purpose baffled the environmental science club members, they were fully engaged.

Again, without a word, Mitchell finished the demonstration and set the glass aside. He picked up a string with a large metal weight tied to one end. Dangling the weight in front of his body until motionless, he slowly moved the string's end back and forth, an inch in either direction. Though his hand moved, the weight barely stirred. In over-exaggerated disgust, he shook his head. He stilled the weight, as if resetting the demonstration.

Mitchell stared intensely at the weight, helping to focus his audience's attention onto the object. This time, he rapidly moved the end of the string back and forth, vibrating the string the same inch in both directions. However, the weight did not move.

With dramatic flair, Mitchell again shook his head, obviously disappointed with the result. Next, he started moving the end of the string the same distance, but at a moderate rate. The weight began to swing. After a few seconds, the swinging grew higher. Mitchell smiled and nodded his head in affirmation. As he continued this swing frequency, the weight continued to increase its height until nearly horizontal, first in one direction, and then the next.

Apparently pleased with the result, Mitchell set the weight down. He quickly turned on a projector that showed a video on the front screen. Harrison leaned forward in his chair while Celeste squinted to make out the image. "What is that?" she asked.

"It looks like cells," said Harrison, "but I'm not sure why. We didn't cover this in practice."

The teachers and students watched silently as one of the cells slowly swelled and burst open, spewing its contents. A moment later, a second cell repeated the process, and then a third, and a fourth. The destruction continued until all cells in view completely ruptured.

Mitchell stopped the projector. "So," he finally said. "What do all of those demonstrations have in common?"

He surveyed the students' blank expressions. "Anyone? Anyone?"

Still no response. "Ms. Scott?" Mitchell queried.

The group swung their heads around awaiting the answer. "I have no clue, Mitchell."

Mitchell smiled. "The answer is . . . resonance."

"Resonance?" several students echoed.

"Sure. Let me explain." The student became the teacher, and Mitchell clearly enjoyed the role. "First, you have to understand that everything vibrates, whether at a microscopic level, like an atom or molecule that you cannot see, or at a large scale that you can see, like a pendulum."

Mitchell paused to gauge the group's comprehension. Satisfied they were with him, he continued. "Secondly, everything has its own natural vibration frequency. So, depending on the object's size, shape, material, or other properties, there will be a certain rate of vibration, or frequency, associated with the object.

When objects vibrate at their natural frequencies, resonance is created."

Finally, one of the club members commented, "What's the big deal if an object vibrates at its natural frequency?"

The smile stretched wider across Mitchell's face. "I am so glad you asked. It turns out that if you start with a small vibration of an object at its natural frequency, resonance can turn that into large vibrations at that same frequency."

Noting the confused expressions, he continued. Mitchell picked up his trumpet. He buzzed his lips, without touching them to the mouthpiece. "You can hear my lips buzzing, but just barely. Now if I buzz them at just the right frequency, and touch them to the trumpet, the column of air inside the metal tube will start to vibrate at its natural frequency creating resonance and amplifying the sound."

Mitchell demonstrated, blaring the horn once again. "Pretty cool. Huh? Now take the wine glass. If I wet my finger and run it along the rim, friction creates a small vibration of the glass. Too fast, and no sound. Too slow, and no sound." Mitchell demonstrated. "But if I get the vibration to match the natural frequency of the glass . . . voilà, the sound is amplified." The crystal tone sung out once again.

"Now with the string and weight, the frequency required to create resonance is easier to see. Notice how the motion mostly depends on the string length." Mitchell repeated his original demonstration. "Too slow, there's little motion; too fast, and no motion; just right, and the weight swings wildly."

"I get it!"

The exclamation from one of the club members startled everyone, resulting in a chorus of laughter. A second student added, "I think I understand those examples, but what's with the cells?"

Mitchell turned the projector back on. "The cells you see on the slide are cancer cells being exposed to high frequency sound waves."

"Nice," whispered Harrison. Celeste noticed Harrison's look of satisfaction that his student expanded on the concept: every teacher's goal.

Mitchell continued, "The cells have a natural vibration frequency. These researchers exposed the cells to that frequency and created resonance that amplified the vibration until the cells exploded. Using cell resonance frequency may one day be a treatment for targeting and destroying cancer cells."

"That's pretty cool," said a club member, "but what does this have to do with wind turbine syndrome?"

Another club member spoke up, "Is it because the spinning windmill blades create a low frequency vibration that hits whoever or whatever is nearby? And if that vibration corresponds to a person's natural frequency of one of their body parts, a resonance is created and the vibration gets amplified. I would guess that if a part of your body starts to vibrate and you don't know why, you might feel pretty weird."

Mitchell looked at Harrison. "Mr. B., my work here is done."

Harrison nodded.

"HI, MOM," ANNOUNCED Celeste.

"Hi, Sweetie." Celeste's mom gave her a hug, and then addressed Harrison, "Come on in, Harrison."

He hugged her, and she kissed him on the cheek. "Hi, Mrs. Scott."

"When are you going to start calling me Selene?" scolded Celeste's mom.

124

"I'm working on it," replied Harrison.

"Lunch is on the table, so we can eat and talk. I know you have something you want to run by me," continued Selene.

"Mrs. Sc . . . Selene, you didn't have to make us lunch," said Harrison. "We were going to take you out."

"Nonsense. I'd rather sit and chat in my own house than some noisy restaurant."

Celeste nudged Harrison. "Told you."

"Well, thank you," said Harrison. "It looks great." Secretly, Harrison was glad to eat in. A retired gourmet chef, Celeste's mom certainly would prepare a better meal than anything they could get nearby on such a tight schedule. Harrison not only loved Mrs. Scott's daughter; he also adored Mrs. Scott's cooking.

The drive from Brentwood to Selene Scott's house in Sacramento took a little over an hour, so Harrison and Celeste visited often after they got engaged. This visit, however, had an entirely different purpose than the others. Celeste sought answers about the Native American DNA that appeared in her genetic profile.

The three sat and shared small talk while savoring Selene's roasted vegetable and pesto minestrone soup and fresh garden salad with homemade herb dressing. Harrison was in heaven, although he felt challenged to balance eating with talking. As the meal wrapped up, Celeste's mom ladled the last bit of soup into a grateful Harrison's bowl. She turned toward her daughter and steered the conversation toward the visit's intended purpose. "So, dear, what is it you wanted to ask me about?"

"Well, Mom . . ." Celeste began. "Do you remember a while back when you did the DNA test?"

"Of course," Selene responded.

"Your results were pretty much what you expected, right?"

"They were," said Selene with questioning tone.

"I got my DNA results recently," continued Celeste. "And there was something unexpected."

Selene eyed her daughter. "Just spit it out, dear, for goodness sake. What is it?"

"Why do I have Native American DNA?" Celeste blurted out. "There was no Native American DNA in your profile, and dad came to the U.S. straight from Wales, where his family has lived for generations. So what's the story?"

As soon as the question passed Celeste's lips, she realized her tone may have been harsher than intended. Since receiving her DNA results, a multitude of possible explanations accounting for the unexpected ancestry swirled through her mind. "I mean," Celeste continued. "How is it possible for me to have Native American ancestry when you do not, and Dad's family was never on this continent?"

Harrison listened carefully while finishing the soup. He knew Celeste was confused by her DNA results, and he was just as interested as she about the explanation. He also knew that this should be a one-on-one conversation between Celeste and her mom.

Selene gave a knowing nod, as if she expected this question for some time. Selene moved to the family room and sat on the sofa. A faint smile appeared and she motioned Celeste to sit with her. "Harrison," said Selene. "Please join us."

Harrison obliged, though he still felt uneasy about intruding on the personal mother-daughter conversation.

"Well?" Celeste said.

Selene took her daughter's hand. "I cannot tell you the exact details. That will have to come from your grandfather, your dad's father."

Celeste furrowed her brows, growing more bewildered. "Grandpa Lloyd?" she asked.

"Yes. He can give you the exact details and dates."

"For what?" queried Celeste, nearing exasperation.

"You were right about your father coming to the U.S. directly from Wales, but not about his ancestors. I suggest you pull out your cell phone and look up . . . Welsh Indians."

CHAPTER XVI

November 3, 1878

ALL OF NORTONVILLE and most of Somersville, turned out for the early morning church service. And now, a slow, somber funeral procession once again traversed the well-worn cemetery trail. Daniel Abraham and Thomas Oliver walked side-by-side near the front of the all-male processional led by the elderly church pastor, John Price. A horse-drawn wagon guided by the livery stable owner followed close behind. In the wagon lay a simple wooden coffin containing the remains of Rebecca Abraham.

Rebecca lingered for two days before succumbing to her horrific injuries and unbearable pain. The Nortonville physician did his best to keep her sedated. All Abraham could do was sit by her side. He could not touch her, and found it difficult to look at her without falling into fits of tears and anguish. So he read bible passages, and he prayed, and he secretly asked for God's mercy to ease her suffering. When Rebecca finally passed, the small measure of relief could not temper Abraham's agonizing grief.

The afternoon was unusually dark and still. Gray clouds saturated the sky in a fitting backdrop for the townsfolk's drab black dress clothes. Mt. Diablo's rolling foothills, so green and alive during the spring, now looked dull and lifeless. Dried grasses and bare shrubs covered the ground like a burial shroud.

The pastor and wagon stopped just outside the cemetery border. Abraham, Oliver, and two other men carefully lifted and carried Rebecca's coffin to its final resting place. As the men gathered for the interment, the pastor spoke. "No one has ascended into heaven but he who descended from heaven, the

Son of man. And as Moses lifted up the serpent in the wilderness, so must the Son of man be lifted up, that whoever believes in him may have eternal life. For God so loved the world that he gave his only Son, that whoever believes in him should not perish but have eternal life. For God sent the Son into the world, not to condemn the world, but that the world might be saved through him."

The men slowly lowered Rebecca's coffin into the ground.

Flowers to honor the deceased were scarce this time of year. The exception was California Fuchsia, with silvery foliage and vivid scarlet blooms. Abraham gently tossed a handful of the flowers into the grave. The plant's vibrant color seemed an especially appropriate symbol of Rebecca's radiant spirit.

Abraham stared as if he could see right through the wooden box. He looked upon Rebecca one last time, if only in his mind's eye. Her long, straw-blond hair flowed into a pure white dress. Her arms crossed atop her chest clutched the carved love spoon that Abraham had placed inside.

Pastor Price finished a prayer, and the men responded, "Amen." Then they sang. The first verse and chorus of the hymn, *Gwahoddiad*, were slow and soft.

"Mi glywaf dyner lais
(I hear thy tender voice)
Yn galw arnaf fi
(A-calling now to me)
I ddod a golchi 'meiau gyd
(To cleanse myself in precious blood)
Yn afon Calfari.
(That flowed on Calvary)

129

Arglwydd, dyma fi
(Lord I hear thy call)
Ar dy alwad di
(And I come to thee)
Golch fi'n burlan yn y gwaed
(Oh, wash me spotless in the blood)
A gaed ar Galfari."
(That flowed on Calvary)

The second verse crescendoed, and by the third verse, the mournful tune could be heard by the women in town as the Welsh men sang boldly of atonement.

"Yr Iesu sy'n cryfhau
(In Jesus is my strength
O'm mewn Ei waith trwy ras
(Forgiving all my sin)
Mae'n rhoddi nerth i'm henaid gwan
(He gives such power to weakened flesh)
I faeddu 'mhechod cas."
(That I to heaven can win)

Their lyrics filled the barren hills with the Lord's invitation to strengthen a weak soul and beat hateful sin. As the final chorus ended, the last words hung in the air, gradually settling to the ground like a warm blanket comforting the soul.

Once more the pastor spoke. "Now unto the King eternal, immortal, invisible, the only wise God, be honor and glory forever and ever. Amen."

"Amen," responded the group.

Quietly, each man turned from the grave and headed back down the hill. Abraham remained, and Oliver stayed with him.

They watched as two volunteers shoveled dirt onto Rebecca's coffin. Oliver thought about directing Abraham away, but chose instead to simply comfort his friend however he could.

"I know I said this already," said Oliver, "but I am so very sorry for your loss."

"Thank you," replied Abraham. His eyes glistened with tears, blurring the sight of the workers filling the grave. The rhythmic sound of shovels scooping and dumping dirt resonated in his head.

The two men stood in silent reflection. Finally, with the grave nearly filled, Abraham turned toward Oliver. "I don't think it was an accident."

"You don't think what was an accident?" asked Oliver.

"Rebecca's death."

The statement stunned Oliver. "What do you mean, Daniel?"

"If she knocked over a lantern, the kerosene would have fallen away from her, not on her," Abraham continued. Oliver watched his friend's distant gaze transfix on the tragic scene replaying in his head. "And the furniture ..."

"What about the furniture?" asked Oliver.

"Why was it out of place? Drawers open, clothing and blankets tousled? Rebecca was meticulous. She would not have done this before, or after, the fire. No, someone else was there, in our home. I am sure of it."

Oliver considered the allegation. "And you think they murdered Rebecca?"

"Yes."

"But why?"

Abraham broke his stare and turned toward Oliver. "They were looking for something."

"The sword?" said Oliver.

131

"Of course," replied Abraham. "Rebecca must have interrupted. She was supposed to be at the church."

"Someone knew that you would both be out that night."

"Yes," continued Abraham. "They must have been looking for the sword or a clue to its location. Thomas, someone in town knows the sword is here; it cost Rebecca and maybe others their lives."

Abraham's words weighed heavy on Oliver. "If you are right, then my worst fear will be realized. The factions that seek the sword are convinced of its potential power. They will not rest until the sword is in their possession."

"Do you think the sword is safe?" asked Abraham.

"For now," said Oliver. "Only you, Sarah, and I know where it is hidden."

"Do you think we did the right thing telling her? Can we really trust her? "

Oliver stopped walking and turned toward Abraham. He rested his hand on Abraham's shoulder. "I trust her with my life."

"Yes, of course," Abraham replied. "But I am concerned for her safety. She is now deeply involved, and should anyone find out . . ."

"Yes, my friend," interrupted Oliver. "I share your concern, but no one knows of her involvement and God willing, they never will."

The two continued walking the trail back to town. They did not speak for a long stretch. Cadenced footsteps on the rough dirt path were all that disturbed the silence. Suddenly, Abraham stopped.

"What is it?" asked Oliver.

"I must tell you something, Thomas," said Abraham.

Oliver patiently waited for his friend to continue.

"I . . . I have decided to leave," Abraham said.

132

Assuming Oliver's reaction, Abraham continued before his friend could speak. "I know what you must be thinking, Thomas. This is a most difficult decision, but as soon as Rebecca passed, I knew I could not stay in this town. So much love suddenly ripped away has broken me. There is no happiness for me here. Knowing that my role with the Knights may have caused Rebecca's death is too much to endure. I cannot be responsible for the fate of the sword or the Knights of Pythias or for anything or anyone."

Abraham's torment distressed Oliver deeply. "I understand your grief, Daniel," replied Oliver. "But is leaving for the best? Your friends are here. The brotherhood is here to comfort you and help ease your pain."

Abraham looked directly into Oliver's eyes. "There is no way to ease my pain, Thomas."

Oliver nodded sympathetically. "Where will you go?"

"I hear that Washington Territory has coal. I will try my hand there."

"That is a long journey north," added Oliver.

"Yes," said Abraham. "But we have both traveled much further."

"Indeed," replied Oliver.

Abraham paused thoughtfully before continuing. "I am worried, Thomas . . . for your safety."

"This is a dangerous time, my friend, but I will be fine. I will contact the Supreme Lodge in Washington, D.C. for direction. When will you leave?"

"Tomorrow."

"So soon?"

"Yes," said Abraham. "I cannot stay a minute longer than necessary for fear my grief will shatter me completely."

"I understand, Daniel. Is there anything I can do to help?"

"Thank you, no. You have been a great friend, Thomas, and I will miss you."

"Come, let's get back to town," gestured Oliver.

"You go, Thomas. I need a moment alone and will be along shortly."

"Very well. Of course you will say good-bye before you leave tomorrow."

Abraham forced a slight smile. "Of course."

As Oliver headed down the trail and out of sight, Abraham removed a pencil and folded paper from his vest pocket and sat on a fallen log. He looked back up the hill toward the cemetery while he straightened the paper. On the paper, Abraham had sketched the outline of a gravestone. The rectangular image showed a flower at the top. Below that, Abraham had written the words: *In Memory of Rebecca Abraham. Died Nov. 1st, 1878. Aged 18 Years & 4 Mos.*

He took the pencil and carefully placed it near the bottom of the drawing. After a deep breath and somber sigh, he wrote: *Gone but not forgotten.*

Headstone of Rebecca Abraham [11]

CHAPTER 17

"IT'S GETTING DARK. We should start back," said Harrison. "The park closes at sunset, but I don't think we'll get kicked out if we're here a little longer than that."

"Such a nice evening for a Sunday hike," said Celeste. "Thanks for suggesting Black Diamond Mines. Nice to explore parts other than the cemetery. The park really is beautiful."

"There are some other great trails throughout Black Diamond Mines Regional Preserve that we'll have to check out in the future. For now," added Harrison, "let me gather my mutt. Cousteau, come."

Twenty yards ahead of Harrison and Celeste, the mixed black lab pulled his head from the shrubs he had been snuffling and turned toward his owner. "Come," repeated Harrison.

Instantly, Cousteau galloped back along the dirt trail to a squatting Harrison. With unexpected force, Cousteau rammed his forehead into Harrison's chest, nearly knocking him over. "Whoa," said Harrison, bracing himself. "He doesn't quite understand the concept of stopping."

"Well, he seems pretty smart to me," responded Celeste.

"Oh, he's plenty smart. Just a little goofy," Harrison replied.

"Then I see why you two get along so well," smirked Celeste.

Harrison just nodded. "Sit, boy."

Cousteau plopped his rear onto the trail. His swishing tail brushed dirt aside like the single wing of a snow-angel. As he stared up at Celeste, then back at Harrison, Cousteau's dangling tongue and broad smile indicated a thoroughly happy dog.

Harrison attached Cousteau's leash and the three began the return hike toward the parking lot. "I don't think you ever told me where you got Cousteau," said Celeste.

"University of California, Davis," said Harrison.

"You got him from college?"

"Well, sort of. He flunked out."

"Excuse me?"

"You know that UC Davis has the top vet school in the nation, actually named best in the world," Harrison continued. "One way they achieve that rating is to enlist furry assistants to help train the vet students. So, every year they scour nearby animal shelters and collect dogs. Each student is responsible for a rescue dog during the year while they practice taking measurements, giving injections, and other non-invasive procedures. At the end of the school year, students can formally adopt their dog. If a student declines, then the public can adopt the animal at no charge, if the interested party qualifies."

"Sounds like a great program. The students get necessary experience and the dogs get care and, eventually, a forever home. So how is it that sweet, intelligent Cousteau flunked out?" asked Celeste.

"Apparently," Harrison continued. "Some dogs don't do so well as practice animals. I was told that often this is because they are too smart. They realize what is happening and decide they don't want to participate in being poked, prodded, anesthetized, and whatever else comes with the program. Cousteau was one of those, so they put him up for adoption before the school year ended. I happened to be looking for a dog at that time."

"Was Cousteau his original name?"

"Actually, yes. Each year the vet school selects a theme for naming their training dogs. One year they were all Harry

137

Potter characters; another year was characters from Mary Poppins. During Cousteau's year, they were all named for famous scientists. Jacques Cousteau being an absolute hero of mine, the name immediately caught my attention when I searched online for rescue dogs. And, as they say, the rest is history." Harrison scratched the panting, still smiling Cousteau behind the ear. "Isn't that right?"

Cousteau glanced at his owner and leaned into the scratch. As Harrison lifted away his hand, Cousteau took the opportunity to nuzzle Celeste's leg. Happily, Celeste obliged, patting the dog's belly and rubbing his neck. "Alright, alright, Cousteau, I'll give you some love, too."

"The wind is really picking up," said Harrison. "Are you warm enough?"

"I'm fine," Celeste replied. "We'll be back to the car soon. It's my hair I'm more worried about," she added as she pulled long black strands from her face.

"So," Harrison continued. "The whole Welsh Indian story your mom mentioned is pretty fascinating. What do you think about that?"

"Well, I have to admit, though I didn't have time to read much online, I am in a bit of shock. I never knew there was even a possibility that Welsh explorers came to North America centuries before Columbus. And then to have my mom suggest that I might be a descendent is, quite frankly, remarkable."

"That is pretty mind blowing. Like you, I've never heard about early Welsh settlers before. Vikings, yes; Welsh, no. I've been swamped correcting science projects before spring break gets here and have not had a chance to research myself; so what are the details?"

"I've also been catching up on grading papers, but I managed to find out a little. The gist of the story, or legend, or whatever you call it, is that in the 12th century, a Welsh prince left Wales due to some conflict."

"A Welsh prince?" queried Harrison.

"Yes, Prince Madoc," said Celeste. "Supposedly, he fled a conflict with his brother after their father, the king, died. Prince Madoc ended up in what is now America. Over the years, the crew interbred with the natives, creating the so-called Welsh Indians who were light-skinned, blue-eyed, bearded men, speaking a strange Welsh-sounding language."

"That's an interesting tale, but is there any evidence?"

"What I came across so far," Celeste continued, "has to do with written accounts by explorers, some associated with the Lewis and Clark expedition. Some researchers cite physical evidence, like earthen structures in Tennessee and Kentucky that resemble an ancient Welsh fortress and burial mounds. Some symbols carved into stones resemble Bronze Age Welsh letters. And there was something about a boat."

"A boat?" Harrison asked.

"There are descriptions of round boats made of wood and animal hide among this group of natives that look very similar to known boats in ancient Wales."

"I have to admit," said Harrison. "I'm intrigued. Definitely want to learn more. Did you find anything about what happened to this tribe?"

"The tribe was called the Mandan. Like so many others, they were devastated by disease following European expansion into their territory. Tribal members that survived migrated to North Dakota. That's where Lewis and Clark came in contact with them. In fact, it was in a Mandan village where Lewis and Clark met Sacagawea, though she was a captured Shoshone."

"The story gets more and more fascinating. So, my understanding from what your mom said is that she thinks you might be descended from these Welsh Indians?" Harrison asked.

"Yes, she is making that assumption, but to be sure, I need a lot more information," replied Celeste.

"From your grandfather in Wales?" continued Harrison. Celeste nodded. "Exactly."

Harrison stopped walking. He bent down and patted Cousteau who appeared appreciative of the rest break. Celeste paused and turned toward Harrison. "What is it?"

"You know what you have to do now?" said Harrison.

"Sure," Celeste shrugged. "I need to call my grandfather."

"No, I don't think that'll be good enough."

"What do you mean?"

"Spring break is in another week."

"Yes."

Harrison unzipped his fanny-pack and dug behind Cousteau's treats and poop-bags. He handed Celeste two folded papers. Unsure how to respond, Celeste cautiously opened the papers. "Are these . . . tickets?"

"Pack your bags, C, we're going to Wales."

Celeste's look of confusion gradually transformed into a beaming smile. "Oh my, gosh, Barre." Without another word, Celeste grabbed Harrison in a tight hug. She held him passionately, and he held her – until Cousteau intervened. Harrison's dog forced his snout in between the two sets of thighs until Celeste nearly stumbled. "Alright, alright, Cousteau," said Celeste. "A hug for you, too." She knelt and squeezed an appreciative Cousteau around the neck.

"I am so surprised," Celeste continued. "How did you ..."

Harrison interrupted. "I called your mom the day after we left her house. She contacted your grandfather and confirmed he

140

would be around, and then gave me the details on where to find him."

"How exciting. It's been so long. You know, I spent a summer with him when I was in college."

"Your mom told me."

Celeste pulled her hair from her face again as the wind increased. "It will be so great to see Grandpa Lloyd again, and to visit Wales. You will love them both. Thank you so much for making this happen."

"I'm looking forward to them both," said Harrison. He gave a light tug on Cousteau's leash. "Now we better get moving. It's already dark. Here's the entrance to the sand mine so we're almost back. Though too dim to see, that hill to the left is the cemetery."

Celeste suddenly froze.

Harrison immediately recognized her expression, the same expression she had the first time they visited the park – anxiety and fear.

"What, C?"

She grabbed Harrison's hand. "I don't know, I don't know . . . I feel it again."

"What? What are you feeling?"

"Like . . . something terrible is about to happen," Celeste whispered, her voice quivering slightly.

"Come on," said Harrison. "Let's get out of here."

Celeste lifted her wrist to check the time on her Fitbit. "Yes, yes. Let's go. Please."

As Celeste started to lower her arm, she paused. Her look of anxiety turned to something else, an expression Harrison did not recognize. Celeste raised her wrist again and examined her Fitbit closely.

"How is that possible?" she said softly.

141

"How is what possible?" Harrison asked.

"This thing measures every time I take a step. So . . ."

"Yes?"

Celeste turned her wrist so Harrison could see the Fitbit screen. "How if I'm standing perfectly still, is it recording footsteps?"

Harrison clearly saw the Fitbit tallying steps, quickly, as if the wearer was sprinting. He observed for a moment before speaking. "Must be a glitch in the device. I'll get it checked out when we get home." Harrison had no idea what kind of glitch might cause a misreading like that. All he knew was that Celeste was getting more anxious by the minute, and he needed to get her out of there.

He held her hand firmly and began to guide her down the trail.

"I'm so sorry, Barre. I don't know what's the matter with me."

"No worries. The car is just ahead."

Walking as quickly as they could along the dark path, they headed down the final stretch until Harrison had to stop once again. "Cousteau, what is it?"

Harrison's dog, the well-mannered, happy-go-lucky lab, stopped walking. With his ears pinned back and tail down, he had suddenly become as anxious as Celeste. "Come on, boy. Let's go." Harrison tugged gently, but Cousteau would not move. "I've never seen him act like this before," said Harrison.

Cousteau began to whimper.

The hair on Harrison's arms began to stand. Celeste and Cousteau's frightened reaction to some unknown sensation sent a chill through Harrison. "Come, Cousteau!" said Harrison as he pulled harder on the leash. Cousteau began to walk, but Celeste did not.

With her head turned slightly away from Harrison, Celeste appeared fixated on something out of the corner of her eye, something in the direction of the cemetery.

"C, we need to go," insisted Harrison.

Celeste did not respond.

"C," he repeated.

She did not move.

Harrison touched her shoulder. "Celeste! What's the matter?"

Celeste broke her gaze and looked at Harrison, "Don't you see that?" she whispered.

Harrison never saw Celeste's olive complexion look so pale. "What? Where?" he said.

"There," answered Celeste. "On the hill." She turned back toward the cemetery.

"It's gone," she said softly. "I don't see it anymore."

"What? What did you see?" Harrison asked with growing concern.

Celeste reached out and grabbed Harrison's arm as she continued to scan the hillside. "It looked like . . . like . . ."

"Like what?"

Celeste looked back at Harrison. "A ghost."

Harrison swallowed hard. A million thoughts raced through his head, and he sorted through them before responding. He did not see anything unusual, nor did he believe in ghosts. But clearly Celeste saw, and felt, something. "Come on, let's get out of here," he urged. "We'll figure it out at the car."

Harrison tugged again on Cousteau's leash, who now seemed more than eager to move. He took Celeste's hand and guided her down the trail. Within minutes, they were at the parking lot and inside Harrison's car.

"How do you feel?" Harrison asked.

143

Celeste paused to reflect. "I'm much better." She took a deep breath and sighed. "I can't believe that feeling happened again. What is the matter with me?"

"I'm not sure, but whatever you felt, Cousteau reacted, too," replied Harrison.

"And I know you must think I'm crazy, but I swear I saw what looked like a ghost – a glowing white figure drifting over the cemetery. It looked like . . . a White Witch."

"First of all, I don't think you're crazy. You definitely saw something, though I'm not sure what, yet."

"I am just so confused. You really did not see the white glow?" asked an incredulous Celeste.

"Sorry, no," said Harrison, genuinely disheartened that he could not corroborate Celeste's vision.

"Maybe I am going crazy."

Harrison squeezed her hand. "Just sit back and relax while I drive home."

"Thanks, Barre." Celeste leaned her head back and closed her eyes, only to be interrupted by the familiar chime on her cell phone of an incoming message. She pulled her phone from her purse, tapped the screen, and silently read the email.

With startling speed, Harrison watched the color once again drain from her face. "What, C? What does it say?"

Celeste could not speak. She handed Harrison the phone.

The screen showed an image of an upside-down cross. The bottom of the vertical piece ended in a circle, and the upper in a point. Three rays radiated out from each side of the vertical shaft. Harrison had never seen this symbol before. He scrolled down to the text and read aloud. "Stay away from Black Diamond Mines. You will not be warned again."

CHAPTER XVIII

July 4, 1879

BY 10:00 A.M.., THE SUMMER SUN had been up for hours, as had the nearly one-thousand Nortonville residents. Following early morning chores, most now lined Main Street's rough dirt road. Citizens not anxiously awaiting the July 4th parade milled around the livery stable, preparing to take part in the town's largest annual celebration.

The crowd of onlookers huddled under covered wooden walkways. Adults stood in the rear, many leaning against the fire-resistant brick buildings built to replace those destroyed in the devastating blaze. Young children, seemingly impervious to the already stifling heat, sat in front, their eyes fixed in the stable's direction.

Planning for the event took weeks — parade participants and their order of appearance, noon-time orators who appropriately berate the King of England and promote benefits of a free society, picnic arrangements infused with music and children's games, afternoon foot and horse races, the popular Horribles competition where residents dressed in ugly costumes or clown outfits, and, of course, the requisite evening fireworks. The most contentious decision was always selection of the year's Goddess of Liberty, represented by the town's prettiest, most wholesome teenage girl. Debate and all-out bickering consumed the committee as members promoted their favorite candidates, typically a relative or close family friend. Final preparations involved decorations, including the red, white, and blue bunting now hanging from every Main Street building.

Just as the children's impatience grew unbearable, a pistol shot in the distance captured everyone's attention. Faintly at first, but quickly growing louder, the twenty-member Nortonville brass band played and marched as it left the livery stable. A short distance behind, two horses pulled a large, open carriage. Perched high in the middle, under a red, white, and blue canopy, stood the Goddess of Liberty. Her white stockings, long white dress, and curled blonde hair flowing beneath a broad-brimmed hat presented the desired image of purity and goodness. All around her on staggered haystacks sat a contingent of thirty-eight other girls dressed in frilly white dresses, each wearing a satin sash embroidered with a state in the union.

The girls smiled and waved as they approached the crowd. Onlookers cheered and waved back at the passing wagon. The smallest children covered their ears when the band's blaring horns and thumping drums crossed directly in front. Delegates from various organizations followed: uniformed ranks of the Oddfellows, Masons, and Knights of Pythias; Sunday school children's choir; local dignitary horse and buggy processions; and a variety of other Nortonville groups displaying their pride and patriotism.

The parade passed through Main Street and meandered into the hills above, heading toward the predetermined picnic spot – a flat plateau just below the Cumberland mine opening. Observers waited for the last participant to pass, then filed in behind and followed the procession. The band, choir, and speakers proceeded directly to a raised wooden stage installed for the occasion. Most others made their way toward tables where volunteers began setting out food. Picnickers reached for chicken, lamb, or beef, along with a variety of fresh fruits and vegetables plucked from Contra Costa County's prolific orchards.

Traditional fare, including Welsh cakes and speckled *bara brith* bread, were tucked among the choices.

As children sipped on punch and cider, many adults imbibed wine and beer. By the time the Nortonville band took to the stage that afternoon, attendees were joyful and light-hearted, and most adults thoroughly intoxicated. A second large wooden platform served as the dance floor. For hours, married couples and hopeful pairs waltzed and swayed gently to slow, sweet tunes, or stomped and strutted to upbeat jigs and polkas. Cheerful laughter and pleasant chatter added to the festive sounds of merrymaking. All of Nortonville blissfully celebrated the Country's independence – all, save one.

Sarah Norton's stern countenance carried an especially serious tone. For the past several days, she tried to contact Thomas Oliver to no avail. Delivered notes received no response. Several trips to his house proved fruitless. Concerned that he might be avoiding her for some reason, Sarah asked his friends to help locate him, but they, too, were unsuccessful.

Sarah resolved to confront Thomas at the July 4th picnic. As a food volunteer, she did not watch the parade. Rather, she spent the morning cooking and preparing the site. She knew that Thomas would lead the Knights of Pythias procession, so when the parade found its way to the picnic area, she could easily meet with him.

Satisfied that provisions were well stocked, Sarah delegated the area's supervision to other volunteers. Finding Thomas in the crowd should be easy once she located the Knights of Pythias Uniformed Rank. Dressed in dark blue coats with a line of gold-colored buttons, golden epaulets, and shimmering medals, each Knights of Pythias member also wore an embroidered kepi-hat and sabre in a fashion directly reflecting Civil War military style. Though many parade participants donned costumes, the Pythians stood out, and Sarah quickly spotted the group.

Her immediate reaction was one of growing alarm. Thomas was not among the assembly of uniform-wearing Pythians, nor nearby Masons or Oddfellows either. "Can you tell me where Thomas Oliver is?" Sarah asked David Woodruff, one of the older Pythians and the town's undertaker.

Woodruff answered immediately. "He's not here, Sarah."

"I know he is not here. I can see that," Sarah responded, impatiently. "Where is he?"

"I mean, he's not been here at all today," Woodruff clarified.

Sarah looked confused. "Didn't he march with you in the parade?"

"He was supposed to, of course. But he did not show up. In fact, none of us has seen him in three days. Been trying to track him down, but no one knows where he went. Strange that he would not let one of the Brothers know where he was headin'. And sure not like him to miss the big July 4th parade. We figured something important must've come up."

"Yes," Sarah said, trying to conceal her heightened worry. "It must have been something very important for him to leave without saying a word. Or . . ."

Sarah did not finish her thought aloud, but intense unease over Thomas' safety could not be ignored.

"Mrs. Norton!" came a shout from the food tables. "Sarah, we need your help, please!"

As Sarah turned in the direction of the voice, she saw a woman volunteer beckoning her. The search for Thomas would have to wait while Sarah saw to necessary supervision of the festivities. Besides, Sarah tried to convince herself, I'm sure everything is fine.

TWO DAYS PASSED SINCE the July 4th celebration, and still no Thomas Oliver. Sarah questioned everyone who knew him and many who did not. She covered Nortonville from end-to-end, as well as Somersville and the smaller outlying towns of Stewartville, Judsonville, and West Hartley. She even asked over the hill in Clayton. Not a soul had seen Oliver for days, nor heard of his whereabouts. Sarah feared the worst. If something terrible happened to Thomas Oliver, Sarah realized, not only would she have lost a dear friend, but she would be the only one left who knew the location of the Knights of Pythias sacred sword.

As Sarah sought an explanation for Oliver's disappearance, she asked herself another question — a question that grew more profound with each passing day. What, Sarah thought in earnest, if something happens to me?

"You wanted to see me, Sarah?" said Mary Tully.

Mary had long been Sarah's dearest friend and closest confidant. Unwed and childless, Mary Tully arrived in Nortonville shortly before Noah Norton's death. Mary's comforting manner eased Sarah's grief. Sarah soon gained tremendous respect for Mary's honest, unassuming attitude. Sarah's question now was not whether Mary could be trusted with the secret, but given the potential danger, whether she should become involved at all.

"Yes, please come in," replied Sarah. Mary entered Sarah's spacious home and sat comfortably at the table while Sarah poured tea. The setting sun left a warm orange glow filtering through lace curtains. "Something to eat?" offered Sarah.

"No, thank you. I am fine. Your note sounded urgent."

"As you know," continued Sarah. "We are all quite concerned about Thomas Oliver. Disappearing without a word has me deeply troubled."

"The entire town is very worried," said Mary, gently patting Sarah's hand. "But I am sure he is fine. I expect he will return any day now."

"Unfortunately, I do not share your optimism, Mary."

"Why is that?"

"Before he vanished, Thomas shared a secret of extreme importance with me. I believe this secret may have cost the lives of several of our Nortonville residents, and perhaps, that of Thomas, as well."

Sarah's words stunned Mary. A secret that led to lives lost? It seemed incomprehensible to Mary. How could the whole town and she be totally unaware of such nefarious events?

"I don't understand, Sarah. Are you telling me that people have been murdered?" Mary asked incredulously.

With her usual stoic expression, Sarah responded. "I understand your disbelief. I also found the situation difficult to comprehend at first. However, Thomas convinced me of the vital nature of his charge, along with its potential danger."

"What, Sarah . . . what secret could possibly be hidden in our little community that would lead to such horrific acts?"

"That is why I needed to speak with you, Mary. Thomas entrusted me with the information, and now, not knowing when, or if, he will return, I feel that I cannot be this burden's sole bearer. Should my time to depart this earth be soon, whether by nature or an evil hand, I cannot let Thomas's efforts be in vain. He believed his task to be of supreme importance to this country's destiny and I vowed to support his undertaking."

"Of course, Sarah," said Mary. "And you know that you may confide in me and that I will do all that I can to assist you."

Sarah now patted Mary's hand. "I know that, and I am grateful for your loyalty and resolute character. But I need you to be sure you truly understand the potential consequences of becoming involved, as I now am. I believe that men, some of our friends and neighbors, have paid with their lives to keep Thomas' secret concealed."

"I understand the risk. But if you feel that I am worthy of such a responsibility, then I whole heartedly and without hesitation accept."

"Thank you, Mary," said Sarah. "It will be a great relief knowing someone of your quality is willing and able to act, if needed. You know that I am not a religious-minded woman, but I pray that it will not come to that."

For the next hour, Sarah described the situation to Mary, providing as much detail as she could. Mary listened intently. "And so you see, Mary," said Sarah. "Should something happen to me, you will be responsible for the sword."

"I understand," said Mary. "Thomas's belief, and that of the Knights of Pythias, is that possession of this sword may truly impact the moral direction of our country: a noble mission and one that I am honored to assist you with."

Sarah stood and reached for her long overcoat. "Are you ready?"

"Yes, of course," Mary responded.

Clutching a single kerosene lantern not yet lit, the two women slowly trekked through the darkness to the powder magazine. With some effort, Sarah displaced the rock and removed the wooden box. She opened the box, removed the contents, and carefully unwrapped the sword.

"It looks very old," said Mary.

"I believe it is, but I am not sure that even Thomas knows the whole story surrounding this sword. I just know that

151

he insisted no part, neither blade nor handle, be touched by human hands. His belief, and that of many others apparently, is that possession of this sword, holding and wielding it, instills great power and influence upon the bearer."

"Do you believe that, Sarah?"

"I am a practical woman. It is difficult for me to believe such a thing. However, one's perception of power can often be as influential as power itself. Therein lies the danger and the reason I have chosen to help however I can," said Sarah.

Mary helped Sarah replace the sword and reset the stone that concealed the small chamber. They doused the lantern, but as they walked toward the cave opening, Sarah paused.

"What is it, Sarah?

Sarah squinted into the darkness. She cocked her head and scanned the trail, watching and listening. She took firm hold of Mary's arm, leaned toward her, and whispered, "There's someone out there."

Nortonville Welsh Choir [12]

CHAPTER 19

"YOU'RE DOING GREAT," said Celeste.

"Thanks," replied Harrison. "Driving on the left side of the road while shifting with my left hand is harder than I thought. Feel free to holler at me if I start drifting."

"Oh, don't worry," Celeste quickly responded. "I will."

"And what's with all these round-a-bouts?" Doesn't Wales believe in intersections with a stoplight?" Harrison continued.

"I know they can be confusing. Remember that if we are not sure about the exit, just take another lap around. They're actually pretty efficient when you get used to them."

"I suppose," muttered Harrison. "How did you manage driving when you spent the summer here with your grandfather?"

"I didn't," said Celeste. "I took the bus most places, and my grandfather drove on occasion." Celeste paused to stare at her cell phone. "According to the GPS directions, we have about ten miles to go. And only six more round-a-bouts," she added with a smirk.

"Great," replied Harrison sarcastically. "It's nice, though, that your grandfather only lives thirty miles or so from the Cardiff airport. Hopefully we will get the chance to visit the city. It looks interesting."

"Cardiff is beautiful. You'll love it. And being the capital of Wales, there's a lot of great culture showcased. I spent a lot of time there during my summer visit," said Celeste.

"So here's a question," said Harrison as he momentarily relaxed while steering down a straight four-line road. "I noticed that every road sign for Cardiff also has the word *Caerdydd* beneath, though I'm sure I'm mispronouncing."

"That's right. *Caerdydd* will always be alongside Cardiff. Though, it's pronounced more like, kay-r-deethe." Celeste said, easily slipping into a perfect Welsh accent. "Just like every time you see Wales on a sign, you'll also see *Cymru*. In fact, if you look at any of the road signs we're passing, you'll notice they all have both English and Welsh words on them."

"So *Cymru* means Wales, in Welsh?" asked Harrison, with his best attempt at mimicking Celeste's pronunciation.

"Correct. Wales is officially a bilingual country. The language was dying out, so in the 1990s, the government created some regulations to help prevent its further decline. More recently, to preserve the language, schools teach Welsh until students are sixteen years old."

"I had no idea," said Harrison.

"Everyone also speaks English, so it's easy to communicate. Reading the Welsh words, however, is a whole other challenge."

"I did notice that many Welsh words have serious vowel deficiencies. I can't begin to try and pronounce them."

Celeste just smiled. As she began to comment, the GPS interrupted, "In a quarter-mile at the round-a-bout, take the second exit onto A466 toward *Pwllmyric*, Chepstow."

"Oh, good, I was beginning to miss those round-a-bouts," said Harrison with a grimace.

"This one will take us off the main road and into the countryside. If I remember right, the roads get really narrow and windy," said Celeste.

"What can you tell me about Chepstow? Has your grandfather always lived there?" asked Harrison.

"As far as I know," responded Celeste. "I remember my parents wanting him to come to the U.S. when my grandmother passed away twenty-or-so years ago, but he declined. He's eighty-two now and still going strong, so I don't think he's going anywhere. The town itself is modest in size, less than 15,000 people, I think, and is gorgeous. It grew up around Chepstow Castle and alongside the River Wye. My grandfather lives a bit outside the town center in a house built in the late 1700s."

"He lives in an 18th century building? Amazing," replied Harrison.

Celeste nodded. "Coming from California, you really get a whole new perspective on the age of buildings. Chepstow Castle, for example, has a tower and original door from the 12th century. They're considered the oldest castle remnants in the entire UK."

"Well," said Harrison. "I am impressed. And it gets more and more beautiful as we get closer to the Wye Valley with the rolling hills and green forests. I'm anxious to meet your grandfather and see his place."

Celeste glanced at the GPS map on her cell phone. "The good news is . . . not much further. The bad news is . . . we're coming to another round-a-bout."

"Great," muttered Harrison.

For the next few miles, Harrison followed directions announced by Celeste and the GPS on her cell phone. Their route skirted the edge of town along increasingly narrow roadways, occasionally requiring Harrison or an oncoming vehicle to pull over and stop, abutting tightly against bordering shrubs so the approaching car could squeeze by.

"Turn left here," said Celeste.

Harrison complied. Wrapping around a stand of trees, the road led to an open expanse of land adjacent to the River Wye's elevated banks. Colorful flowerbeds and hedges layered half the area, while a sprawling vegetable garden covered most of the rest. In the middle of it all stood a well-kept two-story house. Its stone and mortar walls, gabled roof, and four towering chimneys hinted at the home's prosperous founders over two-hundred years prior. Now, the building's size and stature appeared much more modest, more in tune with history buffs than wealthy elites.

"Awesome," said Harrison with a grin.

"TEA OR ALE?"

"Tea for me," replied Celeste. She turned toward Harrison, "He brews his own ale."

"Ale would be great," said Harrison. "Thank you, Mr. Scott."

"Call me Lloyd," responded Celeste's grandfather. "No need for formalities here." Lloyd Scott strode into the kitchen, leaving Harrison and Celeste perusing old photos in the living room."

"Wow, eighty-two and looks in great shape," said Harrison.

"I know," said Celeste. "He has barely changed since I was here last. Same thick gray hair. Still gets around great, driving when he needs to. I hope to be so lucky at that age."

Harrison did not respond. He stood frozen in front of the fireplace mantel. The thick wooden shelf held an assortment of items: an ornate 18th-century clock, several small porcelain vases, two large brass candle holders, and a single framed black-and-white photograph at which Harrison stared transfixed. "Oh my, gosh. Is this your grandmother? You look just like her."

Celeste joined Harrison at the photo. "Yes. My father always told me how much I looked like her, but I didn't realize how strong the resemblance was until I came here and Grandpa Lloyd showed me all these old images."

157

"Honestly," said Harrison, still mesmerized. "If I saw this photo in any other context, I would swear that was you. It's amazing."

"I guess you noticed how much my granddaughter looks like my wife," Lloyd announced.

Harrison and Celeste turned to see Lloyd returning to the living room carrying a tray and tea service in one hand and two pints of amber-colored ale in the other. Celeste immediately stepped forward and took hold of the tea service, allowing Lloyd to hand a glass to Harrison.

"Cancer," Lloyd blurted with disgust. "Like Celeste's father. An unfortunate hereditary scourge, it seems."

"I am so sorry for your losses," replied Harrison.

Lloyd nodded silently. "Have a seat," said Lloyd, motioning toward a sofa where Celeste poured her steeped tea. He lifted his glass while Harrison and Celeste followed. "To those memories kept dear to our heart and those yet to be created."

Two pint glasses and a teacup clinked. "Cheers," said Harrison and Celeste simultaneously.

"I know that we could have talked over the phone or emailed about what you want to know," said Lloyd, "but I am delighted that you decided to pay me a visit."

"I'm glad, too. It's been too long," Celeste responded. "I really have Harrison to thank. He surprised me with the trip."

Lloyd nodded at Harrison. "Good lad. And have you two set a date for the wedding, yet?"

"Not yet. We're still working on it," answered Celeste.

"Well, don't wait too long. I'm an old man, you know, but I'd sure like to be there."

"Grandpa, you have a lot of years left. But don't worry, we'll make sure you're there."

The small talk continued for the next hour, mostly with Harrison asking questions about Celeste's family, the house they were in, and life in Wales. As Lloyd returned from the kitchen with a second pint of ale for Harrison and himself, and a first glass for Celeste, his tone grew serious. "I suppose it's time we talk about what you really what to know."

"Grandpa," Celeste continued. "Ever since I learned that my DNA contains traces of Native American ancestry, I'm terribly anxious to learn the family connection. Any light you can shed is most appreciated."

Lloyd settled back into his chair and took a long drink. He sat quietly for several minutes, seemingly searching his memory for the details he wanted to share. Celeste and Harrison waited patiently, glancing at each other and wondering if Celeste's grandfather was going to provide any insight at all.

Then he spoke. "The story I am about to tell will seem farfetched, and I have no real proof of its accuracy. But your grandmother believed it with all of her heart, and that was good enough for me."

This was not at all how Celeste expected the explanation to begin. She was now more intrigued than ever.

"In the twelfth century," Lloyd continued, "Owain Gwynedd, one of the greatest Welsh rulers of the middle ages, died. His many sons soon engaged in a ruthless battle for control. Disheartened by his family's bloody power struggle, one son, Prince Madoc, set sail to explore the western ocean."

"Wait," interrupted Harrison, engrossed by the story. "Prince Madoc? This is this Welsh Indian story you told me about," he said towards Celeste.

"In 1170, Prince Madoc and his crew arrived at a previously unchartered land. Impressed with the abundance this new land provided, the prince left behind some crewmembers to

159

begin a colony, while he sailed back to his homeland. Once there, he recruited additional settlers and ships, and soon returned to the new land. He began exploring the many interior river valleys, eventually settling himself in the new world."

"That's over three-hundred years before Columbus," Harrison continued incredulously.

"Quite right," said Lloyd.

Harrison caught his mouth slightly agape. "I'm aware of evidence that Vikings arrived in North America prior to Columbus, but I never heard anything about the Welsh?"

Celeste broke into the conversation. "That's a fascinating tale, but what does it have to do with me?"

"Well, my dear," said Lloyd. "Like your tales of Columbus, Prince Madoc also encountered the indigenous people. But more than just share a meal together - I believe you Yanks call it Thanksgiving - Prince Madoc and his crew intermarried with the natives. For centuries the Welsh settlers and the natives lived together, mostly peacefully, exchanging and integrating cultures and . . ."

The pause frustrated Celeste. "And what?" she insisted.

Lloyd leaned toward her. ". . . and DNA."

Harrison understood immediately. "You're saying that Celeste's Native American ancestry is descended from these Welsh settlers to America."

"Indeed," said Lloyd, "from the Welsh Indians as they were called."

Celeste looked perplexed. "But you were born here, in Wales," she said. "And so was dad. So, how could . . ."

Anticipating his granddaughter's question, Lloyd interrupted. "According to my dear wife, your great, great, grandmother was born in America, but returned to Wales just before the turn of the century . . . the twentieth century, that is."

"So you're telling me," Celeste continued incredulously, "that I have Native American DNA because I am related to the Welsh Indians who lived in America centuries before Columbus. And they are descendants of Welsh settlers brought there by someone named Prince Madoc?"

"That's right," said Lloyd with a shrug. "I told you the story would seem farfetched."

Celeste continued to shake her head in disbelief. "Prince Madoc?"

"Correct. Though you will often see his name written as . . . Madog"

CHAPTER XX

August 1, 1879

SARAH'S GAZE PENETRATED the darkness. Her experienced ears easily distinguished wind-rustled tree branches from footsteps on leaf litter. Someone was out there, concealed by the night, but not far away. Still holding Mary's arm, Sarah slowly walked sideways out of the powder magazine cave. She led Mary off the trail and into the surrounding shrubs and trees. "If we cut through here," Sarah whispered to Mary, "we will connect to the mine trail and can circle around whomever is out there. That trail will take us back to town, hopefully without being seen."

The two women carefully stepped atop stones and soft dirt to minimize the noise. Within minutes, they crossed onto the mine trail. Sarah paused and listened intently for any sound of being followed. Confident she skirted the unknown person, Sarah again held Mary's arm. She dare not light the lantern, as the two quickly, but silently, made their way along the trail visible only by the crescent moon's dim glow.

On the edge of town, Sarah and Mary veered from the mine trail and headed toward Sarah's house. Mary needed to collect some belongings left at Sarah's before returning to her own home. As the two women passed the trailhead leading toward the powder magazine, Sarah abruptly stopped.

"What is it?" Mary asked with concern. She had just begun to relax from the tension of the past few hours. The story of the mysterious Pythian sword and possible murders, the trek to a secret hiding place, and avoidance of a shadowy figure in the dark, all exhausted Mary and put her on edge. She hoped dearly that being back in town would allow her to feel more at ease, but Sarah had other plans.

"I wonder," said Sarah, "if whoever is out there will return along this trail."

"Why?" asked Mary.

"I surely would like to know who is wandering the hills in the middle of the night with no light. If he, or she, was not following us, what were they doing?" Sarah replied.

"Oh, Sarah," said Mary in disbelief. "It is much too dangerous. After all you have told me, you cannot possibly confront a stranger out here with no manner of protection."

Sarah considered the comment. "Firstly, I did not say I would confront them. I just want to see them. Secondly, I will have protection. Wait here."

Sarah trotted into her house and quickly returned. She handed Mary the twelve-gauge shotgun she kept by her bed. A stunned Mary took the gun. "Have you handled one of these before?" Sarah asked.

"I have," said Mary. "But . . ."

"It's loaded and ready. You'll be to the side, behind this oak tree.

Mary thought about continuing the debate, but she had knew that look in Sarah's eyes. There would be no convincing her otherwise. The two women moved back into the shadows and waited. They spoke softly to each other to pass the time. Mary wondered just how long Sarah would stay here, hoping to catch a glimpse of someone who may, or may not, be coming.

The wait was short. "Shh," said Sarah. "Listen."

The faint, rhythmic footsteps in the distance were unmistakable. As the steps grew closer, Mary grew tenser. "This is not a good idea," she whispered nervously in Sarah's ear.

Sarah did not respond. She peered into the blackness toward the trail. Who is that, she thought. Why no lantern? What is this person doing out here? She was dead-set on getting an answer.

A figure came into view, walking quickly, but still too concealed by darkness to identify. Approaching the trailhead, the individual slowed, as if looking for something, or someone.

"Who is it?" said Mary.

"I cannot tell, yet." Sarah turned toward Mary and looked up into her fearful eyes. She patted the shogun Mary clutched tightly, and then, without saying another word, Sarah stepped from behind the tree.

Mary gasped, but managed to withhold the sound. Determined to protect her friend, Mary gently lowered the gun barrel, ready to do whatever was needed.

Sarah, unaccustomed to hiding or sneaking around, walked directly toward the mysterious figure. "Who's there?" she asked boldly.

The figure spun swiftly toward Sarah and jumped, clearly startled by the voice, but there was no response. Sarah stepped toward the figure. Mary directed the gun at the faint outline of the person. Don't get too close, she thought. Her finger edged near the trigger. "Don't get too close," she whispered.

Sarah abruptly stopped. She bent down, rested the lantern on the ground, and in an instant a sparked flint lit the kerosene. She lifted the now-blazing lantern toward the shrouded image and repeated, "Who's there?"

"S . . . S . . . Sarah? Is that you?"

Sarah directed the lantern at the familiar voice. "Ann? Ann! What are you doing out here so late and in the dark?"

"Oh, Sarah. You frightened me," replied Ann.

"I would expect so," scolded Sarah. "Out here all alone is not safe."

"Yes, well . . ." began Ann, who suddenly flinched again at the sight of another person emerging from the dark.

"Hello, Ann," said Mary. Mary approached the two women empty handed. Carrying a shotgun, she reasoned, would only add anxiety to the uneasy encounter, so she left it propped against the tree.

"Why, Mary . . ." Ann responded. "What on earth are you doing out here?"

Sarah anticipated the question and answered before Mary had a chance. "Mary walked me home," said Sarah. "We lost track of time chatting at her place, so she thought best to accompany me home."

Mary nodded, thankful for Sarah's quick explanation.

"And you?" Sarah continued.

"I, uh . . ." Ann began. "That would be . . . bats."

Sarah and Mary shared a puzzled glance.

"I suppose it is more accurate to say guano," added Ann. "You know, bat droppings."

"Yes," said Sarah. "I know what guano is. But just what are you doing?"

"Well, selling honey and candles from my bees is often not enough on which to get by. So, some years ago, I learned the value of bat guano for making saltpeter."

"Saltpeter?" queried Mary.

"Saltpeter is used for making gunpowder," said Sarah, who recalled her husband hiring men to procure and blend saltpeter, sulfur, and charcoal for mining operations.

"That's right," said Ann. "If I find locations with substantial deposits of bat guano, I can sell that information to powder manufacturers. So, I try and follow the bats."

165

Neither Sarah nor Mary was sure whether to be impressed by their friend's adventurous enterprise or stunned by her risky undertaking.

"And were you successful?" asked Mary.

"Not tonight. I'll try again when the moon is brighter. I should be going now. Good night, Mary . . . Sarah," said Ann as she turned toward town.

"It has been a long night," Mary said softly to Sarah. "Time for me to head home, as well." She leaned toward Sarah and lowered her voice further, "Your protection is behind the tree." Mary winked at Sarah and turned toward town. "Ann!" she yelled. "Wait a moment and I will join you!"

THE EARLY MORNING KNOCK on her door surprised Sarah, though she had been up for hours. Perhaps Mary returning to collect something forgotten from last night, she thought. As Sarah carefully descended the stairs from her second floor bedroom, the knock grew louder. "Alright, alright," she said. "Hold your horses."

Sarah readied herself to playfully chastise Mary for her impatience. She swung open the door and stared at the unexpected stranger in front of her. "Yes," said Sarah. "May I help you?"

The man removed his bowler hat revealing dark, neatly trimmed hair that he straightened with a clean, well-manicured hand. Sarah knew everyone in Nortonville and most folks in the surrounding towns. This gentleman certainly did not live in one of the mining towns.

"Mrs. Norton?" he asked. "Sarah Norton?"

Sarah eyed him suspiciously. "Yes . . ."

"I have something for you." The stranger opened his waistcoat and reached inside. Sarah instantly felt a rush of adrenaline shoot through her body. My God, she thought, someone has found out already. Her mind raced. Do I run? Do I fight? Do I scream?

She knew she could not escape this man. Screaming for help was her only hope. Perhaps someone in town would hear and come to investigate before it was too late. As the man slowly removed his hand from inside his coat, Sarah inhaled deeply.

"This is for you," he said calmly. He handed Sarah an envelope. She let out an audible sigh and took the paper. "Good day, ma'am," he said. The stranger immediately replaced his hat, turned, and headed toward a waiting buggy. Sarah watched as he climbed in, grabbed the horse's reins, and rode off without saying another word.

Receiving mail was rare enough, but mail personally delivered to your home was highly unusual. She placed the unmarked envelope on the kitchen table and poured herself some tea. Still suspicious, she carefully peeled open the envelope and removed the letter within. As she unfolded the paper, Sarah instantly recognized the printed insignia – a shield in front of crossed battle-axes, a knight's helmet on top, and the letters F, C, and B on the shield face. This was from the Knights of Pythias.

Greetings Mrs. Norton,

I hope you are well. While I should prefer to exchange pleasantries, I am afraid that recent events require immediate and direct communication. I was informed by Thomas Oliver of your acceptance of and able participation in the just and Godly mission undertaken by the Knights of Pythias. The importance of the origin sword cannot be overstated, and we are forever in your debt.

167

It is now evident that Brother Oliver may have succumbed to an evil hand. It is, therefore, the purpose of this message to warn you of the deadliest peril to which you may now be subject. There is a rogue faction within the K of P that wish to use the origin sword to control our most powerful order for unscrupulous and immoral objectives. We cannot let this occur.

You are the sole bearer of the sword's whereabouts, a fact that remains unknown to even the highest ranking KoP. Wish it I could guarantee this fact held true forever, but sadly I cannot. Therefore, it is my request that you seek a place for the sword to reside in utmost secrecy, perhaps for years, and that you prepare a description of that place in a manner not easily discernable. As soon as you are able, send this notification to one person only – John C. Holmes, Grand Chancellor, Knights of Pythias Sacramento Lodge. The note must go directly from your most trusted messenger into the hands of the Grand Chancellor only; this is of extreme necessity.

Through his letters, it was clear that Brother Oliver trusted you whole-heartedly and espoused your virtue. So know this, the K of P origin sword is more than just a symbol for the leadership and control of our order. It carries a secret that is older and more powerful than all but a very few on this earth are aware. I dare not share this attribute for fear that one additional individual with this knowledge increases the danger one-hundred fold. Your noble actions from this day forward will impact country and humanity.

Be well and God speed.
Justus H. Rathbone
Supreme Chancellor, Knights of Pythias
Washington, District of Columbia, U.S.A.

JUSTUS HENRY RATHBONE,
FOUNDER & PAST SUPREME CHANCELLOR OF THE ORDER OF KNIGHTS OF PYTHIAS.

Justus Rathbone [13]

CHAPTER 21

AT THE MENTION OF MADOG, Celeste and Harrison looked at each other. Celeste raced to her bag and pulled out a small notebook. She flipped to a page near the beginning and sat next to her grandfather. "Not long ago," Celeste began. "A man was murdered in a nearby city. The murder actually took place at an old pioneer cemetery in the surrounding hills."

Celeste paused to gauge her grandfather's reaction. "Go on," said Lloyd, clearly concerned about the story's direction.

"Before he died from a knife wound," she continued, "he wrote something on a headstone." Celeste pointed to the words in her notebook as her grandfather watched. "Madog near. Warn Celeste Scott," she read.

Lloyd sat back, brow furrowed and eyes fixed on the page. "Madog near. Warn Celeste Scott," he repeated in his thick Welsh accent.

"Do you suppose it refers to this Prince Madoc?" Harrison asked.

"Aye," nodded Lloyd, "I expect so."

"But why?" Celeste asked. "Even if the legend were true, how could a centuries-old Welsh prince be near the base of Mt. Diablo in Northern California? And why warn me?"

Lloyd turned toward Celeste. "I don't know the answer to those questions. Your grandmother was the Prince Madoc expert, not me. Perhaps learning more about the Madoc story will shed some light."

Harrison joined Celeste on the sofa and patted her knee. "Fortunately," he added, "we have a bit of practice investigating lately."

170

"I believe the National Library of Wales has a fair amount of literature on the subject," Lloyd replied.

"Fantastic," replied Harrison. "Where is that?"

"Unfortunately, you'll be in for a long drive to the other side of the country," said Lloyd.

Celeste squeezed Harrison's hand. "First, let's see what they have online. I am endlessly amazed at the historical documents now digitized on the web. Plus, that will allow us to hang around here for another day." Celeste rose from her seat. "But right now, I'm exhausted and heading to bed." She leaned over and kissed Lloyd on the cheek. "Thanks, Grandpa. I'll see you in the morning."

"I'll just finish my drink and be up in a few minutes," said Harrison. In addition to not wasting the outstanding homemade ale, he relished the opportunity to chat with Celeste's grandfather with the hope of gleaning new details about the woman he loved and would soon marry.

"So tell me, Lloyd, did you spend much time with Celeste when she was young?"

THE EARLY MORNING AIR was crisp and refreshing. Harrison, Celeste, and Celeste's grandfather strolled through the garden toward raised banks overlooking the River Wye. Following a substantial breakfast prepared by Celeste, all three appreciated a chance to stretch their legs. The dirt path meandered around Lloyd's property until paralleling the river. From nearby woods, green woodpeckers squawked at each other sounding like a treetop laser battle. Rapid-fire nuthatch chirps and grunting ravens added to the morning chorus.

Harrison felt morning strolls in the wilderness were both tranquil and exciting. As an amateur birder, he listened closely to

171

the calls, trying to memorize tones and patterns for later identification, but as soon as the river came into view, Harrison froze.

"Whoa," Harrison announced. "What happened to all the water? When we walked by here yesterday afternoon, this river was nearly full and now there's just a trickle."

A slight smile eased across Lloyd's face. He pulled an antique pocket watch from inside his coat, flipped open the cover, and glanced at the time. Nodding in satisfaction, he replied, "Listen."

Harrison had been listening to the birds. Is that what Lloyd meant? "I'm sorry," Harrison said. "Listen to what?"

Celeste, knowing what was about to happen, gently nudged Harrison, and pointed toward the river. "Listen to the water."

Thoroughly confused, Harrison did as instructed. The water, appearing no more than three or four feet deep, rushed from left to right over boulders and branches with a typical gurgling stream sound. The three stood silently observing the river. And while spending time outdoors with Celeste and her grandfather thrilled Harrison, his burning curiosity made it difficult to relax.

For ten minutes, they watched and listened to the river. Then, as if Celeste's nudge finally hit its mark, Harrison noticed something changing. The water's rushing sound quieted. It quieted, he realized, because the water was slowing down.

This new observation intrigued Harrison and he gave a knowing nudge back at Celeste. The water flowed slower and slower. The river grew quieter and quieter. Once again, Lloyd checked his pocket watch. He nodded toward the river, and as he did, it happened . . . the river went silent.

Harrison stood in amazement. The silence so contrasted with the moving water's noise just moments ago, that it seemed as though the entire forest just took a deep breath. During that mesmerizing stillness, like a doctor examining their patient's heartbeat, one could hear nature's internal sounds — wind pulsing through branches, animals darting between shrubs, distant tweets and chirps.

And then, as if on Lloyd's cue, the water began to move again — the opposite direction.

Harrison stared dumbfounded. Did the river just change direction? Suddenly, he understood the phenomenon he just witnessed. "Is this all due to tidal activity?" he asked.

"Aye," answered Lloyd, staring with satisfaction at the river, now flowing right to left and picking up speed. "Greatest tidal change in the world."

Celeste intervened. "Well, it's not the greatest. Supposedly, the third greatest average tidal range. But definitely the easiest to observe, and I have to believe the most breathtaking."

"The tide in the River Wye rises or lowers thirty-five to forty feet every six hours," said Lloyd.

"Which means the river actually changes direction like this twice a day," reasoned Harrison as he watched the previously fresh water draining from the mountains be overtaken by salt water flowing in from the ocean and estuary.

"Aye," said Lloyd.

"Absolutely incredible," responded Harrison.

Celeste squeezed Harrison's hand. "I thought you'd like that." She leaned her head on his shoulder and all three again stood silently watching the river.

Harrison instinctively reflected on the earth and moon's rhythmic dance which accounted for the spectacle before him.

173

He thought of the many mathematical calculations required by Pythagoras and his followers to describe such events. He listened intently to the rushing water grow louder in harmony with the wind and forest sounds. Harrison wrapped his arm around Celeste and pulled her close. "The music of the universe," he said softly.

"THE GOAT MAJOR?" said Harrison, staring at the large gold-imprinted letters above the arched door.

"My grandfather's favorite pub," responded Celeste. "Hopefully tomorrow, when we're not walking around so much, he can join us. I think he'll be thrilled since he can't get down here to Cardiff as much as he used to."

Harrison nodded. "Sounds great. Thanks for suggesting a morning tour of Cardiff before digging into the Prince Madoc research. I loved Cardiff Castle and strolling through the grounds. And convenient that your grandfather's favorite pub is right across the street."

Celeste led Harrison inside. Dark wood paneling covered the walls and a large bar stretched across one side of the room. Tables with black leather seating spread through the rest of the space. A mix of locals and tourists lined the bar and filled seats during the lunchtime rush. Harrison and Celeste settled at an empty table. As Celeste perused the menu, Harrison pulled out his cell phone, hoping to access a Wi-Fi signal.

"Aren't you going to look at the menu?" Celeste asked.

"Nope. Already decided to go with the special posted outside . . . a pie and a pint. The sign said homemade meat pies and local ales, which sounds fantastic. The staff can recommend the best of each."

Celeste smiled. "I figured you'd like this place."

"Perfect pub atmosphere," Harrison replied. "So what's the story with the name? The Goat Major?"

"All I know is what my grandfather told me. Supposedly, in 1775 after the Battle of Bunker Hill . . ."

"Wait," interrupted Harrison. "You mean Revolutionary War Bunker Hill? In America?"

"That's right," answered Celeste. "After the Battle of Bunker Hill, a wild goat wandered onto the battlefield and led the Welsh battalion. From that time on, I guess a goat was thought of as good luck so the Welsh infantry always had one. Another story tells of a goat leading a Welsh regiment as they successfully charged against the Russians in the Crimean War back in the early 1800's. Grandpa said the goat is not considered a mascot. It is actually an officer; I think a Lance Corporal."

"So the Welsh military has a goat officer," Harrison stated with a smirk. "Who, then, is the Goat Major?"

"The Goat Major is the guy who cares for the goat."

"Got it."

"Hey, the Welsh military takes their goats seriously. The goat officer was formalized in the late 1800's when Queen Victoria gave the Welsh infantry a member of her royal goat herd. Since then, when one goat retires, another is selected and presented by the British Monarchy. The goat gets a name and a rank, marches in parades, and along with regular meals, gets a ration of cigarettes and Guinness. And no," Celeste quickly added, "the goat doesn't smoke the cigarettes. Grandpa says eating tobacco is good for the coat, and Guinness supplies iron — if you can believe that."

"Well, sounds like the Goat Major has an extremely important job," said Harrison sarcastically, "caring for such a distinguished member of the Welsh military and all."

Celeste playfully kicked Harrison under the table. "Okay, okay," he responded, "no making fun of officer goats. Though, they do make the perfect butt of a joke."

Celeste groaned and rolled her eyes. "Oh, thank goodness," she said, eyeing the approaching waiter. "Let's order."

While eating, the two chatted about their morning tour. Harrison thoroughly enjoyed his meat pie. Savory beef and vegetables stuffed into a flaky pastry crust mushroomed out of the bowl like a mini-explosion of hearty goodness. Washed down with an amber ale, Harrison's meal more than satisfied. Celeste chose a vegetable balti with aubergine, courgette, cauliflower and peppers in a mildly spiced curry sauce along with a glass of wine, and was just as pleased.

As they sipped their drinks, Harrison began an internet search for Prince Madoc. Celeste pulled out her cell phone and did the same. Looking like so many of their high school students, Harrison and Celeste stared silently at their phones, tapping and scrolling through websites.

Like seasoned doubles partners, Harrison and Celeste relied on each other to cover positions, or in this case websites, that the other would not. Harrison scribbled notes onto a napkin, while Celeste added details to her notebook. A short time later, after an inordinate number of surprised expressions and murmured interjections, they rested their phones and shared their findings.

"Why don't you start," said Harrison.

"Are you sure?" responded Celeste. "I found some pretty amazing information. It might be best saved for last."

"Well, if it's anything like what I found, we're in for a wild ride. Please," said Harrison, gesturing to Celeste's notebook, "ladies first."

Celeste flipped back several pages. "Alright then, I focused on the Prince Madoc – Welsh Indian connection. I found a lot more details than the first time I searched about this. What my grandfather told us is the prevailing story. Madoc, or Madog, sailed to America in 1169 or 1170 and landed in what is now Mobile Bay, Alabama."

"Really?" said Harrison. "The story is that specific?"

"Oh, I'm just getting started." Celeste continued skimming through her notes. "I know the thing you'll most want to know about is the evidence. So, let me tell you what came up."

Harrison sipped his ale and slid his chair closer to Celeste. "Go on."

"I'll start with people that wrote about their encounters. In 1686, a Reverend Morgan Jones was traveling near Virginia when members of the Tuscarora tribe captured him. Jones was then rescued by a member of the Doeg tribe who was able to converse with the reverend . . . in Welsh. In 1753, a Colonel wrote to the Virginia governor telling of three French priests returning from missionary work in the region with a native who spoke . . . Welsh. In 1801, a military officer was in a Washington, D.C. restaurant talking Welsh to the waiter. A native chief who was in Washington to sign a treaty approached and began conversing in . . . ."

"Let me guess," interrupted Harrison, "Welsh?"

"Yes. And the chief went on to confirm that his whole tribe had been speaking the language for generations. Along with the stories about a tribe of natives speaking Welsh, the tales also describe many encounters with indigenous people having blonde or light colored hair, light skin, blue eyes, and beards. Most of these documents refer to a tribe called the Mandan."

"The Mandan," Harrison repeated, "is the tribe that supposedly interbred with Prince Madoc's crew."

177

"That's right. I'm surprised I have never heard of them," said Celeste. "But similar to what happened to so many other natives, most were wiped out by disease as Europeans encroached on their territory. That's as much as I got so far, but I can't wait to dig into this more. So, what did you find? Anything as interesting as all that?"

Harrison smiled. "Well, I have to admit, that is pretty fascinating stuff. While you researched Prince Madoc moving forward, I decided to see what I could find out about pre-Madoc connections. The online resources at the National Library of Wales are great, and there are many books written about him. The most interesting thing I found so far is his possible connection with another member of Welsh royalty, someone you may have heard of."

"Who's that?" Celeste asked with interest.

Harrison grew serious and his voice lowered dramatically. "A fella by the name of . . . King Arthur."

CHAPTER XXII

September 26, 1879

"HOW ARE MY GIRLS this morning?" asked Sarah.

"Oh, they're fine, Mrs. Norton," Peter, the stable boy replied. "Just about hitched up and ready to go."

Sarah stood in front of two dapple-grey mares she had known for years. "Here you are Mabel. There you go Betsy." The horses eagerly devoured the apples Sarah held in each palm, a routine performed before trekking over the hill.

"Are you sure you don't need someone to come with you?" Peter asked.

"No, no," replied Sarah. "These two have been pulling my buggy for so long, I expect I could drop the reins and take a nap and they'd still get me where I needed to go." Peter helped Sarah into the small, two-person buggy. He set her medicine bag on the seat and handed her the reins. "We should be back by noon," Sarah said as she directed the horses out of the livery stable.

"Sure thing, Mrs. Norton. I'll be wait'n," Peter said, as he patted Mabel on the rump.

Sarah had traveled the three mile journey to Clayton many times. At least half the town's children were born by her hand. The trail snaked through the Nortonville hills alongside a steep ravine as it entered the valley below. Sarah's trust in her calm, sure-footed horse team offset any anxiety about the precarious route.

A stiff breeze blew through the hills. As Sarah neared the Cumberland mine opening, she noticed a deep hum emanating from within, like a jug player tuning his instrument. The resonating tone rose and faded as winds gusted across the mine entrance. Though eerie and unsettling to some, the low whistling was familiar to Sarah and provided a brief, musical milieu that she appreciated.

Often, Sarah's trips over the hill were emergencies and made in great haste as frantic messengers raced to retrieve her skills. Today was less dramatic. Young Abigail Murphy's first pregnancy was going fine, but with the baby due soon, Sarah felt compelled to check on her. Besides, she needed to take her mind off Rathbone's letter.

In the weeks since receiving the Knights of Pythias founder's disturbing message, Sarah thought of little else. She took the warning seriously. There was still no word about Thomas Oliver, so Rathbone's directive remained the sole responsibility of Sarah. She considered dozens of options about what to do with the sword. However, what confounded her most was describing the sword's new hiding place, "in a manner not easily discernible." What exactly did Rathbone mean?

For now, the sword remained stashed inside the powder magazine in a location known only to her and Mary Tully. With Nortonville's population continuing to grow, more and more people utilized the isolated cave. Sarah knew she must soon move the sword. It was only a matter of time before someone would stumble upon the loose rock concealing the Knights of Pythias origin sword and expose its purported power.

"MOVE ALONG, MABEL. Step to it, Betsy. I know it's steep, but we're almost to the top." Sarah continued encouraging her horses as they pulled the buggy up the trail rising from the Clayton valley floor. Abigail Murphy looked well. According to Sarah, the soon-to-be-mother had another two weeks, maybe three, before delivering. Sarah left Abigail's husband specific instructions about what to expect and when to send for her from Nortonville. The late September weather was warm and clear now, but might change any day with the onset of fall. Sarah made sure the couple understood to notify her early if rain looked likely.

The trail hugged a hillside with a rising slope on the left and a deep canyon on the right. The mares' slow, confident pace through the pass allowed Sarah to relax and enjoy the spectacular scenery overlooking the valley. As she admired the view, the serenity was abruptly interrupted by a deafening noise.

Explosions were commonplace in mining towns. Blasting of rock and coal echoed regularly through the hills. Usually these sounds were distant, often deep underground. The explosion Sarah just heard was not. Though accustomed to loud noises, even Mabel and Betsy reacted to the detonation's proximity.

Sarah quickly spun to her left. Immediately she saw it — the hilltop's rocky outcrop had been obliterated. Boulders and debris tumbled down in a mass of churning earth . . . heading straight for her.

Dear God, thought Sarah.

Instinctively, she snapped the reins. "Move it!" Sensing their dire situation, Mabel and Betsy immediately burst into full sprint. The thunderous sound grew louder as rocks plummeted downhill toward the trail. The old mares frantically struggled to haul the buggy uphill over the rough dirt path. "Come on, Girls! You can do it!"

To Sarah's left, the rockslide grew closer, gathering speed and power. To her right lay the steep gully. Just a few more yards, she thought, and we'll be clear. Small rocks sent flying from the explosion pummeled Sarah, the buggy, and the horses. She ignored the painful stings and cracked the reins once more. "Hee-

181

ya!" she shouted. On cue, Mabel and Betsy surged forward. The jolt of speed lurched Sarah backward. She desperately clung to the seat to avoid being tossed out.

Moments later, the buggy reached the ridgeline. Sarah tugged on the reins and the horses gradually slowed. Mabel and Betsy snorted and gasped for air, unused to such exertion. "That's my girls," Sarah praised. "Well done." Sarah turned back toward the falling rocks and watched in disbelief as they continued plunging down the ravine, spewing dirt and flattening shrubs and small trees.

As the dust cloud settled, Sarah sighed. "That was a close one, girls." She looked up toward the explosion's origin high atop the hill. Not a person in site. She pondered why miners would blast in such an odd location, far from any known coal deposits. And why was there no warning, a steadfast requirement before any detonation? She scanned the landscape suspiciously, then turned to Mabel and Betsy, leaned down, and said softly, "Let's get moving, girls. I'm not sure that was an accident."

"GOOD MORNING, Mr. Cox."

John Cox flinched at the sound of an unexpected voice. He spun toward the sound and his surprise quickly turned to curiosity. "Well, good morning, Mrs. Norton. What can I do for you?"

The sun had not yet risen. Two kerosene lanterns and a small fire that Cox was stoking when interrupted cast the only light. A warm glow reflected off the array of hammers, punches, tongs, and other metal tools dangling from every wall. In the center of the wooden building, sat a massive anvil, like a stage awaiting performers to pound, bend, and twist upon its surface.

Sarah rarely had reason to visit the blacksmith shop. A property manager interacted on her behalf to request the repair of broken farm or cooking tools, or to order the manufacture of needed hardware. Since Sarah successfully birthed all four of the Cox children, she assumed, and he agreed, that his services were provided as debt paid.

Cox's tall, wiry frame and bald head created a stick-figure shadow that danced along the walls as he approached Sarah. She cautiously scanned the dark street, entered the shop, and closed the door behind her. "I trust you are well," Sarah began.

"Yes, fine. Thank you," Cox replied. "And you?"

"Quite well. And the children?

"They're all doing great. Joseph, my oldest boy is learning the craft well. He joins me every afternoon, after school, of course."

"Of course," Sarah repeated in agreement.

The pleasantries baffled Cox even more. He had never seen Sarah Norton appear as anxious as she did now. He thought to ask why, but reasoned she would tell him in due time.

Sarah walked through the shop. She handled projects in various states of completion strewn atop tables and workbenches, her intent, though, was to ensure Cox was alone. "I have a favor to ask of you," Sarah finally announced.

"Certainly. How may I help?"

"I'll pay you for your work, so no need to worry about that."

"If you are paying me," Cox asked, "then what is the favor?"

With a dead-serious expression, Sarah looked up into Cox's eyes. "You cannot tell anyone what you are doing for me. Not a soul."

"Of course, Sarah. You know you can trust me."

"I know," she said, patting Cox on the arm. "That's why I'm here. You are an excellent smithy, but I also know that you make fine jewelry. I have seen the rings and bracelets you have crafted and they are quite extraordinary."

"Thank you. You are very kind. So it is jewelry that you would like," Cox stated.

She pulled a paper from inside her coat and unfolded it on the table. Cox grabbed a lantern and held it near. With his finger, he traced the outline of a detailed sketch. "I believe it would best be made into a pendant, perhaps on a thin chain. Can you do it?" Sarah asked.

Cox leaned down close to the paper and squinted in the dim light. "I don't have the facilities to make a thin chain. That will need to be purchased elsewhere, otherwise, yes . . . yes, I can make it. One other question, though," Cox continued. "From what metal would you like it made?"

Sarah had not considered this question. She had been so consumed with the pendant's design, she had not thought about its composition. "Silver," she said. "It should be silver." Before Cox had a chance to comment on the expense of procuring that much silver, Sarah added, "I will provide the ingot for melting."

Cox nodded. "Very well. I will start on this right away. As soon as I pick up bee's wax from Ann, I can start carving the cast. Will there be anything else?"

"One other thing," responded Sarah. She flipped the paper over to reveal the pendant's outline, but with different markings. "This must be on the back."

"On the back?" Cox asked with hesitation. "But no one will be able to see this if it is on the back of the pendant."

"Precisely," said Sarah. She thanked Cox, reminded him once again of his promise not to discuss the project, and then quickly left the blacksmith shop.

Sarah headed straight for the cemetery, hoping to arrive before the sun rose. She slowly climbed the adjacent hill until high enough to view the entire graveyard at once. She sat and pulled a paper from her coat. On it was sketched an exact copy of the pendant she had left with Cox. As the rising sun peaked over the eastern hills, the scattered headstones came into view, as if waking from a long slumber.

Sarah held the paper in front of her. Her eyes darted from the paper, to the cemetery, and back to the paper. Good, she thought, where disturbed earth will not be noticed, and where no one will think to search.

With the morning light spreading over the valley and nearby Nortonville, Sarah stuffed the paper back into her coat and began easing herself down the steep hill. On the slow walk back toward town, Sarah considered her predicament. Once Mr. Cox is done, she thought, I too will be finished with this burden.

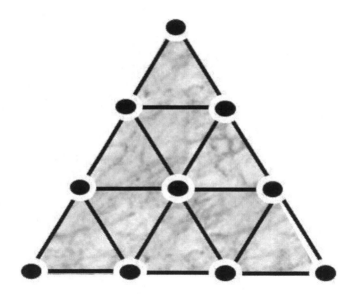

Tetractys [14]

CHAPTER 23

"I'LL BE BACK SOON," said Celeste as she grabbed her coat. "I'm walking into town to pick up a few things for dinner."

"It's almost dark," responded Harrison. "I'll go with."

"No, no. You finish your game with Grandpa. I won't be long."

Harrison and Lloyd had just started their second game of chess. Lloyd's close game-one victory provoked Harrison's insistence on a rematch. The growing relationship between Harrison and Lloyd thrilled Celeste, and she did not want to interrupt their bonding.

"Not to worry," added Lloyd. "Our little town of Chepstow is as safe a place as you'll find anywhere. Tell the folks at the market you're my granddaughter, and they'll take good care of you."

"I will. Back in a bit."

Celeste headed out, walking along the asphalt path leading to the town center. The evening air was cool, but comfortable. The rural Welsh countryside's stillness contrasted with her usually active suburban California neighborhood. Celeste inhaled deeply, filling her lungs with the air of her ancestors and hoping a bit of the Welsh spirit would stay with her long after the trip home.

As she walked, she reflected on the strange tale of Prince Madoc and the Welsh Indians. Was she really related to them? It did not seem likely, yet, so far, she had no better explanation for her DNA results. And what about Harrison's King Arthur connection? All Celeste knew about King Arthur was from a few movies. She was not even sure he really existed, much less was associated with Welsh Indians in the New World.

For now, the intriguing stories swirled around her brain like a River Wye eddy. They provided a pleasant distraction for the mile-long walk into town. Down the hill to her left stood the iconic Chepstow Castle. Celeste admired the twelfth-century stone fortress perched atop limestone cliffs overlooking the river. Reputedly the oldest post-Roman castle in all of Britain, the structure's gatehouse, battlements, baileys, and soaring towers served not only as a window into the past, but also as a present-day event center. She attended several concerts and fairs at the castle during the summer spent with her grandfather.

Celeste vividly recalled the directions to the nearest market, but much of the scenery looked different. New housing spread out from the town center further than she remembered. The developments, she assumed, helped meet Cardiff's growing demand for affordable housing. The Chepstow to Cardiff commute was long, but easily manageable, especially when compared to the nightmarish commute traffic she was used to in the San Francisco Bay Area. Celeste was saddened to think of housing developments encroaching on her grandfather's idyllic property.

The sun sat low on the horizon so Celeste quickened her pace. She confidently wound through alleyways not seen in many years, but remembered well. The shortcuts led her onto High Street in the town center. Along the main street and tucked into narrow side alleys, hanging flower baskets dangled from buildings in typical English fashion. The reds, whites, yellows, and pinks of geraniums, begonias, and petunias cascaded in full springtime display. On weeknights, most shops closed early which accounted for the scarcity of people out and about. Celeste knew, however, that the market, a few restaurants, and the local pubs would still be open.

Inside the market, Celeste quickly picked up the few items needed to prepare the night's dinner – Welsh rarebit. Harrison never had the traditional Welsh dish before. Celeste looked forward to sharing her grandmother's recipe with him and her grandfather, who dropped several not-so-subtle hints about his desire for the meal. Most ingredients — flour, butter, mustard, pepper, Worcestershire sauce, ale — were all at her grandfather's house. Celeste just needed cheddar cheese and bread for toasting. Knowing Harrison and her grandfather's affinity for meat, she decided to add a side of sausage.

Celeste stood browsing the meat counter, trying to determine which of the diverse selections should round out her dinner plans. From behind the counter, a stocky, heavily bearded butcher bound up to her. His thick Welsh lilt was as pronounced as any she heard since arriving in the country. "Good evening," he said immediately. "How can I help you?"

"*Noswaith dda*," said Celeste. "I'd like sausage for an easy addition to Welsh rarebit. Any suggestions?"

"Aye, and good evening to you," the man replied with a huge smile at Celeste's Welsh greeting. "If you're going for something more traditional, I'd go with the pork and leek," responded the man.

"That sounds perfect. Enough for three, please."

"American?" he asked as he weighed and wrapped the sausage.

"Yes. Here visiting my grandfather."

"And who might that be?"

"Lloyd Scott. Do you know him?"

"Oh, sure, everyone knows Lloyd — one of our elder statesmen. A good man with a good heart. Always involved in the town's affairs."

"That's very kind of you to say." Celeste watched the man write the sausage weight on a label and affix it to the butcher paper. "Uh, excuse me, I don't think that is correct. You gave me a lot more meat than you wrote down."

The butcher handed Celeste the sausage. "Nope, it's correct. Enjoy your stay." He winked and quickly turned from the counter before Celeste could respond.

"*Diolch*," she called out.

Outside, night had descended. Streetlamps lit the main road, but once Celeste began winding her way through side streets and alleys, she relied on the faint glow from within closed shops and second story flats. In one hand she carried a canvas bag loaded with dinner ingredients and her small handbag. In the other she held her cell phone after having just texted Harrison that she was on her way back.

Beyond the last row of homes, twinkling stars appeared like pinpricks in a black velvet drape as the sky darkened. A quarter-moon reflected enough light for Celeste to easily follow the isolated road home. A rhythmic frog and cricket chorus enhanced the serenity. Celeste slowed her pace to enjoy the setting a few extra minutes. More resonance of the universe she imagined.

Glancing at her watch, she realized Harrison and her grandfather were probably starving. I guess I better . . .

Celeste froze.

A powerful hand suddenly gripped her arm. She felt warm breath in her hair and a massive body pressed close against her back. The cold, sharp edge of a metal blade held tightly to her throat paralyzed her. She could not move; she dared not scream. Celeste was helpless . . . and terrified.

"Do not say a word," the deep voice whispered into Celeste's ear, each word enunciated precisely with a heavy Welsh accent.

A thousand thoughts raced through Celeste's mind. She tried desperately to maintain her wits and not succumb to fear. If he wanted to kill me, he easily could have done it by now, she reasoned. Just a robbery – if I cooperate, I'll be fine.

Celeste nodded in agreement with her attacker's demand. The knife blade pushed into her skin as she motioned her head. Celeste winced, but remained silent.

Slowly, the attacker eased his hold on her arm and lowered the knife from her neck. "Do not turn around," he warned.

Celeste nodded.

"The bag. Hand me the bag."

Though Celeste no longer felt the man's body against her, she sensed him just inches away. She held the bag behind her, and he snatched it from her hand. She heard him dig through the bag, removing articles and tossing them aside. He unzipped her small purse and dropped the contents onto the ground, one item at a time. She had some cash, a few American dollars and some British pounds. He'll take the cash, and then find the credit cards and leave, Celeste prayed.

From the corner of her eye, Celeste saw her purse thrown aside. "Give me your hands," the attacker demanded.

Celeste forgot about her jewelry – a watch on one wrist and several bracelets on the other. She extended her hands behind her. Grabbing her left wrist, the attacker lifted it up, bending Celeste forward in agony as her arm stretched behind her. She squealed in pain, unable to remain silent.

Celeste felt him twist and stretch her watch, but he did not remove it. Seconds later, he threw her hand back down and

191

immediately grabbed and hoisted her right wrist. Again, Celeste cried out. Spinning and twisting the bracelets, he seemed to examine them, but again, left the jewelry. Celeste did not know what to think.

"Turn around."

Celeste did not expect this command. Seeing her attacker's face would put her in more peril, but she had to obey. Slowly she spun. A small flashlight instantly blinded her. She squinted from the glare enough to notice the large knife blade pointing toward her stomach. As her eyes adjusted, she realized the man had no face. A ski mask covered his entire head and darkness obscured his eyes. The figure was tall, six-two, maybe six-three. Celeste mentally registered as many descriptors as she could: height, weight, clothing, accent. Never had Celeste feared for her life the way she did now.

The man moved closer. He shifted the flashlight to his knife hand, easily holding them both. To Celeste's horror, he began touching her. Methodically, he searched her pockets. He found her cell phone, glanced at it briefly and dropped it. The angled flashlight lit the ground around Celeste. Her belongings lay scattered upon the path, including her cash and credit cards. He did not take them. What can he possibly want from me?

Finding nothing else in her pants or coat pockets, he would surely leave, Celeste desperately hoped. The man worked his way up Celeste's clothing, carefully feeling both outer and inner garments until he reached her neck. He took hold of the thin chain she wore and slowly lifted the attached pendant from inside her shirt. With the flashlight, the man carefully scanned the triangle-shaped accessory. The gleaming knife blade now pointed directly at Celeste's face. She stood petrified with fear.

Something about the pendant intrigued the attacker. He sighed heavily, almost sounding relieved, thought Celeste. He looked Celeste in the eyes, then back at the pendant. Suddenly, he yanked on the chain, breaking the clasp and ripping the pendant from her neck. Celeste lurched forward from the force, her face stopping just as the knife point grazed her cheek.

The man stepped back. His whole attention now focused on the pendant. Perhaps he now had what he wanted and she could escape . . . perhaps not. Celeste slowly and silently backed away from the man as he studied the object. Now twenty feet away, Celeste decided this was her chance. She had to run. As she turned, a voice bellowed. "Do not move!"

Celeste spun back to see her attacker running at her, knife held out. Dear God, Celeste thought, he's going to kill me.

Adrenaline surged through her. Fight or flight? What was her best chance at surviving? As she stood motionless, scenarios racing through her mind, something strange happened. A long, thin object darted out of the darkness and knocked the attacker's flashlight to the ground. Celeste stared into the dimly lit night. The clinking of metal hitting metal echoed through the surrounding forest. Someone else, it appeared, attacked the robber.

Arms flailed as the two shadowy figures fought. The fallen flashlight backlit the scene, allowing Celeste to catch glimpses of the battle. She wanted to help, but how?

Before Celeste could react, she saw the shimmer of a long blade slice down on her attacker's hand. He hollered out in agony and dropped her pendant. In a single, swift motion, the other assailant scooped up the pendant and tossed it toward Celeste.

"Here. Take this back to your grandfather's. Quickly," he said.

His voice was calm. Celeste was confused. She saw her silver pendant flying through the air. Instinctively, she reached out and grabbed it. Why this pendant, she wondered? Who are these men?

Without hesitation, Celeste sprinted the short distance to her grandfather's. The sense of relief as she opened the front door was overwhelming. Harrison and her grandfather, having finished their chess games, sat chatting and sipping ale. When Harrison saw Celeste standing in the doorway, he was stunned.

Celeste breathed heavily. Strands of hair crisscrossed out of place. She carried nothing in her hands, and a small scratch blemished her face. Both Harrison and Lloyd jumped up with concern. "Oh, my God," exclaimed Harrison. "Are you okay? What happened?"

"I'm fine," Celeste responded, trying to catch her breath. "But have I got a story to tell you." She inhaled deeply, held it for a moment, and then slowly exhaled. Harrison rushed to her and took her hand. "I was attacked . . . by a man with a knife," she continued, "and saved by another man with . . ." Celeste paused to reflect on the accuracy of the mental image. "With a sword."

CHAPTER XXIV

THE NEWLY CAST PENDANT draped across Sarah's palm. Cox, the blacksmith, delivered the finished piece earlier that day working extra hours carving, molding, casting, and polishing in between his regular smithing jobs. The silver shimmered in the afternoon sunlight beaming through Sarah's windows. She ran her fingers over the triangular-shaped object, carefully touching each of the nine ruby-red garnets inset along the border.

The pendant's shape precisely imitated many of the Knights of Pythias medals and jewels worn by the fraternal order's members — with one exception. A tenth garnet set in the pendant's center would have formed a perfect tetractys, the sacred symbol of Pythagoras, from whom the Order drew its philosophy. Instead, the center of Sarah's pendant showed the raised image of an upside-down torch.

Sarah considered her design. Was the torch's significance too subtle . . . or too obvious? She had no way to know. She was certain, however, that the pendant's real meaning could not be determined by just seeing the jeweled surface. A passing glance, or even intense study, would not reveal the object's obscure message.

Sarah turned the pendant over. She ran her thumb over letters etched near each vertex of the pendant's backside — F, C, B. The Pythian founding principles of friendship, charity, and benevolence represented the Knights only to those with more than a cursory knowledge of the Order. Between the letters, at the center of the pendant's reverse side and exactly opposite the torch on the front, Sarah examined the exquisitely engraved image of a sword. She marveled at Cox's delicate work that precisely duplicated her sketch — a sketch drawn from her memory of briefly glimpsing the origin sword. Sarah knew this symbol was more than just another general reference to the Knights of Pythias, but would anyone else?

The sudden knock on Sarah's door startled her. Quickly, she placed the pendant into a tiny cloth sack that she then closed inside a small, plain wooden box. Sarah peeked through curtains near the front door. She longed for the time when she need not be so cautious and suspicious. Fortunately, her guest was expected.

"Hello, Mary. Come in," said Sarah.

Mary Tully followed her inside. She sat while Sarah poured each tea from a pot already steeping in the kitchen.

"Thank you for coming on such short notice," Sarah began.

"Of course," responded Mary. "Your note sounded urgent. I expect I know what this is about."

"And you would be correct."

Sarah always bore a serious, composed demeanor, but her obvious consternation greatly concerned Mary. "Please, Sarah, tell me how I can help."

The small box holding the pendant lay inconspicuously on a table next to the two women. Sarah picked up the box and rested it on her lap before proceeding. "I have a tremendous favor to ask of you, Mary. Normally, I would do this myself; however, due to recent events, I believe that my success with this task is in question."

"Of course, Sarah. What can I do?"

"Before you agree, Mary, I need you to be certain of the risks involved."

"Risks? No one knows that you told me anything. I feel perfectly safe, Sarah."

Sarah nodded. "That is what I thought, as well . . . until three days ago."

"I don't understand," Mary responded with growing worry.

"I did not think anyone knew of my involvement with Thomas Oliver's mission," Sarah continued. "Now, I fear that I was mistaken."

"What happened?"

Sarah recounted the rockslide incident on her way back from Clayton. Mary listened intently. "I am so thankful that you were not injured," said Mary. "Do you think the rockslide was intentional?"

"I spoke with Morgan Morgans, the mine supervisor. If any companies were blasting in that area, he would be informed. He said he would check around and let me know if he heard anything, but I suspect he didn't believe the rockslide was caused by an explosion. More likely a natural slide, according to him. But I know what I heard . . . and felt."

"If, as you think, the rock slide was not an accident, your life is in grave danger. I'm so frightened for you, Sarah."

Sarah patted Mary's hand. "Now don't you worry about me. I'll be staying close to home for a while. I feel completely safe in town. But that is why I need your help. I need something delivered . . . discreetly."

"Of course," Mary responded. "I am happy to assist. What needs to be deliv . . . wait, you don't mean the sword? Do you need me to take the sword somewhere?"

"No, no. The sword will remain hidden. But the item is something related to the sword." Sarah handed Mary the small box. "It is best you not open it. Safer that you don't know what is in there. Do you promise?"

"Certainly, Sarah. Whatever you say."

"Excellent." Sarah handed Mary a note. "This is to whom the box must be delivered and to no one else."

"John C. Holmes, Grand Chancellor, Knights of Pythias Lodge, Sacramento." Mary looked up at Sarah. "I understand; tomorrow I'm heading to Sacramento."

"Thank you, Mary," said Sarah, again patting Mary's hand. "Thank you."

"EVENIN', MA'AM,"

The voice startled Mary. In the darkness, she did not see the man leaning against a small wooden building. "Good evening, sir. Are you waiting for the steamboat?"

"No, Ma'am. I'm the dock attendant," the man replied as he approached Mary. "I believe you're the only passenger onboarding here tonight. May I take your bag?"

Mary instinctively pulled her carpet bag close to her body. "No, no thank you," she said, a bit louder than necessary.

The attendant quickly recoiled his arm. "Of course. May I check your ticket, please?"

"Certainly," said Mary. She handed him the folded paper from her coat pocket.

The attendant walked toward a large kerosene lantern near the dock's edge. Mary cautiously followed. "Yup, you're in the right place. The Chryssie should be along shortly."

In the light, Mary now noticed a tag hanging from the man's coat that read California Steam Navigation Company, the same as on her ticket. "The Chryssie?" asked Mary.

"You know, the Chrysopolis. You didn't know you were catching the Chrysopolis?

"Well, no," answered Mary. "A friend bought me the ticket."

"Nice friend," said the attendant as he returned Mary's ticket. "Only the most famous, most magnificent steamer on the entire Delta. Not to mention the fastest. Ever ridden her?"

"No," said Mary. "I have not."

The attendant tipped up the wide brim of his floppy hat, exposing his face for the first time. The young man's kind eyes and sweet smile instantly set Mary at ease. "Well," he continued. "You're in for a treat."

"I am looking forward to the experience."

"Where you from?" he asked.

"Nortonville," said Mary. "Across the water." She went on to explain how she rode the Black Diamond Railroad out of the hills earlier that afternoon. At New York Landing she caught a ferry across the delta waters to Collinsville. For the past several hours, she ate and passed time at one of the Collinsville hotels.

"So what do you think of our little town?" the attendant asked.

"It's a fine town," said Mary.

The young attendant stared toward the water, now just a black abyss in the night. "Yeah, well I can't wait to get out of here. That's why I work for the steamer company and not the salmon cannery. Everyone else in town works for the cannery, but not me. I'm getting out of here. Another couple months and I'll get to work on board one of the steamers. They just go between San Francisco and Sacramento, and some on your side of the delta head up the San Joaquin River to Stockton. I ain't never been to any of those cities. Eventually, if I work hard, maybe I'll captain my own steamer. Then, I'll head east and pilot paddleboats on the Mississippi, like that writer Mark Twain. You know he used to live in San Francisco. Folks here in Collinsville met him years ago when he rode the Sacramento River steamers. That Tom Sawyer book is my favorite."

Mary just listened as the attendant rambled on about Mark Twain stories, piloting paddleboats, and escaping small town life. She enjoyed the attendant's youthful enthusiasm and adventurous spirit. She recalled encounters over the years with other similarly restless young men in Nortonville. Life in the mines would never satisfy their souls; as soon as they were able, they left.

"Here she comes now," the attendant announced.

In the distance, Mary saw dim lights not previously visible. The faint, rhythmic chugging of a steam engine grew steadily louder with the quickly approaching vessel. The attendant lit a second large kerosene lantern and hung it near the water's edge.

"Two lanterns means pick up a passenger. Just one lantern and they'd keep on going," the attendant explained.

"I see," said Mary. "Thank you. But how can you tell that is the Chrysopolis? I can't even see a boat, yet."

"First of all, the time is right. The Chryssie left San Francisco at six-thirty. She makes a short stop at Martinez, and gets here to Collinsville five-hours later. So, she's right on time. You'll have another six hours up the river to Sacramento. Plenty of time to sleep, if you like."

"Oh, I don't think I'll be doing much sleeping tonight," Mary responded.

"But even if I didn't know the Chryssie's schedule, I know that's her headed our way," the attendant continued.

"How's that?" Mary asked. "You can't see her."

"No, but I can hear her."

200

The attendant paused as Mary and he listened closely to the chugging steam engine. "She's a side-wheeler, two-hundred-and-forty-five feet long and forty-feet wide. Can carry a thousand people. I'd know that big engine anywhere. And if you can't tell the Chryssie by her engine, you sure can by her whistle."

"Her whistle?" Mary queried.

As if on cue, a blast from the boat's steam whistle shattered the silence. Mary flinched heavily, catching herself on the attendant's arm. He steadied her and smiled broadly. "Yup, her whistle. I figure there are a hundred steamers on the delta, and I bet I can identify nearly all of 'em by their whistles."

Mary had no doubt about the attendant's boast. This young man clearly lived and breathed steamboats, and Mary delighted in his passion. "That is really quite impressive."

"Well, like I said, I aim to be a pilot someday."

For the next few minutes, Mary watched in awe as the huge Chrysopolis effortlessly glided up to the Collinsville dock. Deckhands raced to hang protective buoys from the side while the young dock attendant tied off several ropes tossed to him from the steamboat. A long wooden plank slid out from the Chrysopolis deck and landed onto the dock. The attendant quickly secured the walkway and reached his hand toward Mary. "All aboard, Ma'am," he said with a welcoming grin.

Mary stared up at the twin steam stacks towering high above the multilevel decks. Two giant paddlewheels, each over thirty-feet in diameter, clung mid-ship onto each side of the vessel. Mary let the attendant guide her onto the steamboat's deck. "Thank you," she said. "Perhaps I'll see you when I return."

"I hope so," he replied. "You have a nice night."

The attendant returned to the dock and Mary watched him fade into the night. She handed a uniformed steward her ticket. "Right this way, Ma'am," he said. "I'll show you to your room. May I take your bag?"

Again, Mary declined the offer. She followed the steward through a large dining room. Crystal chandeliers, rosewood paneling, and plush red upholstery defined the luxurious setting. A few passengers still lingered at meals on white linen-covered tables, even though it was approaching midnight. "The kitchen is always open if you're hungry," said the steward. "Or you may enjoy an early breakfast when we dock in Sacramento."

"Thank you," Mary replied. "Just my room for now."

"I understand," said the steward.

He led her up a polished wooden staircase to a small, but comfortable stateroom. "Is there anything else I can do for you?"

"No, thank you." As the steward left, he closed the door behind him, and Mary immediately collapsed onto the bed. She felt the gentle movement of the Chrysopolis pulling away from Collinsville and heading upriver toward Sacramento. She still clutched her carpet bag to her chest. She closed her eyes and visualized the bag's contents: a change of clothes; money Sarah had given her for at least two nights of hotel stays, meals; a return steamboat ticket; and a small wooden box.

The object inside the box remained a mystery, but that did not bother Mary. She just wanted to help her friend. Hopefully, Mary thought, finding John C. Holmes, Grand Chancellor, Knights of Pythias Lodge would be a quick undertaking. Then, perhaps, she might tour the city for a day. She had never been to Sacramento. For now, as the crew fed Black Diamond Mine coal into the Chrysopolis' boilers, the steamer's rhythmic chugging and soothing sway quickly lulled Mary into a peaceful slumber.

Chrysopolis [15]

CHAPTER 25

With the police report finished, Lloyd followed the two officers to the door and bid them good night. Earlier, Celeste led everyone to the location of the attack. Evidence of a scuffle was clear, but there were no signs of either the knife-wielding perpetrator or her sword-bearing rescuer. Celeste's belongings still lay scattered along the path. Harrison helped her gather them all, including the Welsh rarebit ingredients.

The evening's intense emotions completely suppressed any thoughts of food. By midnight, they finally began to relax and realized no one had eaten dinner. Ignoring Harrison and her grandfather's wishes for her to rest, Celeste insisted on preparing the Welsh rarebit. Cooking was calming, she explained, and the men finally relinquished the kitchen.

"What I still don't understand," Celeste began as she grated cheddar cheese, "is why that guy was so interested in my pendant and not my money, credit cards, or other jewelry?"

"Where did you get the pendant?" Harrison asked.

"From my father. It belonged to my grandmother and is quite sentimental. Although I rarely wear it, I brought it with me for our Wales trip to remember and honor my family."

"Let me see this pendant," requested Lloyd.

Celeste handed her grandfather the item from her pocket. The clasp broke when ripped from her neck, but the rest of the artifact was unscathed. "Does it look familiar?" Celeste asked.

Lloyd carefully examined both sides of the triangular jewel. He studied the red garnets on the front and ran his fingers over the etchings on the back. "I don't recall ever seeing this before. Are you sure your father got it from Grandma?"

Celeste whisked together the butter, Worcestershire sauce, mustard, and cheese as she spoke. "That's what he said. He gave it to me when I was a teen. I distinctly remember him telling me that he got the pendant from Grandma, and it was of great importance, so be very, very careful with it. That's why I usually keep it stashed away."

"And you have no idea why it might be important?" Harrison asked Lloyd.

"I have no idea . . ." Lloyd paused. He flipped the pendant and stared at the backside. "Unless . . ."

"Unless what?" Celeste asked anxiously.

"Well," Lloyd continued. "These letters etched into the back, F, C, and B. I wonder if they could refer to the Knights of Pythias."

Harrison and Celeste looked at each other in disbelief. The beer Celeste was adding to her mixture continued streaming from bottle to sauce pan.

"Uh, do you think that's enough?" said Harrison, gesturing to the beer.

"What?" Celeste answered, still stunned by her grandfather's comment.

"The beer!" said Harrison.

"Oh, right." Celeste quickly regained her composure. "What did he say?"

Harrison turned toward Lloyd. "Did you say Knights of Pythias?"

"I did. F, C, B — friendship, charity, benevolence."

"How do you know about the Knights of Pythias?" Celeste asked.

"Well, your father was one, of course," he said matter-of-factly.

A loud clang echoed from the kitchen as the whisk fell from Celeste's hand, bounced off the counter and onto the floor. "Excuse me?" she said, ignoring the lost utensil.

"I'm sorry, Dear. I thought you knew," responded Lloyd.

"I had no idea. He never mentioned it. Nor did Mom." Celeste paused for a moment. "Does she know?"

Lloyd considered the question. "I assume so."

Celeste retrieved the whisk and tossed it in the sink. She continued her food preparation, smothering lightly toasted bread slices with the cheese sauce and sliding them under the oven's broiler. "I am stunned right now."

"Well if your father being a member of the Knights of Pythias surprised you, you might want to sit down for this," added Lloyd.

Harrison and Celeste leaned in as Lloyd continued, "So was your grandmother."

Celeste set the oven timer and raced toward her grandfather. She plopped next to him on the sofa. "All right, now you're freaking me out. You're telling me Grandma was a member of the Knights of Pythias fraternal order?"

"Sure, well sort of," said Lloyd. "She belonged to the sisterhood, of course, rather than the brotherhood. Sometime during their history, the Order began allowing women into a separate chapter called the Pythian Sisters. Your grandmother was a member before we met. Membership was something she did on her own. I had no interest in joining the brotherhood. I had plenty of friends. But your grandmother enjoyed socializing and participating in charity activities. She even went to meetings and occasional events in other countries. The first time she ever visited America was for a Pythian event in Sacramento."

"I have goose bumps right now," said Celeste, rubbing her arms.

206

"I don't understand why it's such a big deal," Lloyd responded.

The beeping oven timer interrupted the conversation. "I'll get it," said Harrison immediately. "You two finish the conversation."

"Thanks, Barre. Just set the rarebit on the counter and I'll be there in a minute," Celeste responded. "So, Grandpa, it's a big deal because Harrison and I spent the last few weeks researching everything we can find about the Knights of Pythias. Now to learn that both Dad and Grandma were members is rather shocking. How, and why, did they keep this from me?"

"It is a secret order," Lloyd smirked.

Celeste glared, not amused.

"In fact, your father was a part of some super-secret sect of the Order, called the Drama-something. I don't recall the details. Too long ago."

"The Dramatic Order of the Knights of Khorassan?" Celeste queried uneasily.

"That sounds right," answered Lloyd. "No idea what was special about them; neither he nor your grandmother discussed it with me."

Celeste continued shaking her head in disbelief as she rejoined Harrison in the kitchen. The two plated the grilled sausage and Welsh rarebit. The sausage and lightly browned rarebit cheese sauce aroma permeated the whole house, enhancing everyone's overwhelming hunger. "Let's eat," Celeste announced.

With everyone at the kitchen table, Harrison and Lloyd immediately dug into their meals. "Oh my, gosh, C, this is so good," Harrison announced after swallowing his first ever taste of Welsh rarebit.

"Mmm, excellent," Lloyd followed. "Just like your grandmother's."

"Might be a little heavy on the beer," Celeste added. "Sorry about that."

"Works for me," said Lloyd.

Harrison nodded. "Me, too."

"Well, thank you both," said Celeste. "And now that we're eating, back to the topic at hand. I still have a million questions for you, Grandpa."

"May I see the pendant?" asked Harrison.

Celeste handed Harrison the jewel. He studied it while Celeste continued to grill her grandfather about his knowledge of her father and grandmother's role with the Pythians. To her frustration, Lloyd could provide few details.

"Well, what do you think?" Celeste asked Harrison, desperate for any insight into the pendant's significance.

Harrison held the object in front of him as he spoke. "If your grandfather is right that the F, C, and B letters signify the Knights of Pythias, then it's that the red gems on the front should portray Pythagoras' sacred tetractys. However, rather than a tenth gemstone in the center, there is what appears to be an inverted torch. A quick Google search tells me the upside-down torch is a common symbol used in cemeteries."

At this new interpretation, Celeste grew excited. She slid closer to Harrison, urging him to continue.

"What I find really interesting," Harrison said, "is this sword etching on the backside. Why?"

"Why what?" Celeste asked.

"Why is it there? We know the sword is significant to Pythians, but why engrave it on the pendant side where it's not visible when worn, especially when the sword is crafted with such precision? Clearly the sword symbol is significant. You know, the image reminds me a little of that weird email warning message you got the other day; the one we thought had some kind of cross symbol. Instead of a cross, I wonder if the symbol was actually a sword."

Lloyd immediately intervened. "What warning, Dear? Were you threatened before tonight?"

"Yes, I suppose I was. I received an email warning me to stop searching around the Black Diamond Mines; the place I told you about where the dead body was found with my name written on a headstone. As Harrison mentioned, there was an odd symbol attached to the email. The police were not able to trace the sender, and with no more threats I pretty much forgot about it."

"You told me about the body and the headstone message, but not about a direct threat. Do you still have the email?" Lloyd asked.

"I think so." Celeste pulled out her cell phone and quickly scanned through to the warning message. With two fingers, she enlarged the screen image for her grandfather and handed him the phone.

Lloyd read the message. "Stay away from Black Diamond Mines. You will not be warned again." He then scrolled down to the inverted cross symbol.

Celeste knew immediately that something was wrong. Lloyd's face grew pale and his lips tightened. "What, Grandpa? "What is it?" Celeste asked nervously.

"You remember how I told you that your grandmother didn't discuss her work with the Pythian Sisters?" Lloyd began.

"Yes?"

"That wasn't quite accurate. There was one thing about which she made sure I was aware. Along with the social events and charity deeds, some Pythians helped protect against the nefarious activities of a secret order."

"Wait a minute," Celeste interrupted. "Another secret order?"

"Yes. One that's been around for centuries, much longer than the Knights of Pythias is my understanding."

"You say nefarious activities," said Harrison. "For what purpose?"

"Power," answered Lloyd. "The goal is power. The method is fueling discord."

"Discord?" asked Celeste.

"Or as your grandmother would say . . . 'disruption of harmony'. The same method has been used to gain power by oppressors for centuries. When there is social discord, people often look for someone to create stability, and they willfully follow a despot. Think Hitler or Stalin whose countries' economic and nationalistic turmoil allowed their dictatorships to thrive. There are present day examples, as well."

"Some pretty close to home, I'd say," added Harrison, nodding knowingly at Lloyd's reference.

Lloyd continued, "Without social discord, those seeking power must create it. A small crack in social harmony may allow a popular tyrant to exploit the divisions. That is what these Pythians protect against — the disruption of harmony that allows evil to take hold. The Pythians believe human greed and ego leads to imbalance and dissonance. Given the number of ruthless rulers over the centuries, the Order has not always been successful. I don't know if your grandmother, or your father for that matter, was involved with this secretive mission of the Knights of Pythias, but she thought it important enough to tell me."

Celeste gestured toward her phone. "And the symbol?"

"I've seen the symbol before," said Lloyd. "Harrison is correct; it is not a cross. The symbol is a sword. The rays radiating out of the blade represent power. This is the symbol of the Caledfwlch Society."

Harrison and Celeste turned toward each other in silent disbelief. "I am not familiar with the term *Caledfwlch*," said Celeste. "What does it mean?"

Lloyd sat back in his chair, considering his pronouncement's magnitude. He then stated with some concern. "*Caledfwlch* is the ancient Welsh term for Excalibur, King Arthur's sword."

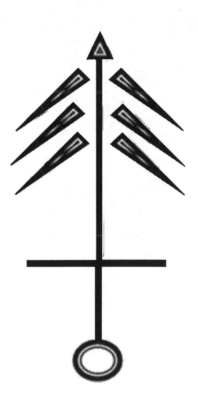

Caledfwlch Society Symbol [16]

212

CHAPTER XXVI

October 5, 1879

"WHY, GOOD MORNING, SARAH," said Ann, opening her door to the knock.

"Good morning, Ann," Sarah replied. "I'm sorry to disturb you so early, but I wanted to catch you before you head off to church."

"It's quite alright," countered Ann. "Please come in. What can I do for you?"

"I'd like to purchase a few jars of honey. I'll be visiting some ailing folks in town today and need to prescribe a healthy dose of tea and honey. I just realized this morning that I used up my last bit."

"Of course," said Ann. "Have a seat while I fetch some from the back."

Ann disappeared into a rear room where she kept the honey and made bee's wax candles. The honey's sweet aroma wafted through the entire house. Sarah was unsure whether the scent arose from the burning candles in the front room, or the fresh honey stored in back. Either way, she appreciated the soothing fragrance.

Sarah perused Ann's front room. During the nearly four years Ann lived in Nortonville, Sarah had never been invited inside Ann's house. Ann rented the tiny shack cheaply as it was set further toward the hills, apart from the main street. This location proved ideal for tending the beehives. In addition, the isolation provided Ann an added sense of privacy, which, Sarah reasoned, Ann preferred.

In Ann's sparsely decorated front room hung a single painted landscape over a small writing desk. As Sarah approached the desk for a closer view of the painting, she noticed an open letter. She did not intend to pry into Ann's personal business, but the brief and unusual wording caught her attention. Time is short. You must act quickly, were the only words. Rather than a signature, Sarah noted a symbol stamped at the bottom. At first, the image looked like an upside-down cross, but after a moment, Sarah realized that the symbol was a sword, with rays emanating from the blade. An unusual symbol, Sarah thought, one she never saw before. Such a cryptic message with no signature seemed odd.

As Sarah reached for a closer view of the letter, she was interrupted. "Here we are," said Ann. The voice startled Sarah, and she instinctively stepped away from the desk. Ann quickly placed the honey jars on an end table and subtly lifted the letter from the desk. Ann slid the paper into her pocket without comment.

"How much?" Sarah asked.

"Seventy-five cents," answered Ann.

Sarah began digging into a small coin purse concealed inside her handbag. "I must say," she continued. "Quite a lovely scent throughout your home. Does it always smell so sweet?"

"I'm afraid so," said Ann, "one of the consequences of the work I do."

"Do you not like the smell of honey?" asked Sarah.

Ann took Sarah's three twenty-five cent pieces. "Oh, I like the smell just fine, but it can get overwhelming at times. Even my clothes smell like honey. Too much of a good thing, as they say."

"Indeed, though surely better than if everything smelled of guano," said Sarah in jest.

"I beg your pardon?"

"The bat guano you search for is most foul-smelling. It is a good thing that odor does not stay with you," explained Sarah, surprised that Ann seemed unaware of the reference.

"Oh, yes. Right," said Ann hesitantly.

"Well, good day to you, Ann. Thank you for the honey."

Ann escorted Sarah out the front door and watched as she headed on foot toward town.

"Mrs. Norton, Mrs. Norton!"

The shout came from the opposite direction Sarah walked. Ann looked on with interest as a middle-aged man she did not recognize quickly approached on horseback. He rode by Ann's front door and dismounted next to Sarah.

"Thank goodness I found you," Ann heard the man tell Sarah. "My name's Grady Murphy, cousin to Abigail Murphy in Clayton. I was sent to get you. They think somethin's wrong with the baby. Can you come now, Mrs. Norton?" Grady pleaded breathlessly. "Right now?"

Grady barely breathed during his conversation with Sarah. Ann continued to watch as Sarah calmed him and assured him she would ride to Clayton to check on Abigail. First, Sarah explained, she needed to make brief stops at two very ill residents. She directed Grady to ride to her home, pick up her mid-wife bag, and then head to the stable to harness a buggy for the ride to Clayton. Sarah would meet Grady at the stable as soon as possible. Grady climbed back onto his horse and sprinted off toward Sarah's house.

Ann waited for Grady to ride past her door, and then quickly disappeared inside her home. She pulled the mysterious letter from her pocket and read it once again. Ann had just received the letter late the previous night, she now leaned over one of the honey-scented candle flames, lit the letter on fire, and watched it burn until she could no longer hold the remaining ash. Ann quickly grabbed her hat and dashed out the front door.

"WHAT DO YOU MEAN Mabel and Betsy are not available, Peter?" asked an indignant Sarah.

The stable boy explained that Sarah's two trusted buggy horses were called away for use at a church function. "One of the choir boys came running over and said he was told to bring the horses right away. I'm sorry, Mrs. Norton, I didn't know you'd be needin' them this morning."

"Any other buggy teams?" Sarah asked.

"I'm afraid not," replied Peter. "They're all out right now."

"Well, Mr. Murphy," said Sarah to Grady. "Any suggestions?"

"We'll use my horse and harness up one of those," said Grady, pointing to a pair of horses at the rear of the stable.

"Whoa," said Peter. "That's not a good idea. Neither of those horses has run as a team. They're racers, like yours probably is, Mr. Grady. Too dangerous to try and team 'em up."

"Nonsense," replied Grady. "I'll keep them in line. It's just a few miles over the hill to Clayton."

"It's your decision, Mrs. Norton," said Peter. "But I sure don't recommend teaming up a racer and a trotter, 'specially if they ain't worked together before."

Grady turned toward Sarah and gently touched her arm. "Please, Mrs. Norton," he pleaded. "Abigail is in such pain. She needs you now."

"Very well," responded Sarah. "Hitch them up, Peter."

Peter reluctantly harnessed together Grady's horse and one from the back stable. The two horses immediately looked

216

uncomfortable next to each other, but Grady gradually gained their control. Peter helped Sarah into the buggy, and Grady directed them out of the stable onto the trail toward Clayton.

Grady worked hard to keep the horses on a steady pace. They continually nipped at each other and frequently tried to sprint. After a mile or so, the horses settled down and fell into an easy trot. Sarah loved to control the buggy and convinced Grady to let her hold the reins. Her prowess with a horse team was immediately evident and Grady eventually eased back in his seat, confident in Sarah's abilities to handle the team, but anxious about his cousin's condition.

"Don't worry, Mr. Murphy," said Sarah, noticing Grady's nervous bouncing knee. "Everything will be fine. I haven't lost a newborn, yet, and I don't plan to start now."

"Thank you, Mrs. Norton. I appreciate the . . ."

A shotgun blast echoed through the valley. The sound originated close by, just behind a rocky outcrop to their right. Sarah saw rock salt hit Grady's horse square on the rump, but there was nothing she could do to restrain the animal. The painful sting instantly set his horse into a frenzy, bolting forward as the terrified creature dragged the buggy and other horse along.

Sarah gripped the reins tightly, shocked by the sudden jolt. Grady, however, had nothing to hold. The buggy bounced violently off the uneven trail sending Grady flying backward out of his seat. Somersaulting in mid-air, he landed headfirst on a stone. With blood oozing from his head, Grady lay unconscious and oblivious to the horse and buggy now careening wildly along the trail with Sarah desperately trying to regain control.

"Whoa!" she cried. "Whoa!"

Unlike Mabel and Betsy, these horses ignored her commands. Frightened and confused, the stable horse tried frantically to pull away from Grady's horse. The tugging created

217

an awkward rocking of the buggy, tossing Sarah side-to-side. She watched her mid-wife bag roll out of the buggy floor and tumble down the ravine.

"Whoa!" Sarah shouted again, but still no response from the horses.

And then she saw the sharp right turn in the trail. At this speed, how could they ever safely make the curve? Summoning her last bit of strength, Sarah yanked back on the reins as the buggy entered the curve. "Whoa!!"

"HEY, JEREMY, WHAT'S GOING on there?" said Josiah to his twin brother.

Josiah shut and latched the livery stable gate where the two young men worked just outside the town of Clayton. He trotted toward the two exhausted horses. Behind the horses, a tangled mass of fractured wooden poles and leather straps dragged along the ground. "That ain't good," said Josiah. "Looks like a buggy hitch, but there ain't no buggy."

Jeremy quickly scaled the stable fence and joined his brother at the horses. "Hey, this looks like Grady Murphy's mare," he said. "Don't know why she's hitched up, but we better go find Grady. You saddle up our horses, and I'll take care of these two."

Within minutes, the brothers were racing on horseback along the trail toward Nortonville. They let the stable-master know the situation before heading out. Their boss's concerned expression sent a chill through each twin as the urgency to find Grady quickly became apparent.

A mile out of town, Jeremy and Josiah slowed their horses. "There's someone on the trail up ahead," said Jeremy.

"Is that Grady?" Josiah asked.

"Can't tell, yet."

The boys sprinted the last hundred yards toward the figure staggering along the path. "Grady! Hey, Grady!" shouted Jeremy, now certain of the figure's identity. One side of Grady's head was soaked in blood. The reddish-brown mixture of blood and dirt coated his hair, face, and neck. Josiah jumped off his horse and caught the stumbling Grady under one arm.

"Grady, you okay?" asked Josiah. "What happened?"

Jeremy joined his brother. They guided Grady to a nearby boulder and sat him down. "Banged your head pretty good," Josiah continued. "We gotta get you to the doctor."

"Sarah," whispered Grady. "Where's Sarah?"

Grady, still dazed and in pain, looked both directions along the trail. "Sarah Norton. Where's Sarah Norton?"

"Was she in the buggy with you?" asked Jeremy.

"Yes, yes. In the buggy. Where's the buggy?" Grady asked anxiously.

The twins looked at each other with growing distress. "Your horse and another made it back into Clayton," said Jeremy. "But the buggy must have snapped off."

Grady tried to stand as the boys braced him. "Sarah Norton," Grady continued. "We have to find Sarah Norton." Dreadful worry overtook Grady. He pulled away from the boys in an attempt to search for Sarah, but stumbled feebly after just a step. Jeremy caught him and sat him back down.

"Alright, alright," Josiah said. "You take it easy now. We'll find Mrs. Norton. Jeremy will get you to the doc, and I'll ride the trail 'til I find her. She can't be far."

Jeremy nodded in agreement with his brother, and the two helped Grady onto a horse. Jeremy led the horse back toward Clayton while Josiah mounted his horse and began trotting toward Nortonville.

Josiah slowed his pace as he approached a sharp bend in the trail. With the ravine on one side, he continued to scan the trail and surrounding hills for any sign of Mrs. Norton. Then he stopped.

A lump formed in Josiah's throat as he rounded the turn. The trail dirt was freshly churned and rutted as if something slid sideways. Toward the ravine, splintered wood fragments lay just outside the trail. Josiah feared the worst.

He dismounted and cautiously peered over the steep drop. A path of flattened grasses and crushed shrubs led to a shattered black mass three-hundred feet below. Josiah tied up his horse and began the slow decent down the hill. Sliding mostly on his rear, he reached the remains of the demolished buggy. The lump in his throat thickened.

Carefully, Josiah lifted the bent and torn buggy cover. He froze, horrified at the vision before him.

Nearly indistinguishable from the mangled buggy, the body of Sarah Norton lay in a twisted heap with one arm and one leg bent into disturbing, unnatural positions. The ghastly image of a milky-white femur bone jutting out from her thigh sickened Josiah. Gently, he turned Sarah's bloodied head to view her face. Instantly he knew.

For twenty-nine years, the Nortonville founder's wife tended to the region's sick and ailing. Over four-hundred lives were delivered by her hand. Now, during a routine ride on an idyllic autumn morning, the pragmatic, occasionally prickly, leader of the Nortonville community was broken . . . and lifeless.

> ### Death of an Aged Midwife.
>
> Nortonville, October 5th.—Mrs. Sarah Norton, widow of one of the original locators of the Mount Diablo coal field, was killed near here to-day, by a runaway horse. She was 68 years of age, and has practiced midwifery for the past eighteen years. During this time she has attended over 600 cases, and never lost one. It was while going on a professional visit that she met her death.

Death of an Aged Midwife. [17]

CHAPTER 27

THE SCHOOL DAY ENDED. Outside Harrison's classroom, students rushed to catch a ride home or meet up with friends. Harrison blinked hard, trying to shake off the lingering jet lag. Stretching Celeste's and his spring break as long as possible meant returning to work the day after arriving home. The eight-hour time difference between California and Wales, following an already exhausting day of teaching, took its toll.

Harrison sipped a rare afternoon coffee and began setting up for his environmental club's after school meeting. Since his student, Mitchell Conder, demonstrated the effects of resonance a few weeks back, Harrison and Mitchell began preparing a second activity. Club members trickled into the classroom while Harrison gathered materials. Mitchell soon arrived and finished the preparations.

"Hey, Everyone," Harrison began. "I'm glad so many of you made it today because, to be honest, I wasn't sure who'd remember the meeting on the Monday after Spring Break. I hope you're all well rested and ready to finish out the year strong."

Harrison waited for groans and under-the-breath comments, especially from seniors, about returning to school. "Before we start discussing our remaining activities for the year, Mitchell wanted to share another demonstration, partly for the interesting science involved, and partly for a project he's working on. Mitchell, all yours."

"Thanks, Mr. B," replied Mitchell. He then turned his attention to the students. "So you guys remember last month when I explained the cause of wind turbine syndrome?"

Most nodded with affirmation. "Resonance," blurted out a club member.

"Correct," stated Mitchell. "The spinning windmill blades vibrate the air, which can resonate with certain body parts. For some people this creates a feeling of discomfort or anxiety, while others feel nothing. After learning about the syndrome, I started researching more about how resonance is related to music."

While the students seemed engaged, they were unclear where Mitchell was heading.

"Anyway, I ended up learning more about a type of resonance called Helmholtz resonance."

"Helm – what?" someone said.

"Helmholtz," answered Mitchell, "named for the guy that described the phenomenon in the 1850's. Now watch and listen." Mitchell lifted an empty old style ceramic jug off Harrison's front desk and put the jug mouth to his lips. Blowing gently, he created a low, smooth tone. "And that is Helmholtz resonance."

"Is that what all those bottles are for?" someone else asked, pointing to a table lined with glass containers of various shapes and sizes.

"Yes, but before you all give it a try, you need to understand the physics." Mitchell began explaining the concept while the group anxiously anticipated playing with the bottles. "When air moves across the jug's opening, some goes inside and squishes the air already inside the bottle. That increases the pressure inside the jug, which forces air back out. But the air racing out of the jug lowers the pressure inside, which causes more air to rush back in." Mitchell paused to gauge understanding. They all seemed with him so far.

"This air rushing in and out causes vibration. Like we learned before, if the vibration is the right frequency, then resonance is created and the vibrations are amplified and we get . . ." Mitchell blew on the jug again, "sound."

223

"So how do you know what the right frequency is?" came a voice from the side.

"Good question, Mr. Barrett," smiled Mitchell. "The resonance frequency will depend on the volume inside the jug, or in your case, the bottle. Typically, a bigger volume will vibrate slower and have a lower frequency, while a smaller volume has a higher frequency."

Mitchell and Harrison distributed bottles, some empty, some partially filled with water. "I know you have all done this before, but there is something I want to try with all of your help," continued Mitchell. "You'll notice the bottles have letters on them. The reason is . . ."

"Musical notes," shouted a member.

"You got it," responded Mitchell. "So first, you all have to see if you can create a sound."

Instantly, Harrison's classroom sounded like the discordic blend between a country jug band and a dying whale. Mitchell checked that each student formed a satisfactory tone with their bottle. "Helmholtz resonance, Mr. B," said Mitchell grinning at Harrison.

Harrison winced playfully at the din. "That it is."

Mitchell quieted the students. "Now, you're only going to play your bottle when I point at you, got it?"

The group all nodded and held their bottle high, lips pursed, ready to blow a note. Mitchell began directing, pointing slowly to various notes and waiting for the proper tone: C, C, G, G, A, A, G – F, F, E, E, D, D, C . . .

Students instantly recognized Twinkle, Twinkle, Little Star's familiar melody. When Mitchell finished the tune, the group applauded. "I can tell you now," Mitchell continued, "the reason I asked Mr. B. to let me do this is that I'm working on a project for my music theory class by forming a band that uses only Helmholtz resonance instruments. I thought some of you might want to help on the project. It gets a lot more complex when I add chords and different types of instruments."

"Sounds cool," said Staci, the club president. "Any more songs we can do right now?"

"I thought you'd never ask." Mitchell grabbed a pen from Harrison's desk and raised it like a conductor's baton. He again pointed to club members and waited for their note: G, C, D, E, E – E, D, E, C, C . . .

"You Are My Sunshine!" shouted several members waiting to play their note. When finished with the song, Mitchell turned toward Harrison. "Well?"

"Alright, you have time for one more. Then we have to get down to business," responded Harrison.

"Nice," said Mitchell. "Okay, let's try this one." He raised the pen and students readied their bottles. Just as he pointed at the first note . . .

"Barre, you have to see this!"

The swinging classroom door and frenzied voice startled the group, including Harrison. "Sorry everyone," said Celeste realizing Harrison was not alone. "I forgot you had a meeting, but this can't wait."

Students were not used to seeing Ms. Scott so excited. They assumed something important happened, as did Harrison. "Uh, Staci, you know what we need to cover. Can you handle the meeting?"

"No problem, Mr. Barrett," Staci instantly replied.

Celeste grabbed Harrison's arm and rushed him out of the classroom. A few hushed whispers from environmental club members assessed the scene.

"I bet it's about their wedding," said one.

"Maybe she decided on a dress," said another.

225

"Or maybe they finally chose a date," added Staci.

HARRISON JOGGED TO KEEP UP with Celeste as they crossed campus toward her classroom. "Is this about the Pythians?" Harrison questioned.

"Yes," she answered enthusiastically. "And a lot more."

"More?"

"A whole lot more," she replied. "You know I've been trying to figure out how I'm connected to all this – the murder in the cemetery, the Pythians, the whole mystery."

"Of course," said Harrison. "And every time we do some research, the story gets stranger."

Celeste nodded. "After what my grandfather told us, I began looking at things differently. Then today, just now after school, I found something remarkable."

"What? What is it?" asked Harrison with growing excitement.

"Here," said Celeste opening her classroom door. "I have to show you."

She raced to her computer and flicked the mouse to wake the screen. "Sit next to me," said Celeste, sliding a second chair up to her desk. "And fasten your seatbelt," she continued, quoting from a favorite old Bette Davis movie, "it's going to be a bumpy ride."

"I can't wait," said Harrison, feeding off Celeste's enthusiasm.

"This is the key." Celeste opened her palm to reveal her tetractys pendant. "At first I didn't make the connection," she continued. "But after my grandfather's story about my father and grandmother belonging to the Knights of Pythias, and the strange attack in Wales, I think I've put the pieces together, as improbable as they may seem."

Harrison leaned in.

"First of all, the association between me and the Nortonville cemetery makes sense now. My father and his mother were Pythians from Wales, and we know some of the coal miners were Welch Pythian members. The tetractys on this pendant must come from the sacred symbol originally described by Pythagoras, from whom the Pythians derive their philosophy."

"I'm with you, so far," said Harrison.

"I can see a connection from 600 B.C. Pythagoras to 1870s Welch miners to present day me. What I didn't understand was everything in between those times . . . until I saw this."

Celeste clicked a tab on the computer screen. "What am I looking at?" asked Harrison.

"In researching the Prince Madoc story about Welsh Indians in America, we read about the evidence, remember?" said Celeste.

"I do," replied Harrison. "There were numerous, including encounters with fair-skinned natives, some ancient Welsh-looking structures and round boats, and old engravings similar to ancient Welsh symbols, among other things."

"These photos are of some of those artifacts engraved with Welsh-looking symbols. Recognize this one on the end, standing alone?" continued Celeste.

Harrison edged closer to the computer as Celeste zoomed in. "Ten dots in the shape of a triangle. That's a tetractys!" As Harrison sat back, he felt a chill shoot through him. "A coincidence?" he said hesitantly.

"Perhaps," Celeste replied. "But the Prince Madoc story tells of a man who believed in friendship, charity, and benevolence that fled his homeland when chaos and conflict erupted. Does that philosophy sound familiar?"

"Pythagoras," answered Harrison. "It's possible that Prince Madoc followed the teachings of Pythagoras. But what does this all have to do with your pendant?"

"Oh, I'm not done, yet," Celeste said with a wry smile. "When my grandfather told us about the Caledfwlch Society, I wondered how that group may be linked to all of this. In the twelfth-century, a man named Geoffrey of Monmouth wrote the Historia Regum Britanniae – History of the Kings of Britain. He traced Britain's rulers back to Brutus of Troy, the first king, and included an account of a sixth-century ruler . . . King Arthur. I was able to find the actual book on the internet."

"Someone scanned the actual centuries-old document?" asked Harrison.

"They did," responded Celeste. "This is a Welsh translation from the fourteenth century. And this . . . ," Celeste clicked open another tab on her screen, "is an image from that document."

Harrison stared at the computer screen. On worn, yellowed parchment was the figure of a red-cloaked figure holding a shield and resting a sword on his shoulder. "Is that a drawing of . . .?"

"Yes," interrupted Celeste, "that's King Arthur."

"Incredible!"

Celeste zoomed in. "Notice anything familiar, below the cross on the shield?" asked Celeste.

Harrison squinted a bit. "Oh my, gosh," he said with astonishment "A tetractys!"

"The same symbol as Pythagoras, Prince Madoc and the Welsh Indians, the Knights of Pythias . . . and my pendant," exclaimed Celeste.

Sitting back in his chair, Harrison thought through the revelation. "When I consider the King Arthur stories, the connection is not so far-fetched. The brotherhood of the Knights of the Round Table and their legendary tales of friendship, charity, and benevolence are all straight from Pythagorean philosophy."

"Exactly," said Celeste.

"But I still don't understand what role you play in a twenty-five-hundred year old philosophy symbolized by a tetractys," said Harrison, focusing back on the ancient King Arthur image.

Celeste picked up her pendant. "That's where I think this comes in. We know about the Arthurian legend, and we learned about the Knights of Pythias and the object they hold sacred. We then found out about a power-hungry secret society. What is the one thing they all have in common with this pendant?"

Harrison watched in awe as Celeste slowly turned her pendant over revealing the isolated etching on the back.

"A sword?" said Harrison.

"Not just a sword, Barre," responded Celeste. "The sword. The sword the Caledfwlch Society has sought for centuries. The sword whose mystical powers are bestowed upon its possessor. The sword wielded by the legendary, King Arthur."

Celeste paused. She turned toward Harrison and squeezed his hand tightly. "I believe this pendant somehow, someway, represents a guide to the hidden location of Excalibur."

15TH Century Image of King Arthur [18]

CHAPTER XXVIII

October 6, 1879

"I DON'T THINK IT'S RIGHT," Mary Tully insisted. "This is not what Sarah wanted."

"Nonsense," snorted Pastor Price. "A proper Christian service and burial are required for the resurrection of her eternal soul."

News of Sarah Norton's death spread quickly through the mining towns and beyond. The evening she died, residents flooded her home for a hastily prepared wake. Although she was not from Wales, the Nortonville town leaders adhered to traditional Welsh customs for the viewing of Sarah's body. Flickering candles scented the room, white lace curtains draped windows and mirrors, and churchwomen laid out spiced wine and cakes.

Some visitors came and went in minutes, just long enough to pay their respects to the wife of the town's founder. Others lingered for hours late into the night, sharing stories of Sarah's often cantankerous, yet always sensible disposition. Dozens of children, young and old, born by Sarah's hand, followed their parents into the parlor where Sarah's body lay on a long wooden table. Dressed in fresh clothing with a white lace cloth covering her badly injured face, Sarah looked peaceful while parents who benefitted from her skillful midwifing gave thanks or said a prayer.

As dozens of mourners wept and prayed during the wake, Sarah's closest friends, along with the town leaders, discussed her funeral arrangements. The conversation provoked debate early into the next morning. The majority of Nortonville dignitaries, including Pastor Price and Justice of the Peace Woodruff, insisted on a Christian service for Sarah, rejecting Mary Tully's suggestion of a simple, non-religious burial. Expecting hundreds of participants, they had already planned a processional to the church, followed by a slow march alongside a horse-drawn wagon up the hill to the cemetery.

"But if you know that Sarah did not want a Christian burial," continued Mary. "I still don't understand why you would force it upon her?"

Mary's pleading was ignored as Pastor Price used shredded bits of paper to mark the bible chapter and verse he intended to quote during services.

Reluctantly, Mary yielded to the consensus. Now, with the morning sun well above the horizon, she helped Pastor Price coordinate the careful loading of Sarah's coffin onto a horse-drawn wagon. The wagon and a small contingent of town leaders headed toward Nortonville's main road. The wind, so persistent across the Mt. Diablo foothills, was unusually calm. A solemn stillness embraced the mining town.

The stable-master guided the horses pulling Sarah's coffin onto the road leading to the Protestant Church. Within minutes, hundreds of individuals fell in behind. Residents of Nortonville and Somersville participated, as did some from the more distant mining towns of Stewartville, Judsonville, and West Hartley. Even people from over the hill in Clayton and down near the river in Antioch made the early morning trek to pay their respects.

As the procession made its way to the edge of town, a chill overcame Mary. At first she thought the shivering cold was in her mind, manifested by distress over the loss of her friend and discomfort at the impending religious services. Eyeing the crowd, however, Mary noticed many townsfolk buttoning coats and hunkering under tightly wrapped shawls. The rapid temperature drop was real, and with it came the wind.

The processional slowly crept east along the dirt path toward the church. Surrounding trees and shrubs now leaned and shuddered. It was not until Mary turned back toward the west that she realized how fast the weather was changing. From behind Mt. Diablo's twin peaks, thick black clouds billowed ominously. Rain was rare this time of year, so the approaching storm caught most unprepared.

A lightning flash in the distance backlit the mountain. Seconds later, hushed thunder rolled across the peaks. The horses fidgeted nervously as the stable-master stroked their muzzles. The crowd mumbled about the unusual sight, but kept moving forward.

The sky continued to darken, like a black veil draping the town. The wind stiffened. Men gripped their hats tightly while women's shawls whipped wildly. Just as the stable-master eased the horses back on track, another lightning flash lit the sky. Instantly, a ferocious thunderclap echoed through the hills. The deafening sound startled the already-tense horses who bucked and pulled. Several men ran to aid the stable-master as he tugged on reins. Others desperately held the back of the wagon, fearing Sarah's coffin might tumble out if the horses ran.

Pastor Price conferred with town leaders about how to proceed, but many in the processional were already breaking line and edging back toward town. Then, as if an unseen hand started pumping water from a heavenly well, rain poured down from above. Another lightning flash and another crack of thunder caused the horses to bolt out of control. The wagon veered from the trail taking with it a group of men desperate to prevent a catastrophe.

Most in the processional disbanded. People quickly headed back into town for shelter from the unexpected downpour. Finally, with few remaining on the church trail, Pastor Price called off the service. "Tomorrow!" he shouted through the wind and rain. "We'll hold the service tomorrow!"

Only Mary and a few town leaders stood near enough to hear the pastor, but they knew word would spread quickly. The storm will surely pass soon, Mary thought, and the trail will dry out. Services can take place tomorrow. Though, in the back of her mind, she could not shake the thought that perhaps . . . this was a sign.

MARY DREW OPEN HER bedroom curtains. Morning sunlight drenched the room. Realizing she slept later than planned, Mary rushed to dress and dashed out the door. Little sleep the night before and an emotional start and stop to Sarah's funeral services the previous day left Mary exhausted, so she was grateful for the extra rest. Now, she needed to get back to Sarah's house.

Pastor Price, Justice Woodruff, and several others were already loading Sarah's coffin onto the wagon and preparing for the processional when Mary arrived. She took a deep breath to calm her nerves and soak in the fresh, rain-cleansed air. The sky directly above looked clear and blue, but to the west, high clouds spread toward the horizon. Nothing to worry about, thought Mary as she joined the preparations.

After the storm broke the day before, runners notified the townsfolk about the rescheduled services. Most people found overnight shelter in Nortonville or nearby Somersville and were now congregating back in Nortonville awaiting the processional. When Sarah's coffin arrived on the town's main street, the gathering once again fell in behind and started the somber walk toward the church.

As the last of the processional reached the edge of town, Mary heard a low murmur sweep through the crowd. She turned back and noticed several people looking upward toward the west. The high clouds had thickened. Charcoal gray swirls already blanketed the peaks of Mt. Diablo like a spewing volcanic eruption. Within minutes, the entire sky once more filled with storm clouds. "Oh, dear God," whispered Mary, "how can this happen again?"

Price and Woodruff said something to each other and then called for the stable-master to quicken the pace. Mary overheard more hushed conversation among the processional. She was not the only one questioning the impending weather's portent.

Suddenly, like the deafening crack of a divine coachman's whip, a massive thunderclap bellowed from above. The horses bolted. The stable-master clung tightly to the reins as the horses dragged him and the wagon off the trail. A dozen men gave chase. Sarah's coffin bounced and slid, and the processional crowd gasped in horror.

Seconds later, the sky opened up with a torrential downpour and whipping wind. People scattered. Some headed into the church for cover; most hurried back toward town. Mary stood motionless. The shock of another thwarted attempt at Sarah's funeral services stunned her. She watched in anguish as the men fought mightily to steady the terrified horses. With water dripping from her rain-soaked hood and wind blasting her face, a fierce determination overcame her. Mary dipped her head and started the hike back to Nortonville. "Not again," she pronounced aloud. "We will not do this again."

PRICE AND WOODRUFF FINALLY conceded. Sarah's body would be laid to rest without a religious service. Pastor Price was the most reluctant. "I cannot bear to condemn her soul to eternal wandering upon this earth, unable to pass into our Father's arms," he declared. Nevertheless, Mary insisted. Woodruff also seemed convinced that the extraordinary phenomena of the past two days were not mere coincidences. His gentle prodding and Mary's resolve finally persuaded Price to concur that Sarah, perhaps, had one more directive to give.

The following morning, Mary woke and raced to the window. She threw open the curtains. Greeted by the sunrise's orange glow saturating the eastern horizon, she smiled. Quickly, she pulled a coat over her nightgown and ran out the boarding house's front door. Barefoot and anxious, Mary stopped and gazed toward the west — not a cloud in sight. She watched the yellow-orange sky gradually transition to azure blue with the rising sun. Mary sighed deeply and smiled. "Yes, Sarah," she said quietly, "you made your point."

Soon, Mary, Pastor Price, and Justice of the Peace Woodruff once again led a processional of townsfolk up the steep hill out of Nortonville. This time, rather than heading toward the church, they veered directly to the cemetery. The crowd carefully weaved their way around existing graves marked by a variety of marble tombstones. Etchings revealed names and ages of the souls buried below.

Mary's heart sank as she reflected on the young ages of nearly half the entombed inhabitants, born healthy by Sarah's hand, only to succumb to horrific disease or disaster. Each headstone displayed carved symbols significant to the deceased or to grief-stricken loved ones left behind. Images of doves, baskets of lilies, or clasped hands adorned the headstones of many

236

women and children, while Mason square and compass or Oddfellow linked rings signified fraternal affiliation on the memorial stones of most men.

Mary followed the Pastor, easing her way around a group of miner's gravesites, each an apparent Knights of Pythias member as revealed by the distinct shield, helmet, crossed battle axes, and F, C, B engraving. She caught up to Pastor Price standing next to the deep hole that would be Sarah's final resting place.

"She chose the site herself," Price said softly to Mary.

"Is that so?" Mary replied. "It seems a fitting location."

"Quite," Price continued. "She was most insistent. She reserved plots for a number of Nortonville residents some time ago and even determined a site that will not receive a body. She made Justice Woodruff and I promise to uphold her wishes, which, of course, we have done. An unusual request, but, as you know, there was no arguing with Sarah once she set her mind."

Mary nodded silently. She stared into the deep, rectangular hole. Sarah's coffin arrived, carried by six men who gently lay it onto the damp ground. As the crowd formed around the gravesite, the men used thick rope and slowly lowered the wooden box into the hole. Pastor Price mouthed some words that Mary could not make out, and then he nodded to Woodruff.

"We lay to rest this day," Woodruff began, "our dear friend, Sarah Norton."

Mary's eyes welled with tears.

Woodruff continued. "A native of Canada, she made a home here in Mt. Diablo's shadow, not just for herself, but for so many others. She delivered countless children into this world and, by all accounts, lost not a one."

237

Parents throughout the congregation patted or squeezed infants, toddlers, and even teenagers that bore witness to Sarah's skill.

"We now release her body and soul," Woodruff continued, "back to whence they came. May she rest in peace for all eternity."

Woodruff nodded to two men with shovels. The thud of wet dirt landing on the wood coffin signaled the end of Sarah's service. Woodruff turned away and the crowd dispersed.

Mary was pleased. Short and to the point, she thought. Sarah would approve.

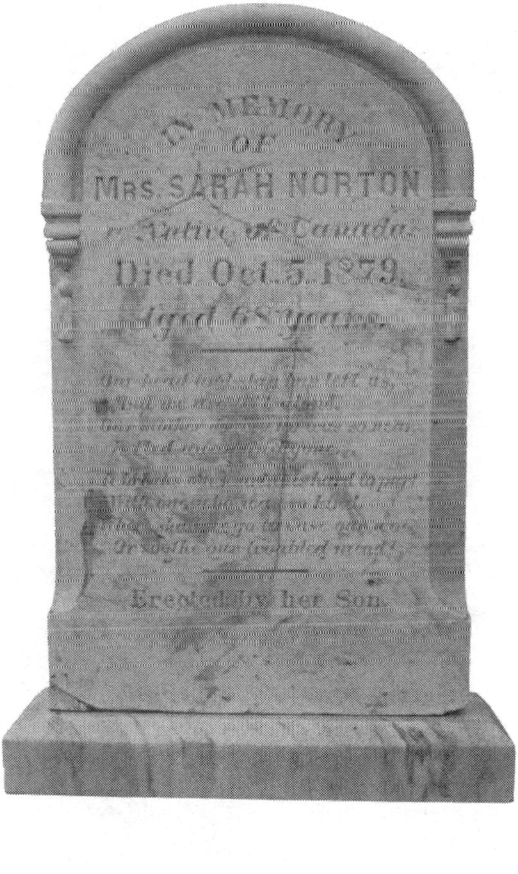

Headstone of Sarah Norton [19]

CHAPTER 29

HARRISON LAY IN BED with his eyes closed.
Celeste's head rested against his shoulder and her arm stretched
across his chest. He inhaled the sweet fragrance of her hair and
felt her warm breath on his neck. He could not be more content.

"Hey," whispered Celeste.

In the dark bedroom with the Saturday morning sun not
yet up, Harrison thought Celeste was still asleep. "Yes?"

"You're wanted," she said softly.

Harrison smiled. "What a coincidence," he said as he
rolled toward her and squeezed her waist. "You're wanted, too."

"I mean . . . someone wants you," said Celeste.

Harrison paused. Someone wants me, he thought? He
slowly opened his eyes. Staring him in the face, just inches away,
was a moist, black nose and long, black snout.

"Ugh," muttered Harrison. "Cousteau, get down."

"I think he wants breakfast," said Celeste as she reached
up and scratched Cousteau behind the ear.

"Clearly, he has not yet learned the difference between a
weekend and a weekday," grumbled Harrison. Sliding out of bed,
Harrison staggered to his closet and pulled on a robe. "I'm gonna
feed him and then get some breakfast started for us."

"Sounds good," said Celeste. "I'll be there in a bit."

Harrison shoed Cousteau off the bed and headed toward
the door.

"Hey, aren't you forgetting something?" asked Celeste.

Harrison immediately spun around. He climbed back
onto the bed, crawled to Celeste, and fell into her open arms.
They kissed and held each other tightly. "Good morning,"
whispered Harrison.

"Good mor . . ."

Celeste was unable to finish her greeting during their usual morning embrace. Standing on the bed with a front paw on Harrison's back, Cousteau grunted.

"Okay, okay," said Harrison. "He can be pretty insistent sometimes."

"I can see that," smiled Celeste.

Harrison reluctantly got back up. Cousteau leapt off the bed, paused a moment for a vigorous shake, and trotted out of the room behind Harrison.

Following a leisurely breakfast, Harrison and Celeste took their coffee to the family room sofa. Scattered upon the coffee table lay dozens of wedding venue brochures. In addition, Celeste's laptop displayed a myriad of other potential locations. Though spiritual by nature, neither Celeste nor Harrison was especially religious. They agreed to find a local outdoor setting that was beautiful and serene, and could accommodate a few friends and family.

"As you know," Celeste began, "before we set a final date, we need to secure the venue. So let's not leave the house today until we've decided. Agreed?"

"Agreed," affirmed Harrison.

For the next several hours, the couple sifted and sorted through venue options. Wineries, private mansions, and historic estates made the top-twenty list, as did country clubs and outdoor gardens. Harrison tried adding Oakland's Chabot Space and Science Center, arguing that getting married under the stars inside a planetarium might be considered an outdoor venue. Celeste appreciated Harrison's unique perspective, but vetoed the choice.

"Some of these wineries are stunning," commented Celeste. "But unless you rent the entire place, I'm not thrilled

241

about having the public wondering around nearby. I'd prefer something more intimate."

Harrison nodded in agreement. "We could, of course, rent out the whole facility if you find a place you really love. Otherwise, I agree with you about a more private venue, perhaps one of the historic mansions."

"It would be incredible if we could use the old John Marsh Stone House," said Celeste.

Harrison grinned broadly. "That would be awesome. Back to the scene of the crime, so to speak, and our first adventure together. Unfortunately, the restoration work has a ways to go, and I don't want to put off marrying you any longer than I have to."

Celeste patted Harrison's knee, leaned over, and kissed him on the cheek. "Me either."

"Here," she continued. "This is my favorite, so far." She handed Harrison a brochure.

"The Grand Island Mansion," read Harrison. "I love that place — a private Italian Renaissance villa from the 1920's right on the Delta. It has my vote if we can find a date that works."

Harrison opened the brochure. "What are these markings?"

"Oh, I was just sketching out possible table arrangements on the dining room photo."

"It appears you've already made your selection," said Harrison.

"I admit, it has been my first choice for a while, but I want your opinion. It's much less important to me where I wed, as whom I wed," said Celeste, playfully nudging Harrison.

"Well, this place absolutely works for me. I think it will be great," responded Harrison, still staring at the brochure. "I . . ."

Harrison paused unexpectedly.

"What is it?" Celeste asked.

"I notice that you aligned possible guest tables in the shape of a triangle. I assume the point of the triangle is where our head table would be, with eight guest tables radiating out from that."

"Yes," said Celeste. "I just like the way that arrangement makes it easier for everyone to see the head table."

Harrison continued examining the brochure. "But no guest table in the center of the triangle?"

Celeste cautiously answered the question, unsure about Harrison's intent. "No, that's where we would roll the cake; in the center where everyone can see." She recognized the intense contemplation in Harrison's expression. "What, Barre? What is it?"

"Excuse me a minute, I'll be right back."

Harrison abruptly left the sofa and headed out of the room. Celeste sat silently, perplexed by Harrison's reaction. Was he not sincere about liking the venue?

Harrison returned quickly. He handed a different brochure to Celeste. "Take a look at this," he said enthusiastically.

Celeste looked at the front page and read aloud, "Rose Hill Cemetery at Black Diamond Mines." She turned toward Harrison, her brows furrowed and face frozen in a stunned gaze. "Barre, we are not getting married in a cemetery!"

Harrison froze in confusion. Then, suddenly, he burst out laughing. "Oh my, gosh, no, no, no . . . I'm sorry," he began. "I'm all for the Grand Island Mansion. No, this is about your pendant."

He sat back next to Celeste. "The sketch you made of the tables got me thinking." Harrison opened the Grand Island Mansion brochure once again and pointed at the table markings.

243

"Notice anything special about the shape and arrangement that you drew?"

Celeste, now intrigued by the conversation, replied, "No, nothing special."

"What if I turn the tables into dots, like this? Now we have: one, two-three, four-six, seven, eight, nine, ten," counted Harrison.

"What happened to five?"

"Five would be in the middle, where our cake is – like this," Harrison said as he added a dot.

Celeste turned to Harrison. "A tetractys!"

"Yes, I assume that's not what you intended, but your subconscious may have gotten the better of you," Harrison said with a squeeze of her hand. "The table arrangement made me think of your pendant with the gemstones aligned in a tetractys except for the center piece. Your wedding tables are leaving space in the center for the cake. What if the pendant gems are leaving space for something, too?"

"There is the upside-down torch symbol in the center of the gems. Is that the missing piece?" Celeste asked.

"That's what's in the center on the front side, in full view," Harrison continued. "But what is hidden in the center on the back side of the pendant?"

"A sword," answered Celeste. "Possibly the sword, Excalibur."

"That's right. And we learned that an upside-down torch is commonly used to represent a cemetery. So . . . ."

Before Harrison could continue, Celeste grabbed his arm. "I get it!" she exclaimed. "If the torch represents a cemetery – Rose Hill Cemetery, and the missing center gemstone indicates the location of Excalibur, then somewhere in Rose Hill there should be a tetractys. Find the tetractys, and we find Excalibur!"

244

"Now it's just a theory, of course," said Harrison. "But all the clues sure seem to point in that direction."

"We need to head back to Black Diamond Mines and the cemetery," Celeste said as she started to rise off the sofa.

Harrison touched her shoulder. "Hold on a second. That's what the brochure is for. If you open it up, there is a map of the cemetery plotted out. It's at least a place to start."

Celeste unfolded the Rose Hill Cemetery brochure onto the coffee table. Stretched across the entire trifold paper was a detailed diagram of the cemetery. Exact locations of gravesites were marked by numbers. Below the drawing, a key indicated the person's name interred at that site.

"So these are all of the people buried there," said Celeste. "They look randomly placed. Nothing that looks like a tetractys, anyway."

Harrison carefully scanned the diagram. "Yea, you're right. Nothing stands out. Whose plot is this one near the corner, number six?"

Celeste ran her finger through the long list of alphabetized names until she came to number six. "That would be Sarah Norton." stated Celeste. "We saw her headstone on one of our visits. Sarah Norton . . . the supposed White Witch?"

"That's right," answered Harrison. "And I'm glad you said supposed. I have a theory about the legend of the White Witch, but that's for another time. Can you tell me which number plot is William Gething, the coal miner whose headstone the murdered man wrote your name on?"

"He is number forty-six."

Harrison found and circled the site with a pencil. "The writing said, Madog is near."

"If Madog is near references Prince Madoc," Celeste began, "and he is linked to the legend of King Arthur, then our assumption is that Excalibur, the mystical object of a centuries-long quest, is near this marker."

A wave of adrenalin surged through Celeste and Harrison. Immersed in their discovery, they both ignored their wedding venue discussion. They fed off each other's excitement like eager school children.

"We know that William Gething was a Knight of Pythias," continued Harrison.

"Yes. His headstone is engraved with the Pythian symbol – a shield, helmet, and crossed battle-axes," confirmed Celeste.

"What was the name of the other Knight of Pythias member that we read about when we visited the Black Diamond Mines Visitor Center?" asked Harrison.

Celeste though a moment. "The only name I can remember is Evan Davies."

"That's right, Evan Davies. So where is he buried?"

Celeste searched the cemetery names. "He is at plot number fifty-three."

Harrison quickly found the number and circled it. "Hmm, pretty close to William Gething. I wonder if that is a coincidence."

"Or something more," Celeste added. "If you're thinking what I'm thinking, then we need to return to Rose Hill Cemetery at Black Diamond Mines to find out which other headstones have a Knights of Pythias symbol."

"And if our theory is right," said Harrison excitedly, "then somewhere in or near that cemetery is a sword thought to be Excalibur."

"The sword wielded by King Arthur, a follower of Pythagorean philosophy," Celeste declared, "saved from the chaos of a crumbling empire by Prince Madoc who fled to North America; protected for centuries by the Welsh Indians until it landed in the possession of Justus Rathbone, who resurrected the original Pythagorean philosophy through the Knights of Pythias; hidden long ago by select Pythians — the Dramatic Order of the Knights of Khorassan — who guard its secret from the Caledfwlch Society, a clandestine organization that seeks to use the sword's fabled power for evil. All of which . . ." continued Celeste, shaking her head in disbelief, ". . . is embodied by a single pendant given to me by my father."

"Yup," said Harrison, enthralled by Celeste's extraordinary account. "That about sums it up."

CHAPTER XXX

November 9, 1879

COYOTES YIPPED AND HOWLED nearby. The quarter moon brightened the night sky just enough for Ann to explore the hills. She directed her candle-lit mining lantern away from town as she walked, careful to avoid drawing attention to her activities. For hours, she searched in and around the powder magazine, but now the approaching morning sun once again forced her to douse the lantern and turn back toward Nortonville.

Ann swelled with frustration and anger as she headed home. *So very close,* she thought. *After four years of toiling in this pitiful town, I am so very close to returning Caledfwlch back home — back into the hands of the rightful rulers of Wales.* Voices from Ann's past echoed tales of glory and power bestowed upon the one who wielded Arthur's sword. Her lengthy and intense indoctrination into the Caledfwlch Society shaped a singular, sacred purpose. "Soon," she said aloud, "the Red Dragon will once again reign supreme."

The night Ann followed Sarah Norton and Mary Tully into the hills, she knew Sarah showed Mary the sword's location. She cursed herself for not getting close enough to see the exact site. Now resigned to scouring the area for the sword's hiding place, she desperately combed through overturned stones, faded footprints, and disturbed soil. Ann recently discovered the removable rock in the powder magazine wall, and if not for Sarah's forethought to move the sword just before her death, the Caledfwlch Society's centuries-old quest would be over.

Ann's modest house on the town's edge not only proved convenient for her bee's wax candle and honey making business, but also allowed her to easily slip in and out unnoticed after sunset. Still concealed by darkness, Ann entered her front door. She pulled a matchstick from her overcoat and quickly lit a nearby candle. The small flame allowed Ann to navigate through her furniture toward the bedroom. As she hung her coat near the door, Ann suddenly froze. Perhaps she saw a faint outline from the corner of her eye, or heard a muted breath. Somehow, Ann sensed . . . someone else was in the room.

Slowly, Ann turned toward a shadowy figure seated in the corner. She stood in silence, facing the unknown intruder and tightly gripping the burning candle she would use to defend herself.

"We need to talk."

Ann immediately recognized the deep, resonant voice. She eased her grip on the candle knowing it would be useless against this man.

"You do me honor with your presence, my Lord," Ann said nervously. She understood that no other pleasantries would be exchanged during this encounter.

The man rose from the chair. A black overcoat draped neatly over an expensive suitcoat and vest. Revealing chiseled facial features softened only by a well-groomed mustache and beard, he towered over Ann as he approached her.

"The Society is disappointed in your lack of progress," he said.

Ann swallowed hard. "I understand, my Lord. I nearly have it."

The man glared intensely at Ann, and then turned away. He pulled back the lace curtain and gazed out the window into the darkness. "We know the sword is near, but there are those who wish to replace you. They feel the Raven has become ineffective; perhaps she has lost her desire to fulfill our destiny."

"My Lord, you know that is not true," insisted Ann, resenting any notion of disloyalty. "I have done what needed to be done here. When the Society trained and released me as the Raven, the members knew then that I would never waiver from our goal. Sent from our homeland to this country, may I remind you that it was I who grew the discord among the Knights of Pythias in the east; I tracked the sword across a continent; I whittled away those Pythians with the sword's knowledge until there are but a few remaining; and I swear to you that I will bring *Caledfwlch* home."

"There is no denying," the man responded, "that you, indeed, have sacrificed much for our cause. But the Society is impatient."

"I just need a little more time. I will find the sword."

The man continued to stare out the window without speaking. Ann waited silently.

"Very well, you have one week. Let me now remind you, Raven, the consequence of failure is severe."

Without another word, he fastened closed his overcoat, left Ann's house, and disappeared into the night.

Ann remained incensed that Caledfwlch Society leaders questioned her loyalty and ability. She knew, however, that she must act quickly, and boldly. Searching the hills would no longer suffice. No, thought Ann, looking deeply into the flickering candle flame, I must confront the last remaining source.

MARY TULLY TOOK THE ENVELOPE from the boarding house owner. "What is this?" she asked.

"Delivered earlier today," the owner replied. "A boy brought it by and said to give it to you."

"Did he say who it was from?"

"I asked," replied the owner, "but he didn't know."

"Thank you," said Mary as she passed through the parlor and into her room. She sat at a small writing desk and slid open the envelope with her finger. Unfolding the paper inside, Mary read the note:

Sarah's death was no accident. If you want to know the truth be at Upper Black Diamond mine tonight at midnight. Come alone.

The cryptic message stunned Mary. She leaned back in her chair and breathed deeply. "Dear, God. It is as I feared."

Scared and confused, Mary collapsed onto her bed. She anxiously considered the invitation. Upper Black Diamond mine was a mile walk uphill. The mine's entrance was the only one accessible by foot, as all of the other mines required a hoist to lower workers into the shaft. The time and location meant that Mary would be isolated, far from town, and far from help.

Mary thought of all that Sarah Norton had done for the people of this and surrounding towns. If she truly was murdered, learning the killer's identity would be the very least Mary could do to bring justice and peace to Sarah's soul. The town owed nothing less to the woman who gave them so much.

I have to do anything I can, Mary thought, to honor Sarah's memory. With growing determination, she glanced at the wall clock. Hiking to the mine entrance took at least an hour, maybe more in the dark, but there was still plenty of time to eat and rest. She refolded the note and slid it up her sleeve out of sight. "Midnight tonight," Mary whispered. "I'll be there."

251

She slid open the bottom drawer next to her bed and pushed aside the small stack of undergarments. Carefully, she reached down and retrieved a single-shot Remington derringer. The small pistol was given to her by her son, James, the last of her grown children to move away. He insisted she have something for protection now that she was alone. For the first time in her life, Mary felt protection might be needed.

LACY VEILS OF CLOUDS DRIFTED across the moon like as Mary cautiously approached the Upper Black Diamond mine entrance. She waved her kerosene lantern side to side, scanning the area. With no sign of anyone, she stepped inside the mine tunnel. In the distance, a dim light caught her attention. The thought of continuing further into the coalmine terrified her, but turning back was not an option.

Mary followed the mining car tracks toward the light. Her heart raced. A faint, sweet smell of honey made her pause. Strange, she thought, to smell something so pleasant inside the dank confines of a coalmine. A few more steps and Mary found the light source, a small candle burning inside a mining lantern that hung on a wooden beam. The distinct honey aroma wafted off the beeswax candle.

Suddenly, Mary stopped. The rhythmic crunching of gravel from behind could only be footsteps. Mary spun back toward the mine entrance, but saw nothing. Slowly, she lifted her lantern. Inside the tunnel, between her and the mine entrance, a murky figure approached. Dear, God, Mary thought, I'm trapped. She quickly reached into her coat pocket and pulled out the derringer. Her hand trembled as she pointed it toward the faint image.

252

The figure stopped, too far away to identify. Mary stood motionless.

"I am so glad you came," said a voice. "This makes things much easier."

A wave of relief washed over Mary. She sighed deeply and returned the derringer to her pocket. "Ann. Oh, Ann, I am so thankful it's you. I was dreadfully afraid for a moment, not knowing who sent me that note. Please, tell me, what do you know about Sarah's death?"

Ann moved closer. Her black dress and overcoat were nearly indistinguishable from her shadow, all of which blended eerily with the coalmine walls. Ann stopped several feet away from Mary. One hand hung by her side, and the other angled behind her back. "I can tell you for certain, Mary," Ann began, "that Sarah Norton's death was not an accident."

"How do you know this?" Mary asked nervously.

Ann calmly responded. "Because I caused her death."

"I . . . I don't understand," said Mary.

"Then let me explain," replied Ann. Her voice changed. The gentle, Welsh lilt was gone, replaced by a dark, menacing tone. "She managed to avoid the first time I created an accident," Ann continued. "The explosion just missed sending her down the ravine. So, the next time I overheard her travel plans to Clayton, I made sure her regular buggy horses were not available. Then, I simply waited on the trail and fired salt pellets into the racing horses. Once they bolted, tumbling to her death was inevitable."

Mary remained frozen, gripped with horror at the revelation. Blood flushed from her face and she grew faint. With one hand, she steadied herself against the rock wall next to the mining lantern. "Wh . . . why?"

Ann remained cold and emotionless. "She was next in line."

253

"I don't understand." Mary's voice quivered as she spoke. "Next in line? Were there others?"

The question seemed to amuse Ann. "Of course. It became clear soon after I arrived here, that the only way I could learn the sword's location would be to thin the herd, as it were. I could not follow all of the Knights of Pythias, but once I began eliminating members, I knew those with the knowledge would be revealed. First, I dealt with the lot in the mine explosion. My long candle burned for hours before the flame hit the dynamite wick wrapped around it."

Mary's stomach churned. "So many innocent men. And their families . . . how could you do such a thing?"

"Would you like to hear more, Mary?" Ann stepped closer, her right hand still concealed behind her back.

Mary could not speak.

"Let me tell you about the rest." Ann's crazed manner intensified. She seemed to draw pleasure from reciting her heinous actions. "One of those wretched Pythians survived; what was his name, Evan Davies? I had to grind and leach quite the batch of toyon berries to extract enough cyanide from the seeds to poison his tea. Then there was the fire . . ."

Mary fell back against the wall. "The fire?"

"My intention was only to destroy the Knights of Pythias meeting hall. This incompetent town let the rest of the buildings burn. I must say, though, that incident really put fear into the Pythians. I saw them squirming. I knew one of them would soon reveal the sword's location."

Each new confession felt like a knife penetrating Mary's flesh. So much destruction, so much pain caused by this one woman.

Ann took another step forward. "And then there was the Abraham girl. I suspected her husband, a Pythian leader, knew of the sword's hiding place. The girl interrupted as I searched their home. Unfortunate for her."

The vision Mary had of Rebecca Abraham's charred body writhing in pain sickened her. And all because of this unspeakably evil woman's quest for a sword. Mary felt her fear gradually transform into anger. A seething burn began to fill her body and mind.

"When Daniel, Rebecca's husband, fled town like a coward, that left just Thomas Oliver and Sarah Norton who knew of the sword. Once Thomas was out of the way, I could easily focus on Sarah. I suspect no one will ever find his body." Mary felt Ann's satisfying smirk tear at her soul.

"And then," Ann continued. "Sarah told you."

Ann took another step closer. Slowly, she brought her right hand forward from behind her back. In it, she held a Colt six-shot revolver. The gun barrel pointed directly at Mary's chest.

Mary gasped.

"Do you really think I was searching for bat guano the night I ran into you two? True enough that I use the guano to make saltpeter and mix my own gunpowder, but I have no need to wander the hills myself. No, I followed you and Sarah that night, and I know that she shared her secret with you. Sarah Norton is dead," Ann continued, "and you, Mary Tully, are the last Nortonville resident to know the sword's hidden location, which you will now tell me." Ann cocked the pistol and lifted it closer to Mary's heart.

Mary still did not understand the sword's true significance. As far as she knew, the sword was just the sacred object of a fraternal order. Its true heritage and power remained a mystery to Mary, which made Ann's monstrous actions all the more inconceivable. The one thing Mary was certain of at this moment was that Ann would never let her leave the mine alive.

As panic and fury boiled inside her, Mary thought about reaching for her derringer. But she could never get off a shot before Ann's already cocked pistol fired. Mary lifted her head high and summoned the courage for one last question. "Who are you?"

Ann's gaze penetrated Mary as if she already fired the gun. "I am called the Raven. For a decade, I tracked the Pythian origin sword across this country. Once you tell me where it is hidden, I will finally be able to return to Wales. That is my quest. Now, Mary Tully, where is the sword?"

Helpless and exhausted, Mary succumbed. It is, she thought, just a sword. It cannot be worth so much misery. This horror must stop. "It is hidden behind . . ." Mary paused.

Ann tilted her head, listening with anticipation.

"Behind a rock in the powder magazine."

"Liar!"

The declaration bewildered and terrified Mary. "It is true. I saw it there myself," Mary insisted.

"I found that rock days ago," said Ann growing enraged. "The space behind it is empty! Where is the sword!

"I . . . I don't know. That is where it was. If it is not there, then Sarah must have moved it. I swear, I don't know."

Could it be possible, thought Ann, that Sarah moved the sword without telling anyone? And now Sarah Norton, the last person who knew the location of *Caledfwlch*, King Arthur's Excalibur, was dead. Recognition that the sword, once again, slipped through her grasp, sent Ann into an uncontrollable rage. "Nooo . . .!" she screamed.

Ann raised the pistol higher. She pointed directly at Mary's head . . . and pulled the trigger.

The pistol did not fire.

The primer charge inside the bullet casing did not ignite.

256

Instantly, Mary grabbed the mining lantern with one hand and threw it on the ground, extinguishing the flame. Holding her own kerosene lantern in the other hand, she spun around and raced into the tunnel. She hoisted her skirt the best she could and ran along the tracks deeper and deeper into the blackness. Her lantern provided just enough light to see the passageway.

Mere seconds passed by the time Ann removed the faulty bullet casing and recocked her pistol. She took aim at the light moving down the tunnel and fired.

The gunshot echoed through the mineshaft as the bullet whizzed by Mary's head, spattering dust into her eyes when it hit the wall.

Mary stopped and turned. She grabbed the derringer from her coat, pointed it in Ann's direction and fired.

Ann's scream penetrated the darkness. Was she hit? She had to be hit. But how bad? Mary could not tell but she knew what she must do. She immediately doused the lantern and froze.

The blackness that enveloped Mary was unlike anything she ever experienced. She held her hand directly in front of her eyes . . . nothing — total and absolute darkness. Mary considered her perilous situation. Unable to see or move without stumbling, she sat down, tight up against a crevice in the tunnel wall.

A sudden bright flash of Ann's pistol startled Mary. The sound of footsteps on the gravelly tunnel floor grew closer. Dear, God, thought Mary, she's still alive.

Another gunshot flashed just yards away, but Ann did not notice Mary's trembling body curled on the ground nearby. Mary dare not breathe. Passing inches away from Mary's feet, Ann continued probing her way down the shaft. Another gunshot, but further away. She did not see me, thought Mary, perhaps . . . I will survive this night.

The noise created by trying to escape the tunnel was too risky, so Mary remained silent and motionless. Another gunshot, fainter still. Physically and emotionally exhausted, Mary leaned back against the tunnel wall and closed her eyes.

CHAPTER 31

"HOW ARE YOU FEELING?" asked Harrison.

Celeste scanned Rose Hill Cemetery. "So far, so good. Thanks."

To avoid the afternoon heat and typical weekend crowds, Harrison and Celeste drove to the Black Diamond Mines Regional Preserve just after sunrise. The anxiety Celeste felt on several previous park hikes was absent, allowing her and Harrison to thoroughly enjoy the morning. The pepper and Italian cypress trees stood motionless, bearing stoic witness to another day of cemetery visitors, as they had since their planting more than a century ago by Nortonville residents. A raven interjected his deep, rasping call into the otherwise tranquil landscape. Harrison pulled the cemetery brochure from his fanny pack. He unfolded the paper and matched the map image with cemetery plots.

"Well," said Harrison, "here we go."

The map showed the circled Knights of Pythias gravesites from the prior day's conversation. "First of all," said Harrison, "let's find the two graves we know about. William Gething should be over there." Harrison pointed toward the cemetery's southern border.

The couple quickly found Gething's headstone. Celeste reached down and touched the engraved emblem. "As we thought, the Knights of Pythias symbol."

"Check," replied Harrison.

"Next is Evan Davies," said Celeste.

"He should be this one right over here," said Harrison.

Celeste examined the marble headstone. "Yes, a Pythian symbol."

"Another check. And now . . ." Harrison began.

"No Pythian symbol on these," interrupted Celeste, already inspecting other headstones.

"Okay, got it," Harrison said as he crossed the plots off his brochure map.

Harrison followed Celeste as she meandered through the cemetery, stooping next to each headstone and closely examining the engravings.

"Here!" Celeste called out. "Here's another with the symbol."

"Who is it?" Harrison asked.

"The name is David Griffiths."

Harrison skimmed through the alphabetized list. "He is number forty-six." Harrison circled the plot on his map. "Who's next?"

Celeste continued to search. She stopped suddenly and brushed dirt from a headstone. "This one," she announced. "Theophilus Watts."

"Plot fifty," said Harrison. "Got it." He continued to cross off gravesites that did not contain a Knights of Pythias symbol as Celeste announced them.

Celeste paused again. "William Williams."

"Plot fifty-two." Harrison circled the number.

"Evan Smith," announced Celeste.

"Forty-eight."

"Theophile Dumas."

"Forty-seven."

Celeste stopped. She stared at a blank marble slab lying flat on the ground. "We may have a problem."

Harrison caught up to her after circling the last name. "What is it?"

"There are a lot of plots with missing headstones. While the base is still intact for some, the headstone is gone."

"Yeah, not surprising. I remember the naturalist telling us about all the vandalism here prior to the area becoming a regional park," said Harrison.

"Right," replied Celeste. "That's going to impact our search."

Harrison reviewed the cemetery map he held. "How about we finish checking all the available headstones, and then see where we are."

Celeste immediately continued walking. "This one. The name and symbol are a bit faded, but it looks like Watkins Williams. Is he on the list?"

"Watkins Williams, Watkins Williams," Harrison repeated as he ran his finger over the names. "There he is, plot fifty one."

Celeste and Harrison wandered among the remains of Nortonville residents, carefully studying each headstone. Before long, they had crisscrossed Rose Hill Cemetery ending back where they started. "How many headstones did we identify," Celeste asked anxiously.

"Eight," replied Harrison. "Eight headstones engraved with a Knights of Pythias symbol. Not quite what we hoped for."

Harrison handed the brochure to Celeste. "Hmm," she said as she surveyed the map. "I wonder . . ."

Celeste paused.

"Yes?" asked Harrison.

"This brochure lists quite a few gravesites with unknown people where there's a plot number, but no name."

"Like those bases with no headstone," said Harrison, "there's no way to know who's buried there."

"True. But what if this grave right here, one that you did not circle, was a Pythian? Then you have . . ." Celeste took Harrison's pencil and circled plot forty-five. "Oh, my gosh."

"Unbelievable," said Harrison. "A triangle, just like the wedding tables you sketched out: nine points outlining a triangle shape, or in this case, nine graves. And if you add a point right about here," Harrison circled a blank spot on the brochure's cemetery map, "you have . . ."

"A tetractys!" exclaimed Celeste.

The map image left them both stunned.

"This is unbelievable," Harrison continued. "If we add this unknown plot and this empty space in the center, these Pythian gravesites form a perfect tetractys."

"Which means the center of the tetractys," said Celeste, excitedly, ". . . is somewhere around here."

She dashed to an area of the cemetery between Pythian headstones and among other scattered gravesites. "Standing here, it's hard to tell where the exact middle is located."

Harrison thought for a moment and then raced off. "I'll be back in a minute," he shouted toward Celeste who stood bewildered.

She watched as Harrison left the cemetery perimeter and stopped just off the trail. He bent down, but Celeste could not see what he was doing. A few seconds later, Harrison jogged back. In his hands, he held a bunch of vivid orange flowers.

"Hey, those are California poppies. You're not supposed to pick those," chastised Celeste.

"Yeah, yeah, I know. Don't worry, I didn't pick the whole plant, just some of the flowers. We need to use them?"

Celeste cocked her head. "For what?"

"To mark the headstones so I can see them better," Harrison replied.

"See them better from where?" asked Celeste.

Harrison turned and pointed toward the top of an exceptionally steep hill towering over the cemetery's northern edge. "From there."

Harrison recognized Celeste's expression as her non-verbal way of telling him that she thought he was crazy.

"You're going to place some of the flowers on each of the Pythian gravesites," Harrison continued. "From up there, I can direct you to the exact center of the tetractys."

"Okay," Celeste said cautiously, "but be careful."

Harrison jogged out of the cemetery to the foot of the hill. After pausing briefly, he began climbing. The hill's steep angle required him to lumber on all four limbs, grabbing clumps of grass and pulling upward with each step. Satisfied with Harrison's progress, Celeste located each Pythian gravesite and laid several brightly colored poppies on top.

She finished and waited several more minutes for Harrison to reach the peak. As she watched him turn and sit in the tall grass, she felt her phone vibrate. Looking at the screen, she instantly recognized Harrison's number. "Hi, Barre."

"I figure this is easier than shouting from the mountain top," he said.

"Can you see the marked graves?" Celeste asked.

"I can. The bright orange really stands out."

Celeste made her way toward the middle of the gravesites. "Okay, where to?"

"Try four steps straight ahead," said Harrison over the phone.

Celeste complied.

"Okay, one more step forward, and then three steps to your left."

Celeste followed the directions and then paused. "Well?"

263

"Almost," said Harrison. "Take one more step forward and then one more to your left."

With her phone held to her ear, Celeste took the steps.

"Stop! Right there," shouted Harrison. "Sorry," he said after seeing Celeste recoil the phone from her ear. "I got excited."

"That's okay. Is this it?" Celeste asked anxiously. "Is this the center of the tetractys?"

"Yes. You're at the exact center. Mark it with something, and I'll be down in a couple minutes."

Scanning the area, Celeste found a large stone and placed it at the spot she was standing. Sweating and out of breath, Harrison soon joined her. He quickly located two large sticks, crossed them together, and partially buried them in the dirt to be less conspicuous, but easy to find later.

Harrison and Celeste stood silently staring at the ground, their minds and bodies filled with anticipation. Harrison took Celeste's hand in his and the two looked at each other. "X marks the spot," he said with a smile.

HARRISON PULLED HIS CAR into the dirt parking lot just outside Black Diamond Mines Regional Preserve's locked gate. Celeste fastened closed her coat and slipped on a knit cap before exiting the passenger seat into the night air. "Not as cold as I thought, but windy," she stated.

Harrison scanned the area. Little was visible in the late night darkness, obscured even more by a cloudy, moonless sky. A strong breeze rustled through huge, twisted oak trees creating background static in the otherwise soundless night. "Yeah, it's the wind that I'm worried about," said Harrison.

"What do you mean?" asked Celeste.

264

"I'll explain later."

Celeste shot Harrison a playful glare.

From his trunk, Harrison removed a large electronic box that he then strapped over his shoulders and around his waist. On top of the box, he rested a computer display screen. He connected one end of a cord to the computer and the other end to a metal rod that fastened onto a thick metallic disc. Harrison pushed a toggle switch and watched as the display monitor came to life. A smear of florescent green and blue lit up the screen. He took a small folding knife out of his pocket and dropped it on the ground. Slowly waiving the metallic disc over the knife, Harrison and Celeste watched with fascination as the display showed a perfect bright red, three-dimensional image of the knife's contours.

"All systems go," said Harrison. "Would you mind carrying the flashlight?"

"Of course. Where did you say Schumacher got that thing?" asked Celeste.

"Borrowed it from Lawrence Livermore National Laboratory, where he works during the summers. I think he has been doing education and research programs there almost as long as he's been teaching. So, apparently, when he asked to borrow a high-definition, three-dimensional metal detector, they had no problem."

"Did you tell Schu why you wanted it?"

"Yes and no," responded Harrison. "I told him about searching for an old weapon; I just didn't say what weapon."

"Probably best," said Celeste. "He'd think we were nuts."

"Yeah, that's kinda what I thought, as well." Harrison handed a flashlight and a shovel to Celeste while he grabbed a pick-ax along with the metal detector. "Shall we?" he said, gesturing toward the trail leading to Rose Hill Cemetery.

The now familiar hike sloped gradually upward, and then angled into a valley before snaking steeply upward on the final stretch to the cemetery. Celeste and Harrison chatted casually about, once again, trespassing during one of their adventures. Of more concern to Harrison, however, was Celeste's condition. As they approached the cemetery, and the wind picked up, he noticed a distinct change in her tone. Her pace slowed. In the darkness, he could still easily notice her growing distress.

"You're feeling it again, aren't you?" Harrison asked.

"Yes," said Celeste meekly. "But I'm sure I'm just anxious about what we may find."

"Perhaps," Harrison responded.

They paused at the cemetery perimeter. "What time have you got?" asked Harrison.

Battling the extreme unease overwhelming her body, Celeste glanced at her Fitbit. "Almost 2:00 a.m."

She continued staring at the display on her wrist. "What is it?" asked Harrison.

"It's happening again."

Celeste's trembling voice sent a chill through Harrison. "What?"

"The footsteps. It's recording footsteps while I'm not moving."

Harrison gently took Celeste's wrist and turned the Fitbit screen toward him. He watched as the counter recorded steps though he held her arm perfectly still. "Interesting. C, I want you to look at me," said Harrison softly.

Slowly, Celeste raised her eyes to meet his. In that instant, Celeste's gaze turned from anxiety . . . to fear.

"You see it," said Harrison. "The ghost?"

Barely able to speak, Celeste responded. "Yes."

"Tell me what you see?"

Celeste grabbed tightly onto Harrison's arm. "The White Witch," Celeste whispered. "She's . . . she's floating over the cemetery. A white glowing light with a flowing dress . . . just floating there."

Calmly, Harrison pressed a button on a separate electronic box he carried just below the metal detector display. He held Celeste's arm firmly as she trembled with fright. "I'm going to try something," he said. "Keep looking at me, but tell me if anything happens to the White Witch."

Confused and terrified, all Celeste could do was nod.

A faint, very deep sound began emanating from Harrison's box. As he turned a knob, the sound grew deeper and deeper until it disappeared. He continued to hold her gaze while carefully turning the knob with no apparent effect until . . .

"Stop!"

Celeste's cry startled Harrison.

"She's gone! She just disappeared," exclaimed Celeste.

"I thought she might," said Harrison.

CHAPTER XXXII

November 11, 1879

Ann crept along in the total darkness of Upper Black Diamond Mine. Now out of bullets, brief flashes of light from her gunfire no longer guided her through the tunnel. The warm trickle of blood dripping from her shoulder had soaked her blouse and she knew the wound needed treatment.

Her mind churned through the possible consequences of leaving Mary Tully alive. By the time she raced home and retuned with a lantern, the mining crew would be starting its shift, but she had few other options.

Running her hand against the rough sandstone wall for support, Ann followed the coal car tracks back toward the mine entrance. She began the long jog downhill with one thought . . . Mary Tully must not live to talk.

Anger and determination intensified as Ann burst through her door and ran to the back room. Wincing in pain, she tore open her blouse and stuffed a cloth against her injured shoulder. She then strapped a belt around her chest and arm to hold the dressing in place.

Her rifle leaned casually against the wall between honey jars and candles. She grabbed the weapon, loaded it with bullets and dashed back out of the house carrying a new kerosene lantern. The morning light had begun to slowly warm and brighten the hills. Ann trekked back along the long, steep trail to Upper Black Diamond Mine, walking and jogging as quickly as possible. By the time she neared the mine opening nearly two hours later, she was exhausted.

Ann carefully moved off the trail and hid behind scattered trees and shrubs. As she quietly approached the mine entrance, her worst fear was realized . . . the entire mining crew stood outside, preparing to enter for the day. Mary Tully was nowhere in sight.

Ann set her lantern on the ground. She could not hope to enter the tunnel undetected. There were now two possible options, Ann reasoned, either Mary was still hiding in the mine and, once found by the miners, would be escorted out. Or, Mary already escaped the mine and headed back to town. Ann cocked her rifle and took position behind a tall pine tree. For now she would wait. Whether here at the mine entrance, or back in town, thought Ann, Mary Tully will be silenced.

"ALRIGHT, BOYS," ANNOUNCED the foreman, "let's be safe in there!"

The ten-man crew and two knobbers finished adjusting gear and igniting lanterns. The foreman took a final head count and began to sing loud and slow. "I'm a little *collier* . . ."

". . . and *gweithio* underground," the crew responded in unison, a ritual performed each day the men began their perilous work.

"The *raff* will never *torri*," continued the foreman.

". . . when I go up and down," echoed the crew.

"It's *bara* when I'm hungry."

"And *cwrw* when I'm dry."

"It's *gwely* when I'm tired."

"And *nefoedd* when I die."

The crew walked methodically into the depths of the tunnel. Some men carried picks and shovels; others pushed coal cars along the tracks. The two knobber boys, as usual, lead the way. Though they carried no lantern, the boys were undeterred by the darkness. Trotting along the tracks and playfully nudging each other into the walls, they adapted easily to their subterranean world.

The crew, now deep into the mine tunnel, approached their targeted coal vein. The knobbers, sensing they neared the work site, raced ahead and disappeared into the blackness. The men chatted casually about the upcoming *Nadolig* festivities, including who would carry this year's *Mari Lwyd*. The conversation took place mostly in English, interspersed with Welsh and occasional Italian from the two Italian crewmembers that enjoyed teasing their Welsh peers for their strange customs.

Suddenly, the men froze. The high-pitched scream echoing from the tunnel depths startled them. "That sounds like the Dumas boy," said the foreman. Fearing one of the knobbers was injured, the miners raised their lanterns, directing the light further down the tunnel. They saw nothing.

The crew rushed into the black void. "John, Thomas, you alright?!" called the foreman. Within seconds, the two boys appeared, running as fast as they could toward the lights. Breathing heavily, they could barely speak when reaching the crew.

"There's . . . there's . . . there's something in here," Thomas, trembling with fright, finally spit out.

"Now settle down," replied the foreman. He put his hand on Thomas's shoulder. "What happened? What's in here?"

"We . . . we were running to the coal vein like always," continued Thomas, "and tripped over something on the tracks. Landed flat on my chin. When I reached over to find out what it was, I felt . . ." Thomas breathed deeply to regain his composure.

"What?" one of the crew asked. "You felt what?"

"Hair," answered Thomas. "Long hair."

270

The men looked at one another. "Likely an animal," said one.

"Probably another fox, "replied another. "Remember when the whole town thought Empire mine was haunted because of eerie noises and glowing eyes? Turned out to be a poor fox chased into the mine by a dog. Had everyone all a-jitter for days."

"Morgan Morgans still has that fox," added a third miner. "Keeps it like a pet on his property."

"Alright, Boy," interrupted the foreman, "let's take a look."

As the crew continued deeper into the tunnel, Thomas turned toward the other knobber and whispered. "Ain't no fox I felt."

Moments later, the foreman stopped. He held up his hand and the crew stood silently behind him. "There's something up ahead. Low across the tracks. Don't look like it's moving."

The men quickly grew anxious. Anything unexpected this deep in the mine was something to be nervous about. "Jenkins, Banks, come with me," ordered the foreman.

Chosen because of the pick-axes they wielded, the two miners followed. The foreman carefully approached the object. Stopping several feet away, he squatted and held out his lantern. "Dear, God," he exclaimed, "it's a woman."

Shocked and confused, Jenkins and Banks quickly joined the foreman and all three stood over the crumpled body. The foreman gently placed his hand on the woman's shoulder and rolled her onto her back. He carefully brushed blonde hair from the woman's face to expose ashen skin.

"Do you recognize her?" asked Jenkins.

"It's Mary Tully," the foreman replied.

Banks lowered his lantern closer. "Is she alive?"

"Not breathing. Ice cold. She's been dead for a while, I'd say." The foreman examined Mary's clothing and exposed limbs. "Not a sign of injury. I expect she succumbed to blackdamp . . . just ran out of air."

The rest of the crew, including the knobber boys, joined the foreman. With mouths agape at the astonishing site, they all stared in complete silence.

"She ain't even got no lantern." Banks finally said. "What in God's earth is she doin' all the way down here?"

The foreman stood up. He removed his hat and placed it across his chest. The rest of the group did the same. Scanning the gruesome scene, the foreman solemnly announced, "Whatever drove this poor woman to such a dreadful and lonesome demise may forever remain a mystery."

Headstone of Mary Tully [20]

CHAPTER 33

"I DON'T UNDERSTAND," said a still visibly shaken Celeste. "What just happened?"

"Science, my dear," responded Harrison with an impish grin. "Science."

He dropped the pick-ax, drew Celeste in, and hugged her tight. "Let me explain," he continued. "While I'll be the first to admit that there are many mysteries in this universe that we can't explain, I could not accept that a ghost hanging out at Black Diamond Mines was one of them. It just took a while to figure out what was going on."

Celeste sighed deeply and relaxed her posture. "Not only is the White Witch gone, but I don't feel the anxiety anymore, either," she said. "Please explain."

"The first clue was your Fitbit," said Harrison. "Those ghostly steps taken while you stood still had to have a physical cause. A tiny accelerometer inside the Fitbit measures each step you take. Usually arm movement while walking vibrates the Fitbit's sensor and a microcomputer calculates steps. However, other sources of vibration, like riding in a bouncing car, may result in false steps. I just needed to determine the other cause of vibrations.

"But wait," said Celeste. "I was totally still when we saw the Fitbit count steps."

"Precisely," responded Harrison. "I thought about what might cause your Fitbit to vibrate even though you weren't moving."

"And . . .?"

"Sound," said Harrison. "Invisible vibrations that can not only impact your eardrum, but also other objects, like an . . ."

"Accelerometer," said Celeste.

"Exactly."

"Just one problem," continued Celeste. "There were no unusual sounds when we saw those false steps."

"None that we heard, anyway," said Harrison, "which confused me . . . until Mitchell Conder came along."

"What on earth does Mitchell have to do with all of this?"

"He's the one that brought up the notion of infrasound," said Harrison. "When I took my environmental science club on the windfarm fieldtrip, Mitchell discussed how turning blades could produce very low sound frequencies that may cause a feeling of discomfort in some people. The infrasound is too low to hear, but not too low to affect certain objects."

"But, Barre, there are no windfarms nearby."

"Yeah, that part puzzled me for some time. Turns out there are other infrasound sources. It was during Mitchell's demonstration of Helmholtz resonance that the explanation dawned on me."

Celeste thought for a moment. "I remember walking in on his talk after school one day."

"He showed my club how blowing across a bottle lip creates a vibration that can cause sound. If the vibration is the right frequency, we can hear the sound. But, if the vibration is a very low frequency, we may not be able to hear the sound even though it's still there."

"Like the wind turbine blades," added Celeste.

"Yup."

"Barre," Celeste said skeptically, "there's no one blowing across a bottle opening out here."

"Actually," Harrison responded. "There is . . . sort of."

275

Celeste again paused, thinking through Harrison's explanation.

"One other clue tied the whole thing together," Harrison continued. "I noticed you did not feel the anxiety or see the White Witch every time we came out here, only on certain occasions."

"Correct."

"What I noticed, was that you only experienced those phenomena when it was . . ."

"Windy," said Celeste. "I assumed that was just a coincidence, but you're thinking there is something more to it?

"I am."

"Of course," Celeste said, grabbing Harrison's arm. "The strong wind is like someone blowing across a bottle's lip, and the bottle itself is like . . . the mines!"

"You got it. But I don't think the coal mines," replied Harrison.

Celeste's momentary satisfaction waned. "Not the coal mines?"

"The coal mines were around for decades before any tales of the White Witch. Based on the articles I researched and stories from students whose families lived in the area for generations, the White Witch legend began between the 1930's and 40's. That coincides with sand mining up here, which fits the bottle analogy. The sand mines have larger openings with much larger caverns, more like a bottle."

"So, you think that strong winds blowing across the sand mine openings cause Helmholtz resonance, creating very low frequency infrasound that vibrated my Fitbit. And I suppose that's the reason for my anxious feelings. What was it called, wind turbine syndrome?"

"Yes," said Harrison. "The infrasound frequency happens to resonate with one or more of your organs, causing that queasy sensation. After reasoning that might be the cause, I found many examples of caves that create infrasound. Apparently, the phenomenon is not that unusual."

Celeste patted Harrison on the arm that she now released. "That is really fascinating, but there is just one problem with your hypothesis, Mr. Barrett. It still doesn't explain the White Witch."

Harrison raised an eyebrow. "Oh, but it does. While learning about cave infrasound, I came across an article called Ghosts in the Machine that describes a scientist working late one night in his supposedly haunted lab. He became struck with an overwhelmingly anxious feeling and saw a white blob of light floating nearby — a ghost. The next day, he was cleaning his fencing sword . . ."

"Wait," interrupted Celeste. "Another sword?"

"They do keep popping up, don't they? With the sword handle in a vice, the scientist observed the tip of the sword vibrating. After a lot of investigating, he determined that the turning blades of a large extractor fan were causing infrasound that resonated with the sword blade, and with . . . his eyeballs."

"His eyeballs?"

"Just as the vibrations of other organs might cause anxious feelings, eye vibrations may cause optical illusions that appear as ghostly figures."

"I see," nodded Celeste. "For all these years, the legendary White Witch of Black Diamond Mines was nothing more than an optical illusion caused by Helmholtz resonance from wind blowing across the sand mines creating infrasound vibrations."

"Yes."

"Then how did you make her, uh, it, disappear just now?"

"This other contraption I'm carrying is an infrasound generator that I also asked Schu to pick up from the lab. I adjusted the frequency lower and lower until it matched the frequency emanating from the mines. The device then calculates a sound wave that is 180 degrees out of phase with the original sound. If the crest and troughs of the two sound waves precisely line up, then the emitted wave cancels out the incoming sound wave, which is the same way noise-cancellation headphones work. Once the frequencies cancel out, there's no more eye vibration, and voilà — no more White Witch."

"That's incredible," exclaimed Celeste. "I'm so thankful I'm not seeing real ghosts."

"I'm pretty happy about that, as well," smiled Harrison. "Now, shall we see about King Arthur's sword?"

Rose Hill Cemetery [21]

CHAPTER 34

"X MARKS THE SPOT," said Celeste. "The sticks are still here where we left them."

Her flashlight lit the spot the couple previously determined as the exact center of the tetractys pattern formed by headstones engraved with a Knights of Pythias symbol. Harrison immediately turned on the metal detector strapped around his shoulders.

"So, when I flip this switch," he explained, "the electricity creates a strong magnetic field in the coil at the bottom. That magnetic field penetrates the ground. If I move the coil around like this and the magnetic field hits metal, then an electric current forms in the metal object, which in turn, generates its own magnetic field. This other coil at the bottom here can detect that other magnetic field and convert it into . . ."

The piercing beep from the device was surprisingly intense.

"Sound?" finished Celeste.

Harrison stood staring at the fluorescent computer display. "Uh, C . . . you need to take a look at this," he said with astonishment.

Celeste gazed at the long, thin, bright red image formed on the screen as Harrison continued to wave the detector back and forth over the ground. She looked at him, and he looked at her, and they simultaneously broke into giddy smiles.

"I can't believe it," Celeste finally said. "That . . . that looks like . . . well . . . a sword."

"This is amazing," responded Harrison. "If that object is what we think it is, we may be about to dig up one of the most significant artifacts of the past two-thousand years."

The couple's smiles stretched into broad grins as they continued to stare at the display screen.

Without warning, a deep voice penetrated the darkness.

"What are you waiting for?"

Celeste immediately recognized the menacing voice. How could she forget? Startled and scared, she and Harrison spun around. Celeste slowly raised her flashlight. The beam reflected off the metal of a small caliber handgun pointed directly at her. Celeste swallowed hard. She lifted the flashlight higher, revealing the muscular body and weathered face of her attacker from Wales.

"It's good to see you again, Celeste," the man said.

Harrison instinctively stepped between the man and Celeste. "Who are you?" he asked.

"You know who I am."

The man's dark, raspy voice terrified Celeste as she remembered his breath on her cheek and knife against her neck when assaulted near her grandfather's house. "The Caledfwlch Society," stated Celeste.

"If I had gotten what I wanted then," the man continued, "we wouldn't be meeting like this."

"You could not have deciphered the symbol," Celeste responded defiantly.

"Perhaps not. But no matter, we are here now."

A dozen scenarios raced through Harrison's mind. None, however, assured him of Celeste's safety. Frustrated and anxious, he tightly clenched the metal detector handle. He needed to comply, for now. "What is it you want?"

"Another silly question," the man responded coldly. "You know exactly what I want. It is just unfortunate for you, that your girlfriend got you involved."

The words sent an ominous chill through Celeste.

281

They could not outrun this man, but perhaps, if Harrison distracted him long enough, Celeste could escape. For years, Harrison wished nothing more than to spend the rest of his life with Celeste. Now, with their wedding so close, and the horrifying realization that he may not survive to fulfill that dream, all he could do was look into her eyes.

Celeste instantly knew Harrison's thoughts: when he attacks, she must run. But how could she?

Staring silently at each other, her eyes said that she could not leave him. His eyes insisted that she must. Harrison gently pushed Celeste back and lifted the metal detector. He needed to last just long enough for her to escape.

Just then, the man stepped back, out of Harrison's reach, and raised his gun toward Celeste. Harrison dare not move.

"Take off the metal detector. Lay it and the flashlight on the ground," the man demanded.

Harrison had to obey. He removed both the detector and the infrasound generator and placed them at his feet. Celeste set the flashlight next to them. With no moon and a cloudy sky, the flashlight beam was the only light in an otherwise coal-black night.

"Now step back," said the man.

Celeste and Harrison did as directed.

The man unexpectedly looked away, to his right, as if he saw something. A strange expression crossed his face.

"What's that?" he said, more to himself than to Harrison and Celeste.

Harrison and Celeste saw nothing and remained silent.

In the dim glow from the flashlight, the man looked anxious. His eyes continued darting between Harrison and Celeste, and something in the distance.

"What is that light?! The man demanded.

Harrison and Celeste stood in stunned silence. Slowly, Harrison took Celeste's hand.

The man grew agitated. "Stay away!" he shouted into the darkness.

Harrison and Celeste still saw nothing.

Then, inexplicably, the man turned away. He pointed the gun to his right and began firing, toward a black void.

Mystified and desperate, Harrison and Celeste fled, sprinting into the cover of night.

"Stop where you are!" the man yelled, a fearful shudder overtaking his voice. Then more shots.

Harrison could not tell if the man called out to him and Celeste or at the approaching apparition. Quickly, Harrison pulled Celeste down behind a large headstone. "Not sure what just happened," whispered Harrison.

"It's like he saw something," Celeste quietly said. "Like . . . a ghost."

Harrison looked at Celeste. "You mean the White Witch?"

"When you turned off the infrasound generator and set it on the ground, the Helmholtz resonance must have affected him the same way it affected me," Celeste explained.

Before Harrison could respond, more shots pierced the darkness, this time, ricocheting off headstones nearby.

Harrison squeezed Celeste's trembling hand, "We can't stay here. We have to make a run for it before he gets any closer."

Celeste agreed. Harrison carefully peaked around the headstone. The man now held the flashlight, aiming it all around him. "I can't tell," said Harrison, "if he's looking for us, or afraid of something looking for him."

"The cemetery entrance is not far, just behind those trees," said Harrison. "We're going to make it."

With overwhelming fear of what might happen, Celeste looked intensely into Harrison's eyes, put her hand to his face, and kissed him, "I know."

Celeste rose into a crouch, still holding Harrison's hand. More shots fired. A bullet impacted their headstone, spraying marble chips.

"That's our cue," said Celeste.

But before they could run, bright rays of light suddenly burst from three directions. The beams lit up the cemetery along with Celeste's attacker, still flailing at the center.

Harrison and Celeste did not move.

A voice in the dark called out, "Drop the gun, now."

Harrison peered from behind the headstone to see the assailant set his gun on the ground. Instantly, three men carrying high-intensity lights and handguns appeared from beyond the cemetery fence and grabbed the man. One of the three turned and said loudly, "Celeste, Harrison, you're safe now."

Cautiously, Harrison and Celeste emerged from their hiding place and walked slowly toward the group. Celeste's attacker's hands were already bound behind his back with a zip tie. One of the three rescuers approached the couple. "I'm sorry we did not get here sooner," he said.

Thankful but confused, Harrison asked, "Who are you?"

Before the man could reply, Celeste responded. "Knights of Pythias." Celeste pointed at the man's ring, a shield with crossed battle axes, knight's helmet, and the letters F, C, and B. "Dramatic Order of the Knights of Khorassan, I suspect."

"That's right," said the man.

"But how did you . . ." Celeste continued. But before she could finish, a woman's voice from behind interrupted.

"Thank God, you're alright."

284

Celeste froze. She spun around, squinted into the darkness, and said with bewilderment, "Mom?"

EPILOGUE

A LOAN SEAGULL SOARED overhead, peering down at the bystanders below. Harrison stood atop the cliff with his back to the cobalt blue Atlantic Ocean. The cloudless sky, soft breeze, and mild temperature were rare for this location on England's southern tip, but Harrison expected perfect weather today. After all, he reasoned, how could the day be anything but perfect?

As Harrison gazed out among the stone outlines of 5th-century buildings, a million thoughts ran through his mind. The past month was a blur. His mind flashed to the confrontation in Rose Hill Cemetery. Attacked by a member of the Caledflwch Society, Harrison was ready to sacrifice his life for Celeste's. Suddenly, an unseen entity distracted the assailant.

Then, members of the Knights of Pythias' secret sect, the Dramatic Order of the Knights of Khorassan, intervened to disarm the attacker. But the most shocking revelation left Harrison, and especially Celeste, dumbfounded. The rescue group's leader, a devout member of the Nomads of Avrudaka, was Celeste's mother.

During the weeks following the incident, Harrison delighted in listening to Celeste respectfully, yet pointedly, confront her mom about the secret life she led for decades. As a protector of the sword, like her mother before her, Selene Scott vowed to do everything in her power to keep the ancient sword hidden from the Caledflwch Society and anyone else that might attempt to exploit its mythical powers.

Celeste spent hours interrogating her mother on every detail. Neither the Dramatic Order of the Knights of Khorassan nor the Nomads of Avrudaka knew the location of Excalibur.

The sword's hiding place had been lost long ago. It was a Knight of Khorassan who had first been murdered in Rose Hill Cemetery when confronting a Caledfwlch Society member who seemed to be getting too close.

Unaware that anyone else knew about the symbolic medallion Celeste's father gave her, Celeste's mother chose not to involve her daughter in the Knight's mission. One day, perhaps, she would inform Celeste. But until then, Selene reasoned her daughter was safer not knowing.

That all changed when the murdered Knight left Celeste's name on a headstone, a desperate warning linked to the Welsh Indian bloodline from which she descended. From that day forward, Celeste was followed by Knights of Khorassan, intervening when she was attacked in Wales, and then last month in the cemetery. The attacker was eventually turned over to the police, but not before Harrison and Celeste, Selene, and the Knights of Khorassan retrieved a long wooden box buried deep underground. The heavy metal object inside, wrapped in decaying cloth, emitted such an overwhelming sense of wonder and awe that no one in the group could bear its touch.

Finally, Celeste's mother carefully unwrapped the object to expose a very old, very weathered, and very breathtaking, sword.

They stared in disbelief.

"*Caledfwlch*," said Selene.

"Excalibur," whispered Celeste.

Celeste and her mother exchanged apprehensive looks. Celeste turned to Harrison, whose gaping mouth embodied his continued amazement. He slowly closed his jaw and said softly to Celeste, "Now what?"

HARRISON FIDEGETED with his bow tie and cummerbund. He turned and smiled at Shumacher who patted him on the back. "You doing okay?" asked Schumacher.

"Could not be better," answered Harrison.

Following the cemetery discovery, Celeste's mother and the Knights of Khorassan took possession of the sword. Only they and a few other select individuals would, once again, be aware of Excalibur's final resting place. Not even Harrison knew. But the question that lingered for weeks was, what about Celeste?

Celeste struggled greatly with the notion of joining the ranks of her mother and the Nomads of Avrudaka. Could she become a keeper of the sword? Should she? She and Harrison discussed the consequences intermittently with their wedding planning. Eventually, as they both grew exhausted from the stress and responsibility, Harrison resolved at least one of their challenges — when and where to get married — and Celeste wholeheartedly agreed.

Harrison now patiently waited on a bluff overlooking Tintagel Castle, the legendary birthplace of King Arthur. Shumacher, his best man, stood by his side. A small group of close family and friends faced them. Celeste's mother's eyes already glistened with tears anxiously anticipating the bride's emergence from a canvas tent erected nearby.

Not only did Celeste think Harrison's choice of location was ideal, but so too, was his selection of a date. July not only landed during their summer vacation from school, but also happened to be the time of a profound astronomical event. For a short time, harmonic resonance aligned all the planets on one side of the sun, an extremely rare occurrence, and one that resonated acutely with the couple's new found appreciation of *Musica universalis*. "It could not be more perfect," responded Celeste to Harrison's suggestion.

A figure appeared from the canvas tent. The woman, Celeste's younger sister, Sophie, waved toward the group. Instantly, a violinist began playing and Harrison began choking up. Is this really happening, he thought? Am I really marrying the most incredible woman I've ever met and the love of my life?

Carrying a traditional cottage bouquet of white roses, pink peonies, yellow carnations, and lavender chrysanthemums, Celeste's sister started slowly walking toward the group. Moments later, Celeste's grandfather, Lloyd, stepped out from the tent. Clutching his arm was Celeste. Her classic white dress danced softly in the sea breeze. Harrison stared, mesmerized.

Wondering tourists watched with delight as Lloyd led Celeste to Harrison and placed her hand into his. Harrison mouthed the words, "I love you." Celeste did the same.

The two teachers-turned-lovers listened intently to brief words from a pastor, one of Lloyd's close friends, who presided over the ceremony. His only quoted biblical scripture closed the pastor's formal remarks, and though neither Harrison nor Celeste had discussed what to say, the verse touched them profoundly.

"From Colossians 3:12 through 14," the pastor began. "Put on then, as God's chosen ones, holy and beloved, compassionate hearts, kindness, humility, meekness, and patience, bearing with one another and, if one has a complaint against another, forgiving each other; as the Lord has forgiven you, so you also must forgive. And above all these put on love, which binds everything together in perfect harmony."

Finally, the pastor uttered the words Harrison longed for. "Do you, Harrison James Barrett, take . . .?"

Smiling uncontrollably, Harrison responded. "I do"

"And do you, Celeste Marie Scott, take . . .?"

"I do," said Celeste, nearly interrupting the pastor's question.

The pastor paused, allowing the couple time to breathe in the moment. He then announced in his lyrical Welsh accent, "I pronounce you husband and wife. You," he said nodding at Harrison, "may kiss the bride."

Harrison, who had not taken his eyes off Celeste the entire ceremony, leaned in. Celeste met his lips half-way, and the couple shared a long, intense kiss, oblivious to their applauding family and friends and the now dozens of cheering spectators sharing the unusual wedding venue.

In a moment of unspoken connection, Harrison and Celeste turned simultaneously to the pastor and thanked him. Then, they both looked up at the towering eight-foot tall bronze statue standing directly behind the pastor. Like a benevolent ruler offering his blessing, the cloaked, sword-bearing figure called Gallos, a regal representation of King Arthur, stared back at them. In a final tribute to their incredible journey to find the legendary sword, and each other, Harrison nodded at the majestic figure and Celeste winked.

Following hugs and congratulations from onlookers, Harrison and Celeste slowly walked hand-in-hand back down the bluffs through the remains of Tintagel Castle.

"It's been an incredible journey, so far," said Harrison. "I can't wait for what's next."

Celeste squeezed his hand. "Hard to imagine we came so close to not making it back at Rose Hill Cemetery. I'm still impressed at your quick thinking to turn off the infrasound generator in case the Helmholtz resonance would affect the assailant, which fortunately, it did. That ghost he thought he saw probably saved our lives."

"Uh, now that we're married, C," began Harrison. "I know that we're not supposed to keep secrets from each other, so, I have a confession."

Celeste looked concerned. "What is it, Barre?"

"Well, when I set the infrasound generator on the ground, I wasn't thinking about the Caledfwlch Society, I was thinking about you. I worried that if I turned off the device, you would start being affected by the vibrations again. So . . . I didn't turn it off."

"What?" exclaimed Celeste. "But it had to be off. How else would our attacker think he saw a ghost?"

Harrison stopped walking and looked into Celeste's eyes, "That, my Dear, is a very good question."

Celeste's stunned expression lingered as the couple continued walking.

"Now that you know my secret," continued Harrison, "can I know yours?"

"What secret is that?" Celeste asked coyly.

"What have you decided? Do you know the location of Excalibur?"

Celeste smiled. "I believe I just answered that question."

Harrison stopped. "You did?"

"No, silly," responded Celeste as she continued walking along the rocky trail of the Tintagel bluffs.

Harrison remained motionless until Celeste looked back, and with an impish wink replied, ". . . I do."

Gallos at Tintagel [22]

Mt. Diablo [23]

END NOTES

The previous story is a blend of fact and fiction. Many elements from the past are based on historical documentation. From Pythagoras to the Knights of Pythias, from Welsh Indians to King Arthur, and from present-day Chepstow, Wales to 19th-century Nortonville, California, the reader is encouraged to explore and discover more about each.

The historical images and text indexed below are reproduced with permission. The reader may find their inclusion helpful in distinguishing real events and characters from fictional ones. And, of course, if you have any questions or comments, please post them at www.danhanel.com or www.facebook.com/InTheShadowofDiablo.

1. Chapter II. *My Fanwy.* 1875. Music by Joseph Parry. Lyrics by Richard Davies.

2. Chapter II. Black Diamond Mine Crew. 1898. Photograph. Collection of the Contra Costa County Historical Society.

3. Chapter IV. *The Nortonville Disaster.* July 29, 1876. Print. Contra Costa Gazette. Collection of the Pittsburg Historical Society.

4. Chapter VI. *Nortonville, California.* 1869. Engraving. With permission from Southport Land and Commercial Company archives.

5. Chapter VIII. In Memoriam of Evan Davies. January 27, 1877. Newsprint. Antioch Ledger.

6. Chapter VIII. Knights of Pythias emblem. Photograph. Public Domain.

7. Chapter X. Sarah Norton (on right) and Gordon family member (on left). Photograph. Circa 1870. Collection of the Contra Costa County Historical Society.

8. Chapter 11. Letter from Abraham Lincoln. Circa 1864. The Pythian Story. *The Pythians: The Order of Knights of Pythias* www.Pythias.org.

9. Chapter XII. Nortonville Main Street. 1875. Photograph. Collection of the Pittsburg Historical Society.

10. Chapter XIV. Nortonville Main Street. Circa 1880. Photograph. Collection of the Pittsburg Historical Society.

11. Chapter XVI. Headstone of Rebecca Abraham. 2018. Photograph. Collection of Dan Hanel.

12. Chapter XVIII. Nortonville's Welsh Choir. 1878. Photograph. Collection of the Pittsburg Historical Society.

13. Chapter XX. Justus Rathbone. Circa 1890. Photograph. Library of Congress. Public Domain.

14. Chapter 23. Tetractys. Image by Dan Hanel.

15. Chapter XXIV. Steamboat Chrysopolis. Circa 1870. Photograph. Online Archive of California. Public Domain.

16. Chapter 25. Caledfwlch Society symbol. Image by Dan Hanel.

17. Chapter XXVI. *Death of an Aged Midwife.* October 6, 1879. Edited print. Daily Alta California.

18. Chapter 27. Image of King Arthur. Drawing. 15th-century. (f.75.v). Welsh language version of Geoffrey of Monmouth's original 12th century *Historia Regum Britanniae.* National Library of Wales. Public Domain.

19. Chapter XXVIII. Headstone of Sarah Norton. 2018. Photograph. Collection of Dan Hanel.

20. Chapter XXXII. Headstone of Mary Tully. 2018. Collection of Dan Hanel.

21. Chapter 33. Rose Hill Cemetery. 1939. Photograph. Zelma Myrick.

22. Epilogue. *Gallos* at Tintagel. Photograph of bronze sculpture. 2017. Collection of Dan Hanel.

23. Mt. Diablo, California. Photograph. 2012. Veronica Hanel.

Made in the USA
San Bernardino, CA
18 March 2019